A

BEAUTIFUL

FAMILY

A

BEAUTIFUL

FAMILY

A Novel

Jennifer Trevelyan

DOUBLEDAY

NEW YORK

FIRST DOUBLEDAY HARDCOVER EDITION 2025

Published by Doubleday, a division of Penguin Random House LLC, 1745 Broadway, New York, NY 10019.

DOUBLEDAY and the portrayal of an anchor with a dolphin are registered trademarks of Penguin Random House LLC.

Book design by Anna B. Knighton

Library of Congress Cataloging-in-Publication Data
Names: Trevelyan, Jennifer, author.
Title: A beautiful family : a novel / Jennifer Trevelyan.
Description: First edition. | New York : Doubleday, 2025.
Identifiers: LCCN 2024026622 (print) | LCCN 2024026623 (ebook) |
   ISBN 9780385551359 (hardcover) | ISBN 9780385551366 (ebook)
Subjects: LCGFT: Bildungsromans. | Thrillers (Fiction) | Novels.
Classification: LCC PR9639.4.T74 B43 2025 (print) | LCC PR9639.4.T74 (ebook) |
   DDC 823/.92—dc23/eng/20240823
LC record available at https://lccn.loc.gov/2024026622
LC ebook record available at https://lccn.loc.gov/2024026623

penguinrandomhouse.com | doubleday.com

PRINTED IN THE UNITED STATES OF AMERICA

10 9 8 7 6 5 4 3 2 1

The authorized representative in the EU for product safety and compliance is Penguin Random House Ireland, Morrison Chambers, 32 Nassau Street, Dublin, D02 YH68, Ireland. http://eu-contact.penguin.ie

For Dad

A

BEAUTIFUL

FAMILY

⊙NE

Driving to the holiday house, I made sure there was acres of empty seat between my sister and me. I sat hard up against the car door and watched the scrub by the side of the road blur past my window. My mother played *Queen's Greatest Hits* on the car stereo and passed around a bag of hard jubes. At an intersection, my father stopped suddenly, spilling the jubes. "Fuckwit," he muttered. I wondered if he'd only just begun to use that word, or if it was a word he'd used for years, which I'd only just begun to hear.

The drive took a couple of hours and we stopped twice: once for corn on the cob and once for an antique shop. My sister Vanessa opted to stay in the car both times, so both times I opted to get out. The antique shop was dark and cool, and my mother bought a teapot to add to her collection.

~~~~~

In the past we had always spent our summer holidays in remote places where there were no fences and the local fruit shop was just an honesty box by the side of the road. That had always been my mother's preference—my father would ask her, around the start of September, when we were just beginning to feel that winter was behind us and spring was coming: where to this year? And he would go down to the street and get the New Zealand road map out of our car, where it lived in the back pocket of the driver's seat, and they would sit down together at the dining-room table and try to flatten out its hopelessly curled edges. My mother liked to lay open a map of the North Island, shut her eyes, and plant her finger somewhere (once, when my parents were "feeling flush," she opened it to a map of the *South* Island). It was funny because sometimes her finger landed in the middle of the ocean, and my father would tease us about hiring a boat. But mostly her finger found land, and if it found a place that was too built-up, or too much like a town or city, she would screw up her face, shake her head, and start again.

This year was different. My father still went and got the road map from the car, but my mother had already made up her mind. She wanted to go to a place with people.

"What people?" my father said. "Which people?"

"Just any people. No specific people."

"Strangers?"

"Well, yes, *people*."

We were all a bit stumped. My mother had been known to rule out a beach on the basis that there was one umbrella already up, or a lone fisherman standing on a rock. She'd bypass a picnic spot if there was a couple kissing on a rug in a far distant corner. (Once, when we were trying to find somewhere for dinner, I saw a restaurant with nobody in it—every table completely empty. I pointed it out to my mother—I was sure that she would love it. She shook her head. Not that one. But it's empty, I said, just the way you like it. It's different for restaurants, she said.)

"Why people?" my father asked. "What purpose will they serve?"

My mother got exasperated then. "Oh, I don't know, for goodness' sake. I just want to try it—a place with *people*. Is that too much to ask?"

My father had only been teasing anyone could tell. We all went quiet for a bit. My mother's face was flushed. Then my father said, "Did you have anywhere in mind?"

My mother nodded. She walked over to the dining-room table where the road map lay. She was wearing an apron and was halfway through cooking dinner. I saw that she had taken off her rings, probably because she was afraid of losing them in the stew. She picked the road map up with oniony hands. "There," she said, putting it down and planting her finger.

My father peered at the point where my mother's finger had left a watery mark. I saw that it was north of where we lived in Wellington, but not by much. "That's a popular spot," he said. "I hope we haven't left it too late."

"See what you can do," my mother shrugged. "It really doesn't matter either way, it's just a suggestion." She turned back to the kitchen, wiping her hands down the front of her apron, alternating front and back. The rest of what she said came to us over her shoulder, in a light, casual voice that barely carried through the open kitchen door. "Wherever we go, I'm sure we'll have a lovely time, so long as the four of us are together."

I reached out, spinning the map around so that I could see it, right way up. My mother's watery mark had dried already. I scanned the coastline but couldn't find the popular spot. My father was getting up from the table—he was stretching his arms, yawning. I hoped he'd taken proper note of where my mother's finger had landed, because I didn't believe what she'd said about it being only a suggestion. I believed that it mattered very much.

~~~~

After the two-hour drive, I climbed out of the car and walked a few steps toward the holiday house with my shorts sticking to the backs of my legs. The garden was big and square and flat. Parched. The ground not dirt but sand you could sink your toes into, cool and fluid like a lake. Big, prickly weeds and little circles of tough, springy grass that felt like plastic. No trees. Not even a bush or a daisy. Just a wooden fence right around, with an opening wide enough to drive a car through. For weeks my father had been telling us how he'd found the most wonderful place, right where my mother had requested. A house all to ourselves. A holiday house, with a lagoon on one side and a beach on the other. But this place had no lagoon and no beach. I turned a full circle in the tough, springy grass. The house sat at the end of a wide, flat road. I wondered if my father was going to get angry. Where was his lagoon? Where was his beach? But my father was unpacking the boot as if it was all exactly as he'd expected.

The house was as plain on the outside as a public toilet and not much bigger. My mother saw it and said, "It looks as if it's been dropped from a great height." She was trying to make a joke, but I could tell she was disappointed too. I felt a pang of longing for our home in Wellington, where all the neighbourhood cats liked to hide in our hedges, and where we'd left our Christmas tree standing in a window with its lights on a timer to ward off burglars.

My sister walked straight to the front door and said, "Key?" She had recently become too cool for us, and for the boring way we spoke to each other in complete sentences. My father threw her the key, which was in a folded-over white envelope and which—surprise, surprise—she dropped. She had a new bag of which she was very proud, with wide navy stripes across it and woven cotton handles. It had come free with a bumper summer issue of *Dolly* magazine, and using some of her holiday money, she had filled it to overflowing with creams and lotions that promised to make her tan without burning, and then promised to soothe the burning that always happened anyway. We all had to wait while my sister rooted around in this bag for the key, which had fallen in. Then we had to wait some more while she tried to unlock the door and, at the same time, tried to look like she was too cool to unlock the door. I chose that moment to follow the fence right around the edge of the section, trailing the tips of my fingers along the unpainted timber (a dumb idea— I got splinters that lasted for days). On the fence I saw a lot of cicadas, which I was careful to avoid. Some of the cicadas were singing very loudly and some, on closer inspection, were not cicadas at all—only their old, discarded skins. At the back there was a little aluminium rowboat lying overturned in the grass with its oars tucked beneath it. I thought about turning it over, but being only ten and a girl, I'd learned that things were often heavier than they looked. I'd learned not to try to lift or throw things in front of boys, because they'd laugh and say, "You lift and throw like a girl." I was standing, looking at the rowboat, wondering if it had a seat in it, when I heard a clicking noise above me. That's when I saw him.

He was standing in shadow on the second-floor deck of the house behind ours. He wasn't wearing a shirt and he had a rounded belly and white hair on his chest. In a mall, behind a plastic picket fence, with a red suit on, he might have made a good Father Christmas. I saw that he was holding something in his hand, which he quickly tucked behind his back. He didn't smile. That's what I noticed—he didn't smile. Adults usually smiled at little girls like me. I didn't smile, and I didn't run away either. I stood there looking him straight in the eye until I heard my mother calling me back, because when you're ten and a girl, it's important not to show your fear. As I walked across the springy grass toward the front door I thought I heard clicking again, but it was hard to tell above the sound of my mother calling, and the singing of cicadas.

～～～

We hadn't been in the holiday house ten minutes before I was pestering to go to the beach. While my father was unpack-

ing the car, and my mother was surveying the small, colourful kitchen, I was getting changed in the little bedroom I was
to share with my sister, where the beds were arranged in an
L-shape—mine by the door, and Vanessa's under the window.
"They haven't actually said yes yet," Vanessa pointed out, but I
wasn't waiting—my togs were on already, the sticky shorts pud-
dled on the floor. In the bathroom, where a collection of winged
creatures lay dead and dying in the bath, I slapped sunblock on
the backs of my knees and across the bridge of my nose. My
mother had switched on the kettle—a terrible sign—but she
knew better than to stand between me and a swim, even if it
was a little late in the day. The kettle was allowed to go cold.
We set off for the beach, the four of us. I tried not to mind that
I was the only one wearing togs.

We walked to the top of the street and crossed to the other
side, where there was a row of houses bigger by far than ours,
with large balconies and glass windows wrapping around, and
beyond that, a high ridge of dunes, dotted with pines. "This
way," my father said. He seemed to know just where to find the
little walkways that snaked between the houses, through the
dunes, to the beach. I grabbed on to his hand, sick with hope
that the beach would be all right; that it would not disappoint
us as the house had done. On the path we twice ran into people
coming the other way, barefoot, wrapped in brightly coloured
beach towels. They nodded hello. I hoped we were allowed to
be there, and that we didn't look like city people, fresh from
our car. When we emerged at last into soft beige sand, I heard
my father let out a low whistle. The beach stretched uninter-
rupted for miles, to the north and to the south. Between where

we stood and the distant water, a strip of dirty black sand was strewn with driftwood and seaweed. Beyond that, at the water's edge, there was an expanse that was dank and grey, hard-packed; the kind of sand that would suck your jandal right off your foot. I looked to my father and saw that he was pleased. "Now that's what I call an adventure beach," he said. But my mother's arms were folded; she was shuddering, muttering that we would not be allowed to swim without a chaperone. I let go of my father's hand. Was the beach all right or was it not? Vanessa was curling her lip, stepping away from us, and my mother was saying that it was the kind of beach that would take no prisoners. I didn't understand—surely taking prisoners was a bad thing? Okay, my father said, but wasn't my sister old enough, at fifteen, to be a chaperone? My mother shook her head. "Adult chaperone," she said. "Case closed." My father didn't exactly roll his eyes so much as cast them sideways. He'd been looking forward to a summer of crosswords and jigsaw puzzles and watching cricket on the television, not chaperoning children at the beach. My mother saw his face and said, "I'll do it. I'll be the chaperone." She still had her arms wrapped around herself; she had not moved more than a foot from the dunes.

"But Mum," I said. "I'm going to want to swim all day, every day."

"Then that's what I'll do, Ally-pally," she said. "I'll sit here all day, every day, if need be. I won't let you out of my sight."

Ally-pally was my mother's pet name for me. When she used it, she meant that we were on the same side, in a thing together. But I didn't believe it; I believed she'd grow tired of chaperoning, and would begin to say, "one swim a day," and "only for an hour." My father sighed, as if he thought the same. I dropped my towel and began to walk toward the water. In the waves I could see heads bobbing about, could hear shouts of fear and laughter. When I glanced around to see if anyone would stop me, I saw that my father and sister were leaving already—they were picking their way back through the dunes. Only my mother remained, standing where we'd first emerged, hugging herself in the cool breeze that flowed under the pines.

TWO·

Early the next morning my father asked me if I'd like to go with him to check out the lagoon. I was the only one up and dressed—my mother was drinking coffee in bed, and my sister was in the bathroom, washing her hair. We walked out onto the street and turned right, away from the beach, following the footpath. It was a clear morning and my father said we were "in for a cracker." He had a long stride and I had to trot to keep up. When we came to a junction in the footpath, I thought we might be lost, but we turned right again. The footpath petered out. We waded through tall grass, down a sloping bank, toward a wall of flax bushes. We *are* lost, I thought, but my father carried on, pushing through the flax, revealing at last the lagoon, flat and quiet as a bath.

"What do we do now?" I asked.

The water was black; clogged at the edges with a mix of rotten branches, flax roots, weeds and mud. A lurid green slime grew in places. On the other side I could see a footpath. On our side there was nothing.

My father frowned. "I have an idea," he said.

I had learned to be wary of my father's ideas. We were standing on uncertain ground, with only jandals on our feet. My naked toes were inches from the water.

"I could go back to the house and get the little boat."

"The . . . boat?"

"We could use it to get to the other side," he grinned. "We could explore the lagoon by boat."

I looked across the black water. On the other side there were tracks where people had launched boats or maybe canoes, but I couldn't see how it could be done on our side.

"Am I supposed to wait here?"

"Yes. It'll only take a minute. Don't move, I'll be right back."

I hadn't been waiting long when across the lagoon, I heard a noise. It was a boy, chubby, with short hair that looked as if it might curl. A Māori boy whose brown skin was pale in places where it had burned and peeled. He was wearing a small greenstone carving around his neck, and he was carrying a long stick with a natural fork at one end. He was close to the water's edge, barefoot, about my age, and alone. I envied him that stick. It wasn't every day you found a stick like that, and when you did, it was rare for your mother to let you keep it. I watched him lift slime out of the water with the forked end of the stick, and then I watched as he flung the slime far across the lagoon. It made a nice *plop* when it landed, sinking under its own weight. Eventually he flung the slime in my direction, and our eyes met. He seemed not to find it strange—a girl hanging on to a flax bush, alone, on the side of the lagoon that was muddy and difficult. No words were exchanged, not even a nod given, but when he went back to his slime-flinging, he was more self-conscious about it. When he couldn't hook a decent payload of slime, or when it slipped off the stick before he could fling it, he muttered excuses under his breath, and once or twice—after a particularly impressive fling, or a really loud *plop*—he glanced proudly in my direction.

I was relieved when I heard my father huffing and puffing on the other side of the flax, and knew I wouldn't have to be the boy's audience any longer.

"Coming through," my father said. With the little aluminium boat balanced on his head, he began to crash through the flax. I closed my eyes because I didn't like to see him fail—especially didn't want the boy to see him fail. Around me, the flax bush shook—I heard its leaves squeaking along the sides of the boat. Then there was a hollow smack. My father had made it through the flax—he'd flipped the boat right off his head and landed it in the water, directly at my feet. "Get in," he said. He had cobwebs in his hair, and sweat trickling down his nose. I looked at the water. My moment to get in was passing. The boat was drifting slowly away from the bank. With an impatient sound, my father stretched one of his long legs out, hooking the boat with his toe.

"Get in," he said again.

I didn't want to get in—I couldn't see how. Across the lagoon, the boy had dropped his stick in the grass and was standing, watching. I reckoned I could guess what he was thinking—*stupid girl isn't brave enough to jump.* I closed my eyes and leapt right off the slippery bank, landing off-centre in the boat. It rocked and rocked, and I thought for sure I was going to lose it, but then I remembered to get down low and grab the sides of the boat with both hands. There wasn't time for celebration though—in the commotion, the boat had moved even further from the bank. My father was busy retrieving the oars from the other side of the flax. I cried out for him to hurry, jerking the boat with my own body weight, trying to move it closer to the bank. But each jerk only seemed to put me further from where I wanted to be. Behind me, the boy was still watching. My father emerged on the bank with the oars. "Okay," he said. "Ready?"

I saw what he was going to do—he was going to throw me an oar. The oars were small, lightweight—aluminium with a bamboo paddle—but still, I was convinced I wouldn't be able to catch one. Not even standing on two feet on firm ground could I ever catch one. "Ready?" he said again. I shook my head and he threw the oar. Bending down low he threw it flat toward the boat, paddle first. It sailed like a dart straight into my shins. "Sorry," he said. It hurt a lot, but I was so glad to have the oar in my possession, I hardly flinched. First thing I did was stick the wrong end in the water. The boat moved further away from the bank. Embarrassed, I turned it over. Still it didn't work—the boat moved another foot in the wrong direction.

"Other side," my father said. "Other side of the boat."

I did as he said, plunging the paddle in on the other side, and to my amazement, the boat moved closer to the bank. "That's the girl," my father said. I felt a surge of pride so pure I could burst. With another push, I came within inches of the bank.

My father stepped out over the water, placing one foot in the boat. He stayed like that for a moment, steadying himself, and then he lifted his other foot off the bank and sat down.

And suddenly all was peaceful. I was drifting on the lagoon with my father's gigantic knees pushed up against mine. "Well done," he said. I thought I had never been so happy in all my life. My father seized the oars and started to row. The little boat that had seemed so unpromising on land, on water, flew. We sailed past the boy on the other side—he watched us all the way down the lagoon and around the corner, with his mouth open and his stick lying at his feet.

~~~~

In the afternoon, my mother took my sister and me to the beach. Vanessa set off with her togs under her clothes, as did I, but somewhere along the way, she lost the urge to swim. I think it was the cool breeze under the pines that did it. I begged, but she wouldn't. "It's cold here," she complained. "It'll be warmer in the water," I pleaded. My mother said nothing, only stood, looking to the south, as if expecting to see someone there, or recognize some landmark. "Please, Vanessa," I said, but Vanessa was spreading her towel, arranging herself for sunbathing. "When I get hot enough," she said. I knew she never would. I knew she'd become, or was becoming, one of those people we thought we'd never become—the kind who walk carefully into water, cringing. At home she was generally horrible to me, but I'd thought out here it might be different—she'd swum with me the summer before. I walked to the water in a mood, sulking as I swam, hoping somehow that my sulking would persuade her.

Before long I saw her stand, shake out her towel, say something to my mother, and disappear back, into the dunes.

I swam more freely then—my mood left me. I paid no attention to the shore. It was okay to be alone. I would never become one of those people. I would never spread my towel for sunbathing.

When at last I came out of the water, my mother was gone too.

I tried not to panic. "Never leave a place," she'd told us, on many occasions. "If we ever get separated, stay where you are. I'll find you." But I wasn't sure—now that I was older—if *I* was supposed to find *her*. Had I been swept south by the tide, or north? Had I drifted, or had she? I'd been in the water a very long time; my lips were numb, I was cold. I walked, looking for a dip in the sand that might have been made by my mother's bottom, but every dip looked the same, every stick of driftwood. I was becoming tearful, shivering. I was sure my mother had been sitting on my towel, and now that was gone too.

"Lost? Need help?"

I turned, swallowing my tears. It was a man in a checked shirt and sunglasses. He was standing higher up, in the dunes. He was off the beaten path.

I shook my head.

He took his sunglasses off. That's when I realized he was the same man I'd seen the day before—our neighbour from across the fence, the one who didn't smile. He wasn't smiling now either.

"You look a little lost," he said.

"My mother's looking after me."

"Is she? Are you sure?" He stepped down off the dunes, glancing left and right. "I can't see her anywhere. Can you describe your mother for me?"

I took a step back. I didn't want to describe my mother.

"That means, tell me what she looks like," he added.

"I know what it means."

"Okay, well then—does she wear a hat? Carry a notebook?"

I frowned. My mother was writing a book. That was why she carried the notebook—to write down her ideas. To make sure nothing was forgotten or lost. But her book-writing was a secret. We girls were not allowed to talk about it, or to ask her how it was going.

Still, I had lost my mother, and I wanted her back.

"Yes," I said, "both of those things."

"Ah, in that case I've seen her. She was right here, in the sand." He pointed to his feet. "She might have needed to stretch her legs. She might have gone for a little walk." He took another step toward me. "I wonder what she keeps in that little notebook? Recipes?"

I shrugged.

"A journal? Some ladies like to keep journals." He looked me up and down. "Little girls too."

I shook my head. *Recipes.*

"The problem is they can be distracting—journals, that is. This is a dangerous beach, even for a strong swimmer like you. Your mother might not realize, but we've lost little ones here before."

I took another step back. My heels were in the dirty sand now—shells crushed beneath them. I said, "I think I'll go now."

"Well, now, I'm not sure about that." He frowned, folding his arms across his chest. "I wouldn't feel right about that. A child running around alone without its mother? Why don't you let me walk you home? I think I have an idea where you're staying."

I was shaking my head, stepping back, across the driftwood and the broken shells. I was shivering all over. He reached out a hand. "Come now," he said. "Your mother wouldn't want you catching a cold." He glanced to the south, and his arm dropped. I turned, and saw my mother approaching slowly. Her eyes were down, and she had my towel in one hand, and her notebook in the other. I turned back to tell the man that my mother had come, and that I wouldn't be needing his help, but I was too late. He'd already gone.

THREE

My favourite game in the water was to pretend I was a dolphin. Diving under the waves and popping up again. Diving under and popping up. Dive-pop, dive-pop. I could do this for hours. I tried to dive low and pop high—I wanted my chin to graze the sea floor, and my hips to clear the water. Sometimes I kept my eyes shut for long periods, becoming completely disorientated. I'd open them to find myself facing the horizon, when I thought I'd be facing the shore, or I'd find myself miles down the beach, staring at the wrong trees, the wrong houses, the wrong-coloured towels lying in the sand.

On the third day, when I'd been at the beach for maybe half an hour, I popped up with my eyes shut and heard a voice close to my ear saying, "Hey."

It was too late to halt my next dive—I was under the water

before I'd had time to react. I popped up again, eyes open. It was the boy with the greenstone carving around his neck. The chubby one from across the lagoon. He was startlingly close, bobbing aimlessly in the water. I looked past him, toward the beige sand. My mother, my so-called chaperone—a pale speck at the corner of my eye—was gone.

"Hey." Slightly louder this time, slightly more insistent.

I dived, but this time I didn't pop back up. I let myself drift a few metres, and then I surfaced lazily on my back. He was still there.

"What."

"You're from the lagoon."

I dived for a third time, and this time, I stayed under as long as my lungs would allow. I wondered if he was impressed by my lung-capacity. I wondered if he would tell his family he'd met a girl who was part dolphin.

"I saw you," he said, when finally I popped back up.

"I know."

"Is it your boat?"

I shook my head.

"Your dad's?"

I shook my head again. "The place we're staying."

He nodded, and began to drift away. I dived, thinking, will he be gone when I come up? He was, and I found to my surprise that I was disappointed. He had turned toward the beach and was meandering away—part doggy-paddle, part breaststroke. He was a clumsy swimmer, nothing at all like a dolphin. Thinking fast, I said, "I like your necklace."

I wasn't used to paying compliments to boys.

"It's not a necklace," he said, touching it. "It's a pounamu. A fish hook."

I reddened, thinking I'd offended him. Taking a deep breath, I prepared to dive again.

"Have you seen the memorial?"

I frowned.

"The wooden cross? With the flowers?" He pointed up the beach.

"Of course," I lied. "I've seen it."

"Wanna look at it with me?"

I did, very much. With my mother walking me to and from the beach, and my sister only interested in sunbathing, I hadn't had much of a chance to explore. I had only the vaguest idea what a memorial was. Something to do with birth, or marriage, or death. Something churchy. We weren't churchy people. I dived again, but I didn't stay under very long this time, and while I was under, I moved toward him.

Pop.

"Well, do you?"

I shrugged. "I guess."

"Good. Stop diving then. Just follow me."

~~~~~

"Her name was Charlotte," he said. "She was nine."

I thought then how small and babyish "nine" sounded, now that I was ten, going on eleven. We were standing in front of a small wooden cross that poked out of the dunes not far from the path through the pines. From a distance I'd thought the cross was a thing a child had made—I thought a child had found an oddly shaped piece of driftwood and stuck it in the ground and thrown handfuls of grass and seaweed at it. Closer up, I saw that it had been made with love and care. You could tell that if you yanked hard on that cross it wouldn't budge, and that if a strong man like my father finally did manage to get it out of the ground, you would find as much of it buried underground as there was visible above, and you would find its buried end sharpened to a point like a garden stake. Above ground, the cross had rounded edges and a smooth, waxed finish, bleached white in places by the sun. The stuff that I thought was grass and seaweed was actually a collection of wild flowers, faded and beginning to wilt. These flowers had been carefully threaded through a piece of wire that looped around the centre of the cross.

"She's buried here?"

"No, course not. It's a me*mor*ial."

I nodded as if I knew what that meant.

"How old are you?"

I thought about lying—I would be eleven in a matter of months. But in the end I admitted I was ten.

"I'm twelve," he said. "My birthday was in October."

I wished I'd lied. I was very cold without my towel. I dug my toes into the sand and clenched my fists to bring feeling back to my fingers. I had a million questions, but to ask them all would have given the boy from the lagoon all the power. He was already a whole two years older than me—if I revealed how little I knew about the cross and what it signified, he would become the one who knew stuff, and I would become the one who didn't. I was already that person at home—always needing jokes explained to me, never allowed to know the full story. To hide my ignorance I turned away and forced a yawn, as if memorials—even ones to nine-year-old girls—bored me.

"Your lips are blue," he said.

"I should probably get my towel."

"Where is it?"

"Over there." I pointed to where Vanessa was lying on her stomach in the beige sand.

"Okay, let's go get it."

We clambered down from the dunes and ran across the sand to my sister. It wasn't a race. I *thought* it was a race, and ran fast, the way I always ran when racing boys—with all of my heart. I sprang off the balls of my feet and pumped my arms, but when I got to where my towel was, I looked behind me and saw that he was well behind, and that the effort of running was all over his face—he wasn't trying to hide it. When he caught up to me, he didn't say, "You got a head start," or "I let you win," he just doubled over and panted a while.

Vanessa raised her head one inch off her towel and opened one eye. "Who's this?"

I didn't know his name and I didn't want him to meet my sister, who liked to torture my friends, or, according to her mood, charm them, and torture me instead. I grabbed my towel and pulled it roughly around me. "Someone I met," I said, by way of an answer. "Where's Mum?"

She propped herself up on her elbows. "Dunno. Gone for a walk, I guess."

"I thought she was supposed to be chaperoning us."

"Chaperoning *you*. I'm fifteen, I don't need a crappy chaper- one. So, does this someone have a name?"

I glanced quickly at him, hoping to warn him. My sister was looking him up and down, deciding whether to torture him, or charm him. I felt we had woken a sleeping lioness, and in doing so, had turned ourselves into fat, juicy prey. But the boy from the lagoon stepped forward and said: "My name's Kahu, and your back is really sunburnt."

"It is?" She twisted around to look at her own back. "Shit, it is too—I fell asleep." I realized that by turning Vanessa's atten- tion to her favourite thing in the world—her own body—Kahu had disarmed her. "So," she said, twisting back to face us, "what are you two doing?"

We looked at each other and shrugged.

"We thought we might hang out for a bit," I said.

Vanessa gave me a look. It was a dead kind of look, empty behind the eyes. I knew it well—it was the look of a cat about to pounce. I had made a mistake. By thinking that my sister was in a good mood, and that Kahu had won her over, I'd walked straight into one of her traps—I'd admitted that I wanted to "hang out" with a boy, and I'd used the word "we," as if he and I were something more than just two dumb kids who had nothing better to do. The last time I'd seen my sister with that dead look in her eyes she'd asked me, in front of our older boy- cousins, if I knew what a vagina was. I lied—I said that I did know what it was. She asked me to point to one. "Go on," she said. "Point to a vagina." I remember the way they burst into fits of giggles—even my older cousins, who were young men of sixteen and eighteen, not usually given to giggling. I was caught in a lie, but it was something more than that—something else about *vagina* that was ugly and sinister, and I didn't know; I hadn't the faintest clue. I remember looking around and, in desperation, pointing toward the window—I thought whatever it was, it was bound to be out there somewhere (to me it sounded like the kind of flower my mother planted in shady spots under trees). I remember that the moment only passed when an adult entered the room to tell us that dessert was ready. I remember eating the dessert, but being unable to taste it, and after that, I felt differently about my boy-cousins. My sister had turned them against me, and the worst part was that I didn't even know how she'd done it—I didn't know what *vagina* was.

Now she was looking up from her towel with the smallest smile on her lips, deciding whether to skewer me in front of my new friend. I braced myself for what was about to come, but then she yawned, closed her eyes, and put her head back down on her towel. "Well? Are you two going to piss off or what?"

We ran—back the way we'd come, toward the dunes. I got the feeling Kahu knew, without me having to tell him, how close we'd come to disaster. This time I slowed down—I didn't try to race. We got to the dunes and sat down. The sand there was cool and welcoming. I was so relieved that Vanessa had decided not to skewer me, I allowed myself a question. "So, where is she buried? This Charlotte-person."

"She's not."

"She's not buried anywhere?"

"She was never found. My uncle said it happens a lot with drownings. He said she ran off to the beach—this was a couple of summers ago. She didn't have permission from her mum, and

the waves were really high that day. That's why you always have
to get permission, even if you know how to swim." Kahu picked
up a stick and dug it into a clump of damp sand, snapping it in
half. I did the same—the sticks that lay in those dunes snapped
easily, and made a pleasing sound when they did. We sat cross-
legged in the sand at the edge of the dunes, snapping sticks,
until we couldn't find any more that were long enough to snap.
Then he stood, brushed the sand off his bottom, put his hands
on his hips, and said, "Wanna help me find the body?"

~~~

All sorts of things might have happened to the girl's body after
it had drowned, Kahu said. It might have been carried out to sea
to be battered by the hulls of large ships and nibbled at by passing fish. Or it might have been eaten whole by a shark, or got
snagged on a boat-wreck, or stuck on a reef. Or it might have
washed up, weeks after the police had stopped looking for it,
or it might simply have got itself lodged somewhere they never
properly looked—like in the lagoon.

"Why wouldn't they have looked in the lagoon?" I asked.

"I don't know—maybe they did. But maybe not very well
because the sea doesn't flow into the lagoon," he said. "They're
pretty much cut off from each other."

"So how would the body have got there?"

"I reckon if it rained a lot and everything flooded, or if high
tide was a bit higher than usual, and the body slipped over. Or if
it slipped through a crack somewhere."

"A crack?"

"An inlet. I asked my uncle, could a body get from the sea to a lagoon? And he was like, 'I don't know, probably. You never know with water.' That's what he said. 'Try keeping water out of anywhere.' My uncle's a fisherman. He knows everything there is to know about water, and fish, and all that stuff. One time, he saw a great white shark. You know what a great white shark is? You seen *Jaws*? They're the worst—the absolute worst. My uncle had one come right up to the propeller of his boat like it wanted to bite the boat in half. He said its eye was like a black hole, real scary, but then the eye rolled back, and that was even worse. My uncle called it a 'brown-trouser moment.' That means he nearly pooped his pants. And another time, he reckons he saw a body. But by the time they circled back, it was gone. Carried away by the tide. He reckoned it was a fisherman who was swept off a rock and never found. That's what he said. My uncle knows everything about boats and tides and stuff like that. But don't worry—I checked the lagoon already. I went right along the edge with a big long stick."

"I saw you."

"Oh yeah, you did. I guess if we could borrow your boat, we could run the stick through the middle of the lagoon. She might have got caught up in the weeds. And another thing we could do is borrow my uncle's dogs. He has two dogs—Dotty and Scottie. German shepherds. We could take one each, and look for the body that way. Whenever bodies get found, it's usually by fishermen and people walking dogs. That's what my uncle told me."

I didn't want to borrow the uncle's dogs. I didn't want the dead girl to be in the lagoon behind our house. I didn't want her to be washed up in the surf, not far from where I swam, and I didn't want to think of her caught on a rock on the sea floor. I thought if I swam over her, her hair would tickle my toes like seaweed. I didn't want her to be anywhere we were looking—but I wanted to keep looking. It was fun. Kahu was fun—he knew a lot, and unlike my sister, he managed to tell me what he knew without making me feel stupid for not already knowing it.

"Why do you want to find the body?"

"Why not? It's interesting. My uncle would be really proud. If we find it, we'll be on the six o'clock news, and the front page of the newspaper, plus, we'd probably get to meet the prime minister and maybe even the Queen. I think there's a special medal you get for finding a body—I'm pretty sure of it." We had reached a part of the beach I'd never explored before, where a large concrete pipe trickled sludgy water into a shallow ditch in the sand. Kahu placed one hand on the top of the pipe and leaned in. "I've never seen a dead body in real life before, have you?"

"No." In my head I had decided I would go no further than this pipe. On the other side the beach looked different—tidier and brighter. The dunes gave way to the row of large houses I had seen from the street—the lucky houses, with views of the ocean from every window, and gates opening right onto the sand. At the same time the beach narrowed, so that there was only the beige sand at the top and the dank sand at the bottom—none of the driftwood in between. I knew I had already gone much further than my mother would allow, and now, I feared that Kahu was going to ask me to look for the girl in the black throat of the pipe. "What is this thing anyway?"

"Stormwater," he said, straightening up. "I'm sure the police would have . . ."

"Yeah, they would have. With torches and stuff."

"And dogs."

"Yeah. Sniffer dogs. And volunteers."

"If I'd been here, I definitely would have volunteered," Kahu said.

"They wouldn't have let you—you're a kid."

He thought for a moment, nodding. "Yeah, I guess. It's only this year I've been allowed to come and stay with my uncle alone. My mum and dad don't get much time off in summer. My uncle's lucky—he's got money *and* he gets time off. He has a boat and everything."

"You said that already."

"Yeah, I guess I did."

Kahu had clambered up onto the pipe and was looking southward, to the brighter part of the beach. It was easy to imagine a body washed up in the debris on *our* side of the pipe, but hard to imagine one going unnoticed under the gaze of those glass-fronted houses. "I think we've done enough looking here," he said.

I was so relieved about not having to go into the throat of the pipe, and not having to go any further than the pipe, that I clambered up on top of it too. "It's different on that side," I said.

Kahu nodded. "I like our side better."

"Me too."

"It's more . . ."

But neither of us had the word for it. More *real*, I thought. More "not taking of prisoners," whatever that meant. We were about to climb down off the pipe when I saw a familiar figure standing on the clean sand further south. How I recognized this figure from such a distance, I'm not sure. It was something about the slope of the shoulders, the particular tilt of the head. My mother, lost in thought. Turning circles in the sand. I squinted down the beach, one hand shading my eyes. Something told me not to yell out. Something told me that this figure, whether it was my mother or not, wanted to be left alone.

"Are you coming?"

"Hang on," I said, waving at Kahu to wait.

The figure I had thought was my mother had been joined by another; slightly taller. I wished I had seen from which direction the second figure had come, but I had missed that part, and now the two figures were embracing.

"You know those people?"

"I'm not sure," I said.

The two figures were becoming one. Their hips and chests had joined so that there was no light between them, and now their faces were joining too.

"Well, who is it?"

The second figure wasn't tall enough to be my father, who was six foot two.

"No one," I said, sliding down off the pipe. "No one I know."

FOUR

Later that day it rained. We drove to a large shopping centre thirty minutes away. My parents planned to stock up on groceries, and my mother also wanted typewriter ribbon, and some more paper for her book-writing. At the holiday house, my mother wrote her book in the afternoons and evenings, on a big heavy typewriter we'd brought all the way from Wellington. My father had lugged it down to the car, where it had sat off-kilter in the boot, on top of the beach towels and pillows, so that every time we went over a bump in the road, it made a little dinging sound. As we were driving to the shopping centre my father said to my mother, "You should really let me photocopy that book of yours." My mother's book existed only in her head, and on the paper that issued from her typewriter. "As insurance," he said. "Should anything happen." But my mother shook her head. "Imagine if you left it on the bus," she said. "Imagine if someone saw it."

While my mother and father went to look for what they needed, Vanessa and I were allowed to roam by ourselves, spending our holiday money.

Despite the promising sprawl of the shopping centre from the outside, inside we found only a chemist, a bookshop, and a tiny toy shop crammed to the ceiling with beach balls and plastic spades. All the other shops sold things like napkins and toasters, or they were places you went to have your power tools sharpened or to get keys cut. Vanessa knew the only thing I was interested in was cassette tapes—I was the proud owner of a fire-engine red Sony Walkman, which I had brought on holiday with me, along with my one and only cassette tape: *True Colours* by Split Enz. My Walkman had smooth, rounded edges, headphones cushioned in foamy black sponge, and on the back, my name etched carefully into its hard plastic shell with the sharp end of a bobby pin. It was my most prized possession in all the world, and more than anything I wanted more tapes to put inside it, more albums by Split Enz. My sister had a Walkman too; blue, with no name on it. It wasn't a thing she cherished. For a few minutes she humoured me, traipsing the mall, searching for a music store, and then she grabbed my hand and pulled me toward the chemist. She had thirteen dollars and she wanted make-up, which she was forbidden to wear. At the chemist, she found a mascara for nine dollars and fifty cents. It was black with gold lettering up one side—a very expensive, very grown-up thing. Our mother's mascara, from memory, had lost all its lettering long ago, and had a bent wand. "Are you buying it for Mum?" I asked. Vanessa just blinked, as if the question was beneath her. Of course, I knew she wanted the mascara for herself—the question was my way of reminding her that she wasn't allowed make-up. "It would be all your money," I said, "or almost all of it." I did some maths quickly in my head. "You'd only have three dollars fifty left." Did I need to remind my sister that if she spent all her money in one go, our mother would be bound to find out, and would want to know where the money went? "I might go back to the supermarket," I said, but Vanessa grabbed my wrist and squeezed it hard. "We're not allowed to split up," she said. I felt myself growing hot. Tinkly piano music was playing over the sound system in the chemist, making me want to pee. The ladies behind the counter had their eyes on us. "Why don't you get a cheaper one?" There were cheaper mascaras in bright purple packaging on a lower shelf. They had fun names like Beach Babe and Party Princess, and they cost only five dollars fifty. *I* could afford one. "They're for babies," Vanessa said.

I looked toward the counter and smiled. Not long ago I had been able to make any shop assistant smile at me no matter what—just by looking at her or opening my eyes very wide, I could make her smile. But not any more; I was growing out of that. One of the ladies behind the counter gave me a look that said, *I'm watching you.*

"Vanessa? Vanessa Owen?"

We turned toward the voice that had spoken my sister's name as if it was a bit of a lame joke. It was the voice of a girl I recognized vaguely as being someone from our neighbourhood in Wellington, who caught the same bus as Vanessa in the mornings, but never walked with her to the bus stop or waited with her on the bus-stop seat. She had long, blonde hair that was cut short around her face—my mother would have called it a "sophisticated" haircut.

"Crystal."

I had never met anyone called Crystal—I didn't even know that name-wise, "Crystal" was an option. I thought my sister was saying out loud the name of a make-up brand or perhaps a perfume. But the blonde girl tossed her hair and came closer, peering at the mascara in my sister's hand. "Is it indigo?"

Vanessa shook her head. "My mum would notice indigo."

"Oh yeah, true, but she'll notice black too. If incognito is what you're going for, I'd get brown."

My sister put the mascara back on the shelf and pulled out another one that looked identical in every way to the first. I was a little lost in this conversation; still grappling with *Crystal*, and now *indigo* and *incognito*.

"Gonna get it?"

"I don't know—it's all the holiday money I have left, plus my pocket money."

Crystal looked briefly toward the counter. "I didn't say are you going to *buy* it. I said are you going to *get* it."

I had been led to believe that I was a smart kid, but Crystal seemed to talk to my sister in a language I barely recognized, with a tone that slid from bored to amused and quickly back again. At first, she had struck me as very pretty, but now I saw that her nose had a bump in it about halfway down, and the skin seemed stretched over that bump as if it might split. I wished then that I could pull Vanessa aside and say, *You're prettier than her, you don't have to do what she says.* But my sister was looking down at the mascara in her hand, listening closely to everything Crystal said. "Um, I don't know," she said.

"Go on, *get* it," Crystal said. "I'll even be your wingman."

"My wingman?"

"Sure." She grabbed a can of hair-lightening spray off the shelf. "Ready?"

Crystal walked directly to the counter, carrying the hair-lightener. In a loud voice, I heard her say to the two ladies there: "I heard this stuff rots your hair." The women leaned forward to take the can from Crystal and pore over the small print on the back—one even reached out to touch a strand of Crystal's hair. "You're a natural blonde, so you won't need much," she said. Beside me, Vanessa suddenly turned and walked away, toward the exit. I was used to my sister abandoning me without a word, so I hurried after her, but it surprised me the way she kept on walking, not looking behind her to check that I was there; not waiting to say goodbye to Crystal. She walked and walked with her hands tucked into her chest and her head down, all the way across the mall until we were about halfway back to the supermarket, and then she veered left and leaned against a wall with her back to me. I wondered if she was trying to get away from Crystal—maybe she'd noticed the slightly teasing way she'd spoken her name: "*Vanessa Owen?*" I hovered behind her, not wanting to see her face in case she was crying.

Then, to my surprise, Crystal was back. She came running up behind us, laughing, and punching my sister's shoulder twice. Vanessa turned, and I saw that she wasn't crying at all—she was laughing. Her eyes were wide and excited. "Oh-my-God-oh-my-God," she kept saying, and then, "Jesus!"

At home we weren't allowed to say "Jesus," and only just got away with "oh my God."

"First time?"

"Yes! Oh my *God*!"

"Such a rush, right?"

Vanessa looked back toward the chemist. I looked too—there was nothing happening over there, and I didn't understand.

"I don't even care about the stuff, I do it for the rush," Crystal said. "There's nothing like it. Well, *almost* nothing."

My sister laughed in that fake way she laughed when, like me, she didn't really understand a joke. I knew then that I wasn't the only one who was struggling to keep up with Crystal. Feeling brave, I said in a sarcastic tone, "What's the big deal?"

Crystal and Vanessa both took a second to look at me, and then both burst out laughing.

"So," Crystal said, "you're here for the holidays, or just passing through?"

"The holidays," Vanessa said.

"Street?"

Vanessa couldn't remember the name of our street, but I could. "Palmer Street," I said.

Crystal shrugged. "Maybe I'll see you round."

She punched my sister on the shoulder one more time, and then she was gone, swinging her hair across the shopping centre. I noticed that her hands were empty—she hadn't bought the hair-lightener. I thought then that I would never understand what had just happened, or any of these words: *wingman*, *indigo, incognito.* But later, I did understand. Later that evening the rain finally cleared, and the sun burst through the clouds, and my father said that if I was quick about it, he'd take me to the beach for one last swim before dinner. I ran to the little bedroom I shared with Vanessa, where I started flinging my clothes around and shucking off my sandshoes. One shoe flew right under my sister's bed. I got down on my hands and knees to retrieve it, and that's when I saw, hidden behind a bed-leg on the floorboards, the glistening black tube of mascara with the gold lettering down the side and the price still attached to it: nine dollars fifty. I stared at it for the longest time, holding my breath, until Dad started calling me, saying we were running out of time to get to the beach. How did that black tube get to be under my sister's bed? And did she know it was there? I thought about it the whole time I swam, and all through dinner and dessert, and then, when we were getting ready for bed and my sister was brushing her teeth, I snuck a look at her wallet and saw that she still had thirteen dollars in there, and I also noticed the way—just before we turned out the light—my sister leaned out over her bed for a moment, touching her hand to the floor very quickly, as if checking something.

I lay awake for many hours after that, listening to my Split Enz tape on repeat, debating whether I should tell my parents. Twice I threw the covers off and swung my legs out. But I knew that if I told them what I thought Vanessa had done, it would change the course of our holiday, and maybe our lives. I was ten—I'd never changed the course of anything. Besides, it wasn't Vanessa who was to blame, it was Crystal. Alone, my sister would never have stolen the mascara.

FIVE

Most nights my father cooked sausages or lamb patties on a little three-legged charcoal burner he'd owned since the first days of his marriage to my mother. At the front door of the holiday house there was a concrete patio, about ten feet by four feet, and my father would stand out there in his yellow plastic apron and tiny shorts, coaxing the coals to life with a glass in one hand and a pair of long metal tongs in the other. I eventually got sick of sausages, but I ate a lot of fluffy white bread and a lot of corn, which my mother cooked on the stove in a chipped enamel pot.

Sometimes my mother would drag one of the kitchen chairs out onto the patio and sit close to the barbecue, out of the drift of the smoke, so that she could talk to my father while he cooked. They'd put a cask of wine on the ground and take turns filling their glasses from the little plastic spout. On those nights,

I usually hung around, sometimes with my headphones on and my cassette tape playing, sometimes not. Sometimes I lay in the grass, cooling my sunburn. Sometimes my parents knew I was there, and sometimes they didn't.

On one such night I was outside, following a grasshopper around the lawn, and I'm pretty sure my parents had forgotten I was there. It was a game of mine to torture grasshoppers—to trap them under a glass and watch their hopping grow frantic, to put my ear down to the glass and listen to the *tap-tap-tap* of their desperate attempts at escape. Once, I left a grasshopper under a glass for three days, to see if it would suffocate. When I lifted the glass on the third day, the grasshopper, which I had thought was dead, leapt right into my hair. In my panic to get it out, I squashed it under my hand.

That night, I was trying to trap a grasshopper when I heard my mother say to my father, "I believe her name was Charlotte."

My ears pricked up. The grasshopper I had been stalking for more than twenty minutes leapt away without a sound. My father said, "You take your eyes off them for one minute . . ."

"They think it must have been a rip," my mother replied. "Or a freak wave."

"Nobody to blame, then."

"Evidently the mother blames herself anyway. The child had a habit of running off. There was a group of . . . what do you call them? People who wander along, looking for stuff on beaches?"

"Scavengers."

"No, that's not it. Something else."

"Drifters, hobos, bums."

My mother chuckled. "Yes, okay, if you like, although I

think you're being a little harsh. I like wandering along the beach—does that make me a bum? No, I'm sure there's another word for it. Anyway, a group of these people spotted the girl heading into the pines—you know that line of trees on the ridge above the beach? They were on the road and they spotted her, but they didn't try to stop her, or ask her where her mother was. I mean, kids run about, don't they? We don't always intervene."

"Where'd you hear all this?"

My mother ignored the question. "That's the last anyone saw of her. Running into the pines in her togs, and all because of a lost Barbie doll, apparently."

"A what?"

"Apparently she'd lost a doll on the beach. A Disco Barbie, is what I heard. She'd been pestering her mother about it but the mother thought it might be at home, and then as soon as her back was turned the little girl took off back to the beach to look for it."

"Beachcombers," my father said.

"What? Oh yes, you're right. The local beachcombing club. Apparently they're quite active around here, cleaning up beaches. One or two of them even have those metal detectors." She chuckled again, but the chuckle had a hollow sound. "I'm sure they must be kicking themselves for letting her run off like that. The family were only supposed to be visiting for the summer, but now the mother lives here alone. Refuses to go home without her daughter. Can you imagine?"

My father, crouching to refill his glass under the plastic spout of the cask, muttered that he could not imagine, and furthermore, he didn't want to.

"I've heard she maintains some sort of shrine to the girl. Somewhere on the beach."

My father tutted, and then reached for my mother's glass, which he began to fill also.

"She puts flowers there, at least once a week. Quite a hopeless figure, by all accounts—the mother, that is. Quite bereft. Shuffles around the place in some ancient coat. I'm not surprised, of course. I'd be the same."

"Best not to think about it. Our girls are strong swimmers. Even Vanessa, when she tries."

My mother agreed, nodding and sipping her wine. Her legs were crossed, and her foot was going back and forth through the air.

"Besides," my father said, "it's not as if they're unsupervised. You're chaperoning them. With you there, I really can't see how anything could go wrong."

My mother's foot went still, just as the grasshopper, dumb as dirt, leapt back into view.

I slapped my glass down, trapping it.

~~~~

"I reckon she was mad at her mum and thought she'd have a go at running away. Is that what you reckon too?"

I shrugged. It was the day before New Year's Eve, and Kahu and I were picking our way through the muck behind some boatsheds—the ground here was cold and marshy and dozens of black, speck-like creatures hopped and darted at our ankles. We were further north than we'd ever been before—we'd passed the part of the beach that was thick with swimmers, and had passed as well a long, shed-like building with a sign on it that said SURF LIFESAVING CLUB.

"Sometimes I get mad at my uncle and I think about climbing out the window," Kahu was saying, "but I just know one of my stupid cousins would see me and rat me out."

I had not yet been to Kahu's house, or met his cousins or uncle. Our arrangement was simple: we would try to meet at the wooden cross every morning. We couldn't be specific about time, and had no way of getting hold of each other. There was a phone at the holiday house, but I wasn't sure if I was allowed to use it, and besides, neither of us knew our phone numbers. Kahu said anyway that the phone at his uncle's house was constantly in use—his aunties spent hours, he said, gossiping to their friends.

So far, the arrangement had worked, and we had spent our mornings together, splitting up around lunchtime. But I felt that there could come a day when it would fail—I would go to the cross and find him missing.

"I think she climbed up on that stormwater pipe and slipped and bumped her head and that was it," I said. I drew a finger across my neck and stuck my tongue out the side of my mouth to indicate: dead. Kahu nodded seriously. He always took what I said seriously—I liked that about him. I had only just thought of the stormwater-pipe idea, but now that I said it I quite liked it. A quick death, carried away by the waves.

"I'm going up there," I said, pointing away from the boatsheds toward higher ground, where the marshy field met the road, and the sand underfoot gave way to dirt.

"You reckon a body'd go all the way up there?"

"Oh yeah, for sure," I lied. "Tides and all that."

I left Kahu frowning in the sludge behind the boatsheds. The truth was that sometimes he was the brave one, and sometimes I was. Only an hour earlier I had convinced him to swim under a rotted-out old jetty with me, feeling our way along the lichen-covered boards in the near-dark. "She's bound to be under there," I'd said. I had truly believed it, and I think so had Kahu, because just before we went under his eyes got really big, and I noticed he stayed behind me the whole time, and when his hand accidentally brushed my foot he made a little yelping sound, which I was careful not to tease him about.

Now, though, I wasn't feeling so brave. The muck behind the boatsheds felt promising. I felt this might at last be it—the place where we'd find the body.

I kept walking away from the boatsheds until the ground hardened and I saw wild flowers growing, and a low fence that bordered the road. Part of the fence was actually a long, hinged gate, and I saw tracks in the grass where cars had been through, and on the gate, facing the road, a sign that said PRIVATE PROPERTY—KEEP OUT. This worried me, but Kahu and I had entered the field from the beach, ducking past the boatsheds and wading through shallow water to get here, so was that trespassing or not? I glanced over my shoulder at Kahu and waved, but he didn't see me because he had his head down, searching. I kept moving forward, watching Kahu and waving, but he never waved back, and when I finally gave up and turned toward the road, there was a figure right in front of me, standing with her back to me in the field near the fence.

A woman, bent over a crop of purple flowers.

I almost cried out. The sign on the fence said KEEP OUT. What if this was the owner of the field, and what if the owner of the field was a witch? Come to think of it, there was something witchy about her. For one thing she wore a long bulky raincoat with a frayed belt that hung from a single loop. The dirty end of the belt lay on the ground like the discarded skin of a desert snake. It was a hot day—I was wearing nothing but togs with a pair of thin cotton shorts pulled over the top. Why did the woman need a coat? In the cop shows I watched on television, bad guys always hid their guns under coats like this one.

I began to back away, carefully, so as not to make a sound. I thought I could back my way down to the boatsheds and then turn and splash through the murky water, shouting, "Kahu! Run!"

But almost immediately the woman in the coat heard me and turned, and as soon as she did I knew exactly who she was.

In her hands she held a small posy of wild flowers. Purple, blue, yellow. Worthless, weedy flowers—some were already beginning to droop. But the way she had arranged the colours was pretty, and it reminded me instantly of something I had seen elsewhere. Looking into her eyes, which were a washed-out greyish green, I saw shock—the shock of me, ten years old but small for my age, barefoot in the field in my togs—and then I saw pain, and the pain seemed to well up and overcome her, pushing the air out of her lungs, so that for a moment she appeared to deflate, and sink backwards into the field. She touched the wild flowers very briefly to her chest, and then I watched as, with a great effort, she forced a smile and said, in a sweet, bright voice that didn't match her eyes at all, "Well, hi there."

I was immediately ashamed of what I did next.

I turned and ran. Sprinted away from her, leaping over weeds and shrubs, panting and gasping. Up ahead, Kahu stopped what he was doing and watched me, open-mouthed.

I ran all the way past him, through the shallow water that trickled between the boatsheds and out, onto the beach, where I saw families playing and couples walking dogs—people doing ordinary things—but I kept running until I couldn't any longer, and then I found a patch of empty sand and sank into it, crossing my legs and planting my elbows on my knees, shading my eyes with both hands. I did this even though I knew the woman in the coat wasn't a witch, or the owner of the field, and I knew also that she didn't have a gun, and didn't want to hurt me in any way.

A few moments later Kahu jogged over to where I sat. "I don't want to do any more searching today," I said, before he could speak. He looked a little surprised, but eventually he nodded and sat down beside me.

The next morning, at the clearing in the pines, there were new flowers tucked into the loop of wire around Charlotte's cross. Kahu hardly noticed them, but I did. They were wild flowers, and they were purple, blue and yellow.

~~~~

Later that afternoon, my sister and I heard, coming from the road outside the holiday house, a loud voice. We were all occupied in our separate ways. My mother was in her room, working on her typewriter, my father was snoring on the couch, and Vanessa was sitting cross-legged on her bed with the December issue of *Seventeen* magazine. I was lying on my back on the kitchen floor, listening to *True Colours* on my Walkman. Learning lyrics. Playing songs over and over until I knew every word by heart.

I turned my music up and waited for the voice to go away, but it didn't—it got closer, and if anything, more insistent. I was annoyed. I believed it was bad luck not to let a song play right through to the end. Some songs finished abruptly, but others faded out gradually, and in those cases, I had to be patient and hear out every last note, even if my mother was calling me to dinner, or I was busting to go to the toilet. I pulled my headphones off and listened. In our bedroom, I saw Vanessa move her magazine slowly to one side and climb off her bed. The voice was right outside our house now. In my parents' bedroom, my mother stopped typing.

We looked at each other—my sister and me. The voice was calling, "Vanessa."

I scrambled up. Vanessa ran to the front door, while I went to the kitchen window. My heart was pounding. I had worried for days that someone would come for her—a store security guard, or a police officer. The black tube of mascara was still lying unopened under her bed—I checked daily. My mother's bedroom door opened. She looked pale and irritated, as she often did when she'd been writing.

"Vanessa . . . ?" she said.

Vanessa threw open the front door and headed out toward the road. On the couch, my father was beginning to stir. It was all about to come out. I felt my hands begin to shake—I had been there that day. I had smiled at the two shop assistants, and had left immediately after Vanessa, trotting to keep up with her. My mother joined me at the window, leaning across the bench for a better look. We watched as Vanessa crossed the grass toward the street. She was barefoot, and wore a white singlet top and tie-dyed shorts. Her hair was mussed at the back because earlier, she'd taken a nap on her bed. Barefoot like that, she looked too young to go to prison, but I'd heard of correctional facilities for children—siblings too perhaps. We watched Vanessa make her way carefully around our parked car, too hot to touch. "Vanessa!" the voice called.

I saw my sister touch her hair.

"Crystal," I breathed.

"What?"

"A girl from school."

My mother frowned. "A friend?"

"Not really. Kind of."

My mother headed toward the front door, muttering. "I've never heard of this *Crystal*. How did she know where to find us?"

I hung back. I still had my Walkman in my hand, and my headphones around my neck. Through the black foam ear cushions, a song was playing distantly. *I* was how Crystal knew where to find us. I was the one who had told her, "Palmer Street." Trying to prove that I was useful in some way—that I knew stuff. I wished like anything I had kept my mouth shut. In the grass beside our car, Vanessa and Crystal were hugging. Crystal was wearing a blue bikini top and denim shorts with frayed hems. Her hair was pulled into a high, side ponytail. She could have stepped straight out of the pages of *Seventeen* magazine. Behind Crystal there was a boy with hair cut short at the front but long at the back and sides, almost down to his shoulders. He was wearing long boardshorts, a beaded necklace, and no T-shirt. I heard Crystal laughing very loudly. She kept laughing even as my mother approached. "It worked!" she was shouting. "I knew the street!" I hated her so much. I hated the brazen way she had yelled my sister's name, and her too-loud laugh. I crept across the kitchen and out onto the lawn. My mother was saying, "You gave us all quite a fright." I was surprised—I thought it was only me who was frightened. I heard Crystal say, "I knew the street but not the number." Next she would blurt out that it was *me* who told her the name of our street. And after that—who knew? Who knew what she was capable of? Aside from Vanessa and me, Crystal was the only one who knew about the mascara.

I turned and began to walk quickly toward the back of the property. It was bad luck, Crystal turning up, and it was my fault. I slipped my headphones back over my ears and tried to whisper the lyrics that were playing, because getting lyrics right was good luck. But it was hopeless, I'd lost my place, I couldn't catch the next line. I ripped my headphones off and pressed "stop"—I didn't even let the song play out. Instant bad luck. I looked up and saw our neighbour. He was leaning over the balustrade of his second-storey deck, his white hair clearly visible in the deepening afternoon shadow. His smile verged on a sneer. "Look out," he rumbled, nodding at Crystal, "here's trouble." I was surprised and annoyed that he'd spotted, immediately, what I thought only I could see—that Crystal was trouble. I wheeled around, back toward the house. That's when Crystal saw me. "Hey!" she called out, waving over my sister's head. "Hey, kiddo!"

Everyone turned to look at me. "Hi," I mumbled.

"Did you spend your money yet?"

"My what?"

"Your holiday money, do you still have it?" She was talking in a high, sing-song voice, as you would to a very small child or a baby.

"Yes, I have it."

"Cool, maybe we can all go back to the mall together. Would that be all right, Mrs. Owen?"

My mother blinked. "Well, sure, maybe one of these days."

"Stuart has a car," Crystal said, pointing at the bare-chested boy. "And a driver's licence. He's seventeen."

"Gosh," my mother said. "Well, we'll see. We might have to—"

But Crystal had turned to me again. "We'll all go along to the mall together," she was saying in that same voice, "I need some stuff from the chemist anyway."

She winked. A long, slow wink, which no one else saw, because Crystal was facing me—she had her back to all the others. Maybe the man over the fence saw it—certainly I felt his eyes on me. Many sets of eyes on me. My mother was frowning. I think she was torn between Crystal's high, sing-song voice, which was a parent-pleasing kind of voice, and the idea of my sister and me riding in cars with shirtless seventeen-year-old boys. I nodded feebly, walking quickly toward the house. Crystal was asking my mother if Vanessa could be allowed to spend some time further up the beach, where teenagers hung out close to the surf lifesaving club. Then she said something else to Vanessa that I don't think my mother heard, or was supposed to hear.

"Tomorrow's New Year's Eve," she said. "The surf lifesaving club will go off."

Inside, my father was sitting up, stretching his arms. I walked straight past him to the bedroom I shared with Vanessa, shutting the door hard behind me. The room was cool and dark. I dropped my Walkman on my bed and got down on the floor on my hands and knees. The stolen mascara was streaked with dust—it hadn't been opened. I grabbed it and climbed onto Vanessa's bed. There was a long casement window above the bed, which we kept open most days because of the heat. I stuck my arm out of the open window and threw the mascara as far as I could. It sailed out across the narrow side-lawn, turning end on end in the air. I wished I'd done it sooner. I wished I'd wiped it for fingerprints first. I waited until I heard it hit the ground with a smack—on the other side of the fence, on the path that led to the lagoon.

SIX

On New Year's Eve, my father wanted to pack up the car early and drive to a waterhole for a picnic and a swim. It was the kind of thing we'd done often on previous holidays, or to mark special occasions. The four of us on a tiny rocky beach at a bend in a river. My father would drive until he thought he'd found a place no one else knew about, and we would try to make our bottoms comfortable on the rocks. Vanessa and I would put aside our squabbling for a few hours, my mother would relax her rules about swimming on a full stomach, and my father would explore the waterhole with us, showing us how to skip stones across water.

This day was different. My father seemed to have a hard time convincing even my mother that the picnic was a good idea. "We've barely spent any time together as a family," I heard him say through the wall between our bedrooms. "The girls have their own lives now," my mother replied. Her voice was cold. She was often tense in the mornings, not saying much until after her daily walk along the beach. For a while there was silence, and then I heard my father's voice. "I really don't know what the big deal is, it's only one day." My mother left their bedroom, walked to the kitchen, and stood with her hands flat on the bench, looking out the kitchen window. I watched her from where I lay in my bed. She seemed to be having some silent conversation with herself. Then she began to set the table for breakfast. "Your father would like to take us for a picnic," she said when we were eating our cereal. Her voice was still cold, but it was bright. Vanessa's shoulders sagged. Her spoon flopped into her bowl, splashing milk.

"Mum," she pleaded.

"I know," my mother said quietly. "I know."

I felt sorry for my father. My mother and sister seemed to want to gang up on him. At school, whenever I saw someone being bullied or cast aside, I would gravitate toward them. I always took the side of the underdog. My father was the underdog now. I resolved not to make a fuss about Kahu, even though I knew he would wait at the cross for me, possibly all morning. Vanessa, on the other hand, decided to make as much fuss as she could. She cried, shouted, stomped and raged, calling it dumb and unfair. She had only just "hooked up" with Crystal, she said, and she wanted to spend the day with her. It was New Years' Eve, for God's sake, she had *plans*—didn't her plans count?

Was this a dictatorship or something?

My father became very angry. In a voice that was barely calm, he threatened to ban Vanessa from seeing Crystal *at all* if she didn't hurry up and get ready.

(That made her get ready so fast she forgot to bring her precious bag full of lotions.)

In the car we were silent. My father's grip on the steering wheel was white-knuckled. We drove for maybe thirty minutes and then he seemed to pick a spot at random, skidding to a halt in a patch of gravel beside the road.

"This'll do," he said, pulling the keys from the ignition.

We stumbled, blinking, into the sun.

Vanessa's mood got better. By the time the picnic hamper was opened for morning tea, and we were treated to the last crumbs of my grandmother's Christmas shortbread, and hot chocolate from a dusty orange thermos, she seemed to have decided that the picnic wasn't such a bad idea. The problem now was my father. I think he was wounded by what had happened that morning. All he'd wanted was for the four of us to have a nice time together in a pretty place. It *was* pretty, but we'd become so used to the adventure beach, with its pounding waves, and all the treasures hidden in its dirty black sand, that we no longer knew what to do with a simple bend in a river. Rock-throwing filled about fifteen minutes, and then we poked around, trying not to look so bored that our boredom would start a fight. Around lunchtime, my father discovered that my mother didn't have her togs with her.

"They're in the car?"

I was standing in ankle-deep freezing water, wondering how much it would annoy my father if I chose not to go any further.

The water, where it got deeper, looked murky and teeming with life. I longed for the cleansing sweep of an ocean wave.

My mother shook her head.

"What? You forgot them?"

She shrugged, waved a hand, and lay back on the rocks. It was clear that she had not forgotten them but had chosen not to bring them. She sat up, moved some rocks around for comfort, and then lay back again. All the time my father stared at her.

"What are you going to do all day without your togs?"

"Lie here. Think."

He stood up. "*Lie here, think*," he muttered. I turned away, lowering my gaze. The murky water suddenly didn't look so bad. Vanessa was standing a short distance away, in the shade of an overhanging tree. She half-turned so that our eyes met.

"I honestly don't know why I bother," he said, throwing his hands up and letting them land back against his thighs with a slap. Then he stomped to the car, losing his footing once or twice on loose rocks. We had parked on a narrow verge of sandy gravel, picking our way down a steep grassy bank to where we had laid our towels. My father took the bank in three strides. I wondered if he was going to drive away and leave us three behind. He had taken angry drives before, but always when I was tucked up in bed, late in the evening, when my parents didn't know that I could hear them fighting. My bedroom at home was under the stairs, just off the hall. From there I heard everything—Vanessa moving around upstairs, the flushing of the downstairs loo, cats hissing on the fence outside my window. Once, after an argument that started in whispers, and ended with the rattle of my father's car keys and the thud of the front door, I thought I heard my mother suck air into her lungs and breathe into the darkness outside my bedroom door, *Keep on driving, why don't you.* But in the morning when I woke, my father was in the bathroom, shaving. He was wearing a neat white shirt, beautifully pressed, and he was humming tunelessly, while at his feet, the sun was making interesting patterns on the floor. I thought then that I must have imagined the thud of the front door, or maybe he'd had to go out for bread, and maybe I'd imagined what my mother said as well—maybe it was just a sigh that I had twisted into something else.

From my position in ankle-deep water I heard my father unlocking our car. I didn't want him to leave us there, in the middle of nowhere with only a half-empty picnic basket and a few tatty old beach towels. On the pretence of looking for a stone to throw, I moved closer to my mother, bending low so that I could see the slope of her cheekbones beneath her sunglasses. There were no tears there, and her forehead wasn't creased. If she thought my father was about to abandon us, she was being very cool about it, lying back on the rocks with her hands folded neatly across her stomach. Up on the gravel at the side of the road, I heard the crunching of my father's footsteps, and the opening and closing of car doors—all of them, one by one, even the boot. I realized then that he was not abandoning us—he was looking for my mother's togs, or something he could fashion into togs. After a while my mother called out, "I know exactly where they are. They're hanging over the towel rail in the bathroom."

There was a brief moment of stillness in which none of us moved and even the cicadas seemed to hold their breath.

"Are you asking me to go get them?"

Even though there was outrage in his voice, I guessed that the correct answer would have been *Yes please, if you would, my dear.* Instead my mother called back, "Of course not, I'm just telling you to stop fussing around in the car. You're not going to find them there."

I swung back to face the water, catching Vanessa's eye again on the way—her eyebrows were up, and she was mouthing something at me—*Here we go*, or *Holy shit*. I pushed off with my feet and plunged head first into that murky water, hardly looking where I was going. It was her fault, all of this. Hers, and my mother's. It was because of them that the day had been ruined. I wasn't going to give Vanessa any comfort, or pretend now that we were friends. I was still on the side of my father.

We arrived home around three p.m. Next door, a party was going on. The deck where my neighbour liked to linger shirtless in the shade was dotted with people, all sitting in the same type of white plastic chair he usually occupied. Pop music was playing lightly, and there was low laughter and a constant rumble of voices. "At least someone's having a nice time," my mother muttered. I couldn't believe she would risk upsetting my father further, and ran ahead to get away from her. As I waited for someone to unlock the door, I thought I saw my neighbour, stooping to fill someone's glass. He was wearing a yellow shirt with short sleeves, and his usually wild white hair was brushed neatly across his head. I stepped inside, feeling dizzy for a moment. The air in the holiday house was stiflingly hot—we'd forgotten to leave a window open. I ran to the bedroom I shared with Vanessa.

As usual, my half of the room was neat and orderly—my bed carefully made, the little suitcase I owned closed and tucked underneath. My nightie folded neatly, stashed beneath my pillow, so that no part of it protruded or could be seen, and my Walkman positioned in the very centre of the bed, with its black foam headphones wrapped protectively around it. Vanessa's side of the room, on the other hand, was chaos. Her sheets twisted and sandy, her pillow off to one side, her clothes strewn about. I kicked off my jandals and jumped onto my bed, happy to be back in the holiday house, which was already beginning to feel like home. I picked up my Walkman and began to unfurl its headphones.

Vanessa walked in, frowning. She moved slowly past my bed—which was by the door—to her bed, under the window. Then she walked back to the door and closed it. Something in the way she moved made me look up from my Walkman.

She pointed to her bed. "What the hell," she said.

I looked. Her bed was so rumpled that at first I didn't see it— I thought it was a crease in the sheets. She pointed again, angrily, at the centre of her bed. "Are you trying to get me in trouble?" I looked harder, and this time, I saw something familiar— something impossible, so that I had to blink several times to believe it. A glossy black tube. The mascara I had thrown out the window, the day before—the one I had watched sail over the fence.

"I didn't . . . I don't . . ."

I had no explanation for it. Vanessa shook me then, hard, leaning over my bed and grabbing me roughly by the shoulders. "You're such a goody two-shoes," she said, through gritted teeth. "You think you're so bloody perfect all the time." I bit my lip—*No, no, I don't, it wasn't me, I didn't touch it*. At the same time, I was confused—I *had* touched the mascara, but only to keep her safe, to keep her out of trouble.

How had it come back?

She released her grip on me, moved over to her bed, and got down on her knees. "If you touch my stuff ever again . . ." she said. I nodded. What she did next I didn't see—I had turned my face away, I was trying hard not to cry. I can only assume that she stashed the mascara back in its original hiding place, on the floorboards under her bed.

SEVEN

It wasn't a good way to end the year. I waited for Vanessa to curl up on her bed with her headphones over her ears and her back to me, and then I slid off my bed and opened the bedroom door. The lounge was empty. My mother was in her bedroom, typing, and my father was outside.

I'd had a whole plan for the day. I'd thought that I'd spend the morning with Kahu, and then lie on my bed listening to music in the afternoon, so that I'd have enough energy to stay up until 12:01, at which point I could say goodbye to 1985, and hello to 1986—the year in which I would turn eleven and enter intermediate school.

Now that plan had been ruined, and I was too restless even to listen to music.

I crossed the lounge and stepped out, into the yard. My father was sitting with his back to me in a chair near the barbecue. He was drinking a beer. I thought about going over to him—clambering up on his knee, nestling into his chest as I'd done so many times before. But the beer made me pause. My father hardly ever drank beer, and never alone. I turned and headed around the back of the house. I would usually have gone to the fence to hide, but the neighbour's party was still in full swing, so I stayed close to the house, hugging the wall, trying to make myself invisible. On the deck next door there were fewer chairs, but the music had grown louder, and those guests that were left were standing, swaying in time to the beat. Around the neighbourhood, I smelled meat sizzling and heard car doors slamming. Other parties were getting started. Kahu had said that his uncle had invited dozens of friends over, and had promised to pay him ten whole dollars in pocket money if he dressed up nicely and helped serve food and drinks. I walked all the way around the back of the house until I reached my parents' bedroom window, at which point I slid down to a sitting position in the grass.

We were not a proper family, I thought, hugging my knees. There was something wrong with us. Inside, my mother was typing furiously. I hated her for it, hated the incessant *tack-tack-tack* of the keys. Was this why she had "forgotten" to bring her togs to the waterhole? Had she been thinking of her typewriter, her unfinished book? My mother had often said that I was a dreamer, just like her. "You'll be a writer one day," she'd say, ruffling my hair. "Just you wait and see." My imagination was as big as a planet, she said, and I spent half my time on this planet—planet earth—and half my time on the other one—planet imagination. I had always loved it when she said things like that—part of me enjoyed, especially, the way it made Vanessa scowl and roll her eyes. (Vanessa was nothing like my mother's side of the family, my mother said, and instead took after my father, who preferred cryptic crosswords to books, and who was good at practical things, like fixing bicycle chains.)

Now I wasn't so sure I wanted to be a dreamer like my mother. Perhaps in 1986 I could be someone new, I thought. A person who was cool and decisive, and better at sports. A person who never got shouted at, or called a "goody two-shoes." Across the fence, the party was winding down, or it was moving on, to some other location. I saw a woman with chin-length grey hair stacking chairs. She looked like someone my grandmother might meet in the city for lunch. She went to pick up the last chair—the one my neighbour usually sat on—but before she could do so, a voice called out from inside. "You can leave that one where it is, Barb," the voice said. "Right you are, Bob," she replied, brushing her hair back from her face. She had a light, pleasant voice, and she was wearing a dress that wrapped around the front. As she turned to go back inside she caught sight of me, sitting on my bottom in the grass.

In 1986 I can be anyone I want to be, I thought.

I dropped my knees and smiled at the woman, who smiled back, and gave a little wave. Then she headed inside, closing the sliding glass door behind her.

~~~~

Later that same night, I woke to find that my Walkman had slipped down between the bed and the wall, and my headphones were tugging at my hair. I sat up, turned my Walkman off, and placed it carefully on the floor beside my bed. That's when I noticed that Vanessa's bed was empty. On her pillow, where her head should have been, there was just a pale depression— no mass of tangled hair, no arm flung out sideways or bent like a frame around her face. The blankets were tidy and flat and the curtains were parted, the window very wide open, so that the room had become chill.

Assuming she was in the bathroom, I waited for the sound of the toilet flushing, or the creak of floorboards between the bathroom and the lounge. If my sister had come down with her period, she might be a long time. She had once locked herself away for more than thirty minutes, while my mother tapped frantically at the door, and had only come out after my mother promised—through the door—to let her skip ballet class.

I waited, but my sister didn't come back, and the more I thought about her, in the bathroom peeing, the more I needed to pee. We weren't close enough to the beach to hear the breaking of waves, but I often *imagined* I heard them. As I tried to stay awake and tried also not to wet the bed, I listened to the waves lapping at our windows even as I told myself it wasn't possible, I couldn't hear them. For hours this seemed to go on, and once or twice I fell asleep and dreamed I had wet the bed in waves, waking with a start only to find the bed dry, my bladder still full, and my sister still not returned from the bathroom.

In the morning when I woke it was 1986 and a beautiful day. I felt between my legs and found them dry. My sister was lying on her side, facing the wall, but unlike last night, our window was closed, and our curtains were pulled. I wanted to say something to her about how long she'd been in the bathroom, but she still wasn't speaking to me after the mascara incident, and besides, she slept so long that day that by the time any of us saw her, I had forgotten all about it.

EIGHT

After New Year's Eve, my sister spent a lot of time with Crystal, hanging out at our place, or at the surf lifesaving club, while I spent a lot of time with Kahu.

The first time I went to Kahu's house we had spent a long morning sifting through debris on the beach, looking for "clues." Kahu thought that somewhere along that stretch of coast there had to be a trace of the little girl, Charlotte, who'd drowned. "You mean like a shoe?" I'd asked, and he'd looked at me steadily for a moment before replying, in a low voice, "No. I mean like a tooth."

I'd looked to the north then, at the miles of dirty black sand that stretched into the distance. How many teeth might be lying there—a whole mouthful? And what about bones? Sometimes we found the brittle bones of birds and fishes in the sand—what happened to the bones of lost humans? Did they wash up one by one—a thigh bone here, a rib—or could a whole skeleton come up more or less intact?

We set about our work, Kahu drawing sections in the sand with a stick he'd found in the debris. *I'll search from here to here—you do that bit, up to that lump of driftwood.* Hours we spent, squatted in the sand, barely talking. My mother passed twice—once heading south, on a walk, and once on her way back. The first time she waved and smiled and the second time she frowned. "Not swimming today?" We were so absorbed in our work that we barely bothered to reply. When we'd gathered enough loot to fill all four pockets of Kahu's swimming shorts, we decided it was time to lay everything out carefully and take a closer look.

"Where shall we go?" Kahu asked. I glanced at my mother, who was sitting in the beige sand. She was staring out to sea, one arm folded across her chest. Her notebook in her lap, her pen in her mouth.

"Your place," I said.

I hadn't told anyone in my family that we were looking for the body of the drowned girl. I felt for sure if I did I'd be laughed at, or told off, or some combination of both.

My mother insisted on walking with us as far as the top of Palmer Street—an agonizingly slow, polite walk, during which she repeatedly asked Kahu if it was all right that I go to his house; would his uncle mind, would there be enough for one extra at lunch, did he want to grab some food from our place along the way? I could feel Kahu growing impatient. His pockets were full of treasure, his answers grew shorter and shorter—I thought I spotted an eye roll. "Mum," I said just once, quietly, to make her stop. Sometimes I hated the way my mother spoke to neighbours and friends, so clearly and smoothly, like a newsreader, or a headmistress directing assembly. As soon as we reached the top of Palmer Street, we waved goodbye to my mother and took off at a sprint.

We need not have worried about "one extra at lunch." When we got to Kahu's uncle's house there were people everywhere— I counted six women in the kitchen, slicing bread and tossing salad, four men in the lounge watching a fishing show on television, and three out in the back garden, throwing sticks for two large dogs while tending a barbecue much bigger and more impressive than my father's. The house was large and bright— a proper house you might live in all year round, with vast leather couches, a shiny white kitchen, and a double garage stuffed full of beach equipment—inflatable doughnuts and waterskis and surfboards. We passed a bathroom where a snorkel set complete with flippers lay discarded on the floor; a spare bedroom where a teenaged boy and girl sat cross-legged and giggling on a single bed (even Kahu seemed surprised to see them); and Kahu's uncle himself, bent low over a freezer in the laundry. "Kahu!" he said, when he spotted us looking for somewhere to lay out our loot. "Where've you been? Your cousins went out on the doughnut without you. They won't be back for hours."

"I don't want to doughnut," Kahu called, pulling me on, toward a room where there was a suitcase open on the floor, and clothes scattered about. "We can work in here," he said quietly, "my aunty won't mind."

We knelt by the bed, arranging our treasure in a wavy line across the blue-and-white striped bedspread. But the haul that had occupied our morning and made Kahu's pockets bulge didn't look like much, spread out on a double bed like that. I'd collected a lot of things that I'd thought were bones, down in the dirty sand. Now, in the soft light of the bedroom, I saw that they were just sticks, bleached white by the sun and polished over time. "They're sticks," I said, rocking back on my heels. "We don't know that for sure," Kahu replied, peering closely at one that was shaped like the letter "T." But I knew that they were sticks, and that Kahu was only trying to make me feel better. Among his finds were a scrap of blue fabric—"It might be from something she was wearing that day"—and a fingernail we got very excited about, but quickly realized was false, and far too big for a little girl like Charlotte.

It was no good, I wanted to say to Kahu. We were just two dumb kids who knew nothing about anything. The little girl probably wasn't even dead. She'd probably washed up in Australia, alive, or been picked up by a ship far out on the ocean.

Behind us, we heard a tutting noise. Kahu's uncle was standing in the doorway, holding a tea towel and a tray of sausages. His hands were pink from the freezer. "Boy, oh boy," he was saying, shaking his head. "Junk and rubbish all over Aunty's bed. What's she gonna say, eh?"

I reached out to begin tidying the bed, stammering apologies, but Kahu put out a hand to stop me.

"They're not rubbish, Uncle. They're clues."

"Clues?" Kahu's uncle came into the room, walked around the end of the bed, and sat down on the other side. The whole mattress tipped in his direction, and several of my "bones" tumbled toward him.

"Clues about that girl who drowned."

"Ah! You're still on the case then. Ka pai, Nephew. It's good to have a project, eh? You two are a proper duo, just like Starsky and Hutch." He waggled his finger between us. "Which one is which?"

"I'm Hutch," Kahu said immediately.

"That makes you Starsky then." He winked at me. I grinned—I had never been allowed to watch *Starsky & Hutch*, which was on after my bedtime, but I was excited to be part of a duo, especially one that included Kahu. Kahu's uncle frowned. "That nail's pretty gross though."

"It's fake," Kahu said.

"Maybe get that off Aunty's bed."

I scooped the nail up quickly, clutching it in my palm.

"Will you be staying for some kai?" he asked.

I opened my mouth to say a string of things my mother had taught me—*Only if that's okay, Mum said it was all right if it's all right with you, Kahu's welcome to come to us instead*—but before I could speak Kahu said, "Yeah, she is."

"Good, good. We've got more than we can eat. Aunty must have buttered a hundred slices of bread, and there's plenty of sausages. I hope you like sausages?"

I nodded that I liked sausages very much, even though I was actually sick of the sight of them; they were all the local shop seemed to stock. Kahu's uncle got up and walked toward the door.

"Did she really drown?" I asked. "And really not get found?"

He stopped. He was still holding the tray of sausages but his hands were becoming less pink. He glanced at me. I could tell he was thinking about what to say—how much to tell me, and how much to keep back. It was a feeling I often had when talking to adults, who said one thing to children, and another thing to each other.

"Waves were this high that day," he finally said, indicating with one hand a point far above his head. "Tangaroa was angry—you heard of Tangaroa?"

I shook my head; I had not.

"Your people would call him God of the sea. The ocean is his place, you see, not ours. Everything we take from it, we take from Tangaroa. Sometimes he takes back. That's why I tell Kahu—you be careful in the water. *Near* the water, even. You never know what kind of mood Tangaroa might be in."

"But why haven't they found her body?" Kahu asked.

Kahu's uncle nodded a while at the floor, pursing his lips. Then he shrugged. "Tangaroa will give her back when the time is right. That's what I think. Other people have their own theories, but I think he's looking after her for now, and he has his reasons. He'll give her back to us when the time is right."

All the way home from Kahu's house, I thought about Tangaroa. Was Charlotte out there still, in the waves? Was she with Tangaroa? I thought about her mother waiting on shore, wearing her drab coat, and tending to the little cross. If I was to vanish, I thought, I wouldn't want my mother to wait for me. I'd want her to write her book and be happy, and I'd want Vanessa and my father to be happy too. I'd want them to pick one day a year—my birthday perhaps—on which to feel sad, and listen to Split Enz songs on repeat, and cry, but otherwise I'd want them to holiday in warm places, wear bright, colourful clothes, and set fireworks on New Year's Eve.

I was thinking about this when I spotted, at a picnic table across the road from the shop, one of my friends from school. A girl called Lucy, except that wasn't her only name. She was Chinese, with a different name her family used for her at home. She was very pretty, with long black hair that she wore in pigtails high on her head, and for lunch every day she brought fried rice or noodles to school instead of sandwiches. For these reasons—the two names, the very high pigtails, and the fried rice—I was fascinated by her. Earlier in the year we had been close enough to play at each other's houses, but then we'd drifted apart—she'd joined a bunch of girls who played skip-rope every lunch hour. I was terrible at skip-rope, which was a pastime I considered dumb and girlish.

Sitting next to Lucy at the picnic table was a small woman with long black hair who must have been her mother. I'd never met her mother, who did the books for a big engineering firm in Wellington. That's what Lucy said—her mother "did the books." I thought my mother would be very interested to hear this, because she loved to read books and was even writing one, but when I relayed this information to my parents, who always liked to know what my friends' parents did for a living, my father said she actually did maths. *Balancing* the books, my father said, as if this explained things. My mother said it was an important job and that Lucy's mother must be very clever to do it. (My father shrugged.) All I knew was that unlike most mothers, Lucy's worked all day at a desk in a big office with her own couch and telephone, while Lucy's father did shift work at the hospital, putting people to sleep with medicine he injected with a needle, often eating breakfast at dinner time, and dinner at breakfast time, and going for days without sleep, but then, to make up for it, going days without having to work at all. My father, who was a manager at the Ministry of Works, viewed the whole arrangement with an air of suspicion—I once heard him say to my mother, after one of my playdates with Lucy, "How much money do those people think they *need*?"

(My mother wasn't having any of that. She said she thought Lucy's mother was "impressive" and "admirable," and that Lucy would grow up with a strong work ethic and "no barriers.")

It was Lucy's father who took care of us when we played at Lucy's house after school—checking every half-hour that I wasn't bored or missing home, and feeding us ordinary stuff like chocolate biscuits (which Lucy loved), but also unusual stuff like haw flakes and White Rabbit candy (which I loved). When Lucy came to my house to play, it was her father who picked her up around five. I remember my mother's surprise the first time it happened—to see a father at the door. He was wearing black shorts much longer than any my father owned, a black T-shirt, and black sneakers with ribbed white ankle socks pulled half-way up his calves. His arms were the colour of weak tea, his legs were hairless, and he wore a thick silver bracelet on his wrist. I remember my mother not understanding at first that he meant to come in—other people collected their daughters with barely a word of thanks (some tooted their horns from the street). Lucy's father talked fast. It was hard to tell sometimes if he was asking, or telling, but any confusion was quickly swept away—he had a loud laugh and he used it often. Once inside the door, he presented my mother with a gift—it was customary in his culture, he said. His gift was a box filled with different varieties of tea. My mother looked at the box, opening it, and carefully examining each of the different flavours, saying, "oh" and "well" and "thank you." She was uncomfortable, I could tell, with this unexpected gift. I felt bad for Lucy's father, because my parents only ever drank coffee, and only kept tea in the house for my grandmother, who drank Earl Grey and nothing else. The teas in the box had names like "Jasmine" and "Oolong," and I felt sure the box would go into the cupboard above the microwave, where my mother kept things she didn't have much use for, like bran flakes and fish oil. "Would you like a cup of tea . . . now?" she asked, and I held my breath in case Lucy's father said yes, because I was pretty sure she was only being polite. "No," he said, "the tea is for you to enjoy. But I'd love a cup of coffee." My mother laughed, which made Lucy's father laugh too. Then Lucy and I got to play a little longer while the adults drank coffee standing up in the kitchen.

The next time my mother saw Lucy's father was a few weeks later, during a special assembly at school. Lucy's father arrived late. He was the only man among a gaggle of mothers. He was wearing jeans and white sneakers, with a soft woollen jersey that hugged his arms. I'd never seen a man dress like this before—my father never wore jeans, only trousers in different shades of brown, usually corduroy, while the only woollen jerseys he owned were the ones my grandmother knitted for him, with big fat cables down the front and scratchy round necks he sometimes pulled at. My mother stood at the back of the assembly hall talking to Lucy's father. Whenever I twisted my neck to look at them, I could find them easily, because Lucy's father was the only man, and the only one whose smooth, pale skin seemed to glow in the shallow light of the school hall. It had turned out that the tea wasn't such a bad gift after all—my mother had got into the habit of bringing the box out every night after dinner, presenting it to my father, saying, "What shall we try next?" I wondered if this was what they were talking about at the back of the school hall—the different types of tea. Soon after that assembly, my mother banned playdates on schooldays because she said I wasn't keeping up with my homework (I was), while Lucy took up skipping, and began to hang out with the girls she skipped with at weekends. Since then I hadn't seen her father, and hadn't seen the tea box either. (I assumed it was sitting in the cupboard above the microwave, emptied of all but the worst flavours.)

I watched Lucy and her mother at the picnic table for a minute, wondering whether I should cross the road and say hello. Would it be possible to include Lucy in our search for Charlotte's body? I remembered, vaguely, that Lucy's parents were stricter than mine. Her house was always quiet, even with her father rushing about; the air always a little too warm. (They had central heating—another thing my father disapproved of. "If you're cold," he'd say, "put on a jersey.")

In the end, I kept walking. Including Lucy in our little gang might complicate things, I thought. To satisfy her parents we might have to pay more attention to our digital watches, and make up stories to account for our time. We might even have to stay dry and clean and bother about things like sunblock. Besides, Kahu and I had only just become Starsky and Hutch— with Lucy around, we'd be Starsky and Hutch and one other.

When I got home my mother was at the kitchen table, typing. I knew not to bother her when she was writing, and I'd already resolved not to tell her anything about Kahu's uncle's house, because I thought she'd be pretty embarrassed when she heard how much food there was, and how she'd wasted her time worrying about "enough for one extra." But I also knew that adults loved to begin conversations with "Guess who I saw" or "You'll never believe who I ran into." My mother and grandmother had conversations like that which lasted for hours, so I walked right up to my mother's elbow and said, "I saw Lucy from school."

My mother always put her hand over her writing when I stood at her elbow like that. I thought it was strange, because it wasn't as if I cared. It wasn't as if I was dying to know what was on the page. She did it now—shifting slightly in her seat, holding her right hand over the few visible lines of type. "What?"

"Lucy, from school. She's here."

There was a moment's pause before she said, "I don't think so."

"Yes, I saw her, at a picnic table, close to the beach."

I could not have been more specific, but my mother shook her head. "I'm pretty sure her mother said something about visiting family for the holidays, and I don't think they have any family in New Zealand, so they couldn't possibly be here."

"Mum, I saw her."

"It would have been a girl who looked like her."

"It wasn't."

"Darling," my mother said, exasperated. "I don't know what to tell you. Chinese people tend to look alike."

I blinked. It was the kind of thing my grandfather sometimes said about Māori people, and when he did, the whole room would go quiet for a few moments, my father would cough, and my mother would look down at her lap. I wanted to stamp my feet and say no, it *was* Lucy I saw, but I said nothing, because my mother was holding her hand impatiently over the lines of type, and because I had a feeling that no matter what I said, I wouldn't win. If I'd dragged Lucy in by the cuff of her shirt, and stood her in front of my mother, saying, *Here, see, it's Lucy*, my mother would have gone on holding her hand up like that, sighing, and saying, *No, darling, it isn't*.

I left her there, sitting at the kitchen table. I walked slowly to my room, thinking about what she'd said. By the time I'd shut the door behind me, she was typing again.

NINE

Crystal had a boyfriend called Josh. He was seventeen to her fifteen. Tall, with long arms and legs, long fingers and feet, and skin the colour of burnt caramel. He wore a woven leather anklet, and he always had stripes of white zinc across his cheekbones, making his eyes seem bluer than they were. He wasn't the boy who'd come shirtless down Palmer Street that day, calling my sister's name. That was his friend Stuart. Josh didn't spend his days trailing around behind Crystal, waiting to hear what she thought they should do or wear or eat or say. He wasn't like that—he was different. He worked at the local surf club as a lifeguard, and he took his job very seriously; guarding the waters between the flags, further up the beach from where Kahu and I swam, and from where the little girl Charlotte had gone missing. If you talked to Josh during the day, between the flags, he would try to answer you (he was a polite sort of person who treated everyone equally, even scrawny ten-year-old girls), but his eyes never met yours—they were always on the water. I hadn't witnessed him rescue anyone, but I believed wholeheartedly that he could.

Josh was a proper boyfriend in the sense that he and Crystal's lives had become interwoven. I learned from my sister that they had been going out for an entire school year, "plus some," and that their families had chosen to holiday close to each other that summer, so that the two of them could be together. Crystal, if she couldn't find her wallet, would say to Josh, "Where's my wallet?" and he would frown, patting his pockets and looking all around him, as if the whereabouts of Crystal's wallet was partly his problem to solve. I thought that this was very grown-up. Crystal and Josh didn't hide the fact that they liked each other—they didn't make constant digs at each other, or stay metres apart when their friends were around. I'd never seen young people behave like this before, and I was very impressed with it. Josh's existence, and the fact that he had tied his existence to hers, made Crystal seem a more definite person—a person to be admired.

Crystal said that the reason Josh was so particularly beautiful—with caramel skin, dark, wavy hair, and blue eyes—was down to his mother being Māori and his father Pākehā. "Like you and Kahu," she said, to my horror, "only the other way around." Josh got his hair from his mother, his eyes from his father, and his skin was the "perfect mix."

"If we have babies," she said, "they'll be perfect too."

("A bit paler," I added, but that got ignored, like a lot of things I said.)

Crystal spoke Josh's name a lot—that was what I noticed. She brought Josh into everything, in any way she could. If you said you liked boiled potatoes, she'd say, Josh hates them, or, we had boiled potatoes at Josh's house last night. If the weather changed, she'd nod and say, Josh said it would, or she'd frown and say, Josh will be getting cold. And whenever Crystal spoke Josh's name, Vanessa would find a reason to touch her hair. If I'd said dumb, boring things about boiled potatoes, or constantly mentioned a boy's name like that, Vanessa would have skewered me, but she never skewered Crystal, or even teased her lightly, about Josh.

For this reason, and for other reasons too—the way she seemed to have trouble looking Josh in the eye, and the amount of time she spent getting ready to go to the beach—I guessed pretty early on that Vanessa had a crush on Josh. I guessed that when she lay on her bed with her headphones on and a look of rapt attention on her face, it was Josh she was thinking about— his arms, pulling her out of a rip, his mouth, delivering CPR.

I think Crystal guessed too. I think that's why she used two coloured zinc sticks to write JOSH on her stomach one morning, out on our lawn, before the sun got high. They did it together—Crystal and my sister. Crystal held my sister's hair back and tightened her stomach muscles while Vanessa wrote the letters J-O-S-H across her skin. My sister took the job seriously, between giggling fits, and was careful to keep the letters uniform, spacing them evenly across Crystal's stomach. Still, I don't think any of us was prepared for the result—those zinc sticks were very effective. They blocked the sun completely, with very little blurring at the edges. By noon you could see that the word JOSH would be visible on Crystal's skin for months—maybe even until next summer. My mother was horrified. She actually gasped—standing at the stove, cooking corn on the cob for lunch in that chipped enamel pot. "Crystal!" she said. "What will your mother say?"

What if he dumps you? was what I was thinking. What if he dumps you tomorrow? In my limited experience, boys and girls dumped each other without warning and without a backward glance. That was the shocking part, for me. My mother was probably shocked by something else—the way the letters drew attention to Crystal's waist, the way they made you want to run your fingers over that section of skin between her tiny bikini top and the belt loops of her frayed denim shorts. But what shocked me was her confidence. To write a boy's name like that on your body—to show the world that you loved him, and to give yourself over to loving him completely. If he dumped her she would be heartbroken, and her heartbreak would be written on her body for everyone to see.

I was on the beach with Kahu when Crystal showed Josh what she'd done. Kahu thought we were heading to the picnic area, but really, I was following Crystal. It was a windy day; the beach flags made a whipping noise as we passed. I watched Josh put his hands on her—his long, tanned fingers—and my heart and stomach did a thing in unison that felt both sickening and pleasant. Until that day, I had only ever got that feeling when watching Neil Finn sing Split Enz songs on *Ready to Roll*. Josh put one hand on Crystal's stomach and one on the small of her back, and I thought it was the most romantic thing I'd ever seen, except that actually, I think Josh was embarrassed. I think he was trying to cover her up, because the next thing he did was take off his red lifeguard jacket and drape it over her, pulling it closed at the front. She was looking up at his face and her hair was blowing everywhere, and he was laughing and shaking his head, red-faced, while Vanessa and Stuart hung back, watching. I think maybe Josh didn't like having his name written on another person like that. I think it was too much, even for him. It didn't matter, though, because the whole exercise was never for his benefit—I believe it was for Vanessa's.

TEN

One evening we found ourselves all at the holiday house together: my sister, me, Crystal, Kahu, Josh and even Stuart. My father rooted around in the fridge and announced that we had enough food for everyone, if everyone would like to stay. Kahu ran off to ask his uncle for permission. I held my breath that he would come back, because I didn't want to be left alone all evening with my sister and her friends, who had already said yes.

He did come back—with a plate of hamburger patties, which my father said were a "godsend." The teenagers by this time were lying on the grass close to the back fence, talking about people they knew from the surf club. Above them, our neighbour was sitting in his chair, drinking from a can and pretending not to watch. (I was certain that he *was* watching, and listening too, because once, when Crystal said something funny, I saw his shoulders shake with laughter.)

Kahu was puffed after his dash home for permission. We sat on the concrete patio, watching grasshoppers leap about the lawn. My father lit the barbecue and dragged two chairs out—one for him and one for my mother. I could tell he was in a good mood because the next thing he did was offer "a smidge" of wine to the teenagers. "No, thank you, sir," Josh said, and Crystal sniggered. "No need to call me sir," my father replied, but I could tell he was pleased, and that my mother and Vanessa were impressed too. A few minutes later, in the kitchen fetching chippies, I muttered to Vanessa, "He's not *your* boyfriend, you know," and she hit me so hard in the side of my leg that tears came to my eyes—I think even she was surprised how hard she hit me. I had to go to the bathroom and rub my leg until the pain went away and my eyes looked normal again.

Outside, on the patio, my mother said to Kahu and me, "Why don't you play?" But we didn't want to go inside and didn't want to "play" in front of the teenagers. My father, being in such a good mood, stood up and said, "Hide-and-seek. Mum's the searcher." He put his wine down and ran, around the side of the house that faced the street. My mother protested at first—she had only just begun her wine. But then she laughed; shrugging, and putting her hands over her eyes. She started counting loudly, "Ten, nine, eight..."

Kahu and I scattered. My first thought was to hide behind the rowboat, because I was pretty sure no one would think to look there. But the teenagers were in my way, and the neighbour was on his deck. Instead, I hid behind our car, which was parked on the grass close to the patio. It was a bad hiding place—my mother found me almost immediately. Then, quite quickly, she found Kahu, who had tucked himself in beside the letterbox (he was wider than the letterbox, and his butt stuck out). There was a protracted search for my father, mainly because he cheated—running around and around the house, switching direction, and staying two steps ahead of my mother, so that she could never quite lock eyes on him. The teenagers by now had sat up and were watching—I bet the neighbour was enjoying it too. My mother had kicked off her sandals. She was getting impatient with my father, and she was in fits of laughter. "You're a cheat! A horrible cheat!" she would shout, and then she would turn and run in a different direction, hoping to catch my father out. This went on until she almost couldn't breathe from all the running and shouting and laughing. Finally, she collapsed back into her chair and said loudly, "I give up." That's when my father emerged from the side of the house, shrugging and grinning, saying, "I don't know why you couldn't find me."

Once my father had stoked the coals and had a sip of his wine I said, "Another game? Please?" because I wanted to prove I could hide better than I had the first time. My mother began to shake her head, claiming exhaustion, but my father smiled at her and said, "One more?"

This time the teenagers wanted to play too. I objected—I said it was too many people, there weren't enough hiding places. But my father said it was only fair we all had a chance to join in. "Vanessa's the searcher," he added. I saw Vanessa glance toward Josh and smile—I think she was looking forward to finding him in some secret place. But as soon as Vanessa's eyes were closed and she was counting, Crystal grabbed Josh's arm and said, "Hide together." I thought Josh looked a bit annoyed—everyone knew it was better to scatter.

I was frozen to the spot, wondering where to hide. The rowboat was out because of the neighbour. I ran to the front door. Inside, Stuart was crouched down behind an armchair—immediately visible. What an idiot, I thought. I was determined to do better. That's when I heard Kahu hissing at me. I followed the sound of hissing and found him in the bedroom I shared with Vanessa—I didn't think it was a very promising place to hide. Outside, Vanessa was almost done. I could hear her counting, "Five, four, three . . ."

Kahu got down on his stomach and shuffled under Vanessa's bed. He was hissing at me to do the same, and I was shaking my head, saying no, I didn't think it would work. But I'd run out of time. I got down on my stomach and slid under my own bed, pushing myself as far into the corner where the two beds met as possible, so that I wouldn't be seen from the door. For extra protection I pulled my little suitcase in front of my legs, and tucked my arms up under my sweater.

Now Kahu and I were hiding together, just like Crystal and Josh.

"It always works," Kahu whispered. "Every time."

"What does?"

"Hiding in the searcher's room. I do it all the time with my cousins. They never think to look in their own rooms, or under their own beds. Watch, you'll see."

I was very doubtful, and a little worried too, that Vanessa would be cross when she found us. Hadn't she told me to stay away from her stuff? And what about the mascara? Was Kahu lying on it? But there was no time to move—Vanessa was in the lounge and had already discovered Stuart, who had laughed loudly when he was found, and was now joining her in her search (I didn't think *that* was fair).

We lay there, under the beds, as one by one everyone was found. First Stuart; then my mother, who was lying in the bath (she made a lot of squeaking noises trying to get out); then my father, who was outside and probably cheating; and then Josh and Crystal, who were also outside, and who shouted, "No!" and "I thought we were going to win!" when they were found.

Kahu and I were the last to be found, and it took for ever. In fact, it took so long that the game began to break apart—my father went back to the barbecue, while my mother made herself busy in the kitchen, preparing bread and salad. I think they might have begun to get worried, except that my mother had already found us—shortly after she'd climbed out of the bath, she'd poked her head in the door and spotted Kahu's foot.

"Pull your foot in," she whispered, and then she winked, and left us.

Kahu was right—it never occurred to Vanessa to look properly in her own bedroom. She did come into the room twice, but only glanced casually across the beds, checking behind the door before wandering off again, muttering, "I think they've run off to the lagoon. I seriously think they're cheating." We lay there whispering and giggling for a long time—we giggled especially hard when we heard my mother say, "Perhaps they've been taken by aliens." At one point Stuart and Crystal and Josh all came in and flopped down on the beds, waiting for the game to end. "This is lame," Stuart said, and Crystal replied,

"Yeah, it is a bit." I worried that by hiding so well, we'd ruined the game. "How long do we have to stay?" Stuart asked, and I heard Josh grunt. "We said we'd stay for dinner," he said. "It'd be rude to leave now." I began to feel bad for Vanessa, who was outside, complaining loudly to my father that Kahu and I were cheats. Without really needing to, I coughed. There was a brief silence, and then Josh jumped off the bed and said, "I'll get her." Moments later we were found.

I think we did ruin the game, and maybe the whole night too. Stuart stuck around for some food and then mumbled something about getting home to his family. Josh politely said that if Stuart was leaving, he'd better be off too. Crystal complained a lot about that, whining, and hanging on to Josh's arm. At the letterbox, where they were supposed to be giving each other a hug goodbye, I heard her say, "I'll leave too then." I was standing at the barbecue with Kahu—we were polishing off the last of the hamburger patties.

"No," Josh said, "stay. You'll upset Vanessa if you leave."

"*You're* upsetting *me*," she replied.

It was the only time I heard them fight.

After the boys had gone, Crystal and Vanessa went into our bedroom and shut the door. Kahu and I ate ice cream and peaches for dessert, sitting on the patio, slapping at the mosquitoes that tried to bite our ankles and feet. When he'd finished his dessert, Kahu stood up and said, "Smell you later," which was his way of saying goodbye. I took the bowls to the kitchen and cleaned them in the sink. My mother and father were sitting side by side on the couch, watching something boring on the television. My mother had a book open in her lap, and my father had one eye on the television, and one on a thousand-piece jig-saw puzzle that had been allowed to take over the coffee table.

I wandered out, onto the lawn. The neighbour's chair was empty—the sliding glass door closed, and the lights inside turned off. It was nice to be in the garden without anyone watching. I ambled about a bit, kicking at the grass, singing softly to myself. The mosquitoes were a nuisance but the air was cool and still. After a while I found myself outside my own bedroom—the one I shared with Vanessa. The window above Vanessa's bed was open, and I could hear the girls talking. I crept over and crouched against the wall, hugging my knees to my chest.

"Did you though?" Crystal was saying. "Did you think there was something off?"

They had ice cream too. I pictured them sitting cross-legged on Vanessa's bed with their bowls in their hands.

"What do you mean, off?"

"I dunno. Like he was pissed off somehow."

"I guess so, maybe. It was pretty boring, that game of hide-and-seek . . ."

"It wasn't that. I actually think I know what it is. I've been thinking it for a while."

"What then? What is it?"

Crystal's voice became muffled, as if she had turned her face from the window, or was talking into her bowl.

"No," my sister said. "I don't believe it. Not Josh."

"Yeah, well, you think he's perfect. Some kind of saint. But *all* boys want it. I mean, he's seventeen. If I don't do it, someone will. There's this girl at the surf club—"

"You don't have to do anything you don't want to do."

"It's not that I don't *want* to do it." Crystal was silent for a moment. Then she said, "There's a surf lifesaving party at the end of January, just before they pack up the flags for the year."

"Okay, so?"

"So I heard it gets pretty wild afterwards. Fireworks on the beach, couples in the sand. I think it would make sense to do it then."

There was a long pause, during which nothing was said, and all I heard was the clinking of their spoons against their bowls. I began to think the conversation was over. But then I heard Crystal say, "You should come. You and Stuart. He'd do it with you, you know. If you let him."

I didn't catch what Vanessa said next. I think she was leaning over to put her bowl on the floor—I heard it go down with a clunk. Whatever my sister said, it wasn't what Crystal wanted to hear. She made a *tsk* sound. "If we made a pact," she said, "we wouldn't chicken out."

They were quiet for a long time. I gathered that they were flicking through their magazines—turning the pages with a slow, rhythmic snapping sound. I stood and crept away from the window. Nothing I had heard made the slightest bit of sense to me. Perhaps I was just tired. Perhaps, if I pestered my father, he would rouse himself from the couch to walk Crystal home. My father always walked Crystal home, and Crystal's father always walked Vanessa home, I guess because they were girls. Kahu, when he left, sprinted off in the dark alone, and we crossed our fingers he made it home okay.

ELEVEN

So far that summer I'd lost two towels and a T-shirt at the beach.
It was hardly surprising, given the long expanse of sand from
the dunes to the water, and given the way Kahu and I spent our
days, scouring the beach for places a body might wash up. We
would make a little hollow in the sand, and leave our things in
a heap there, promising my mother that we would not go too
far, or lose our bearings, but then one of us would notice an
object far off in the distance that resembled an arm, or perhaps
a "torso." (Kahu had taught me this word, which I found particularly grown-up and gruesome—*torso*.) "There, look!" we'd
yell, and off we would sprint, hearts racing, even though deep
inside, we knew it was probably just a gnarly piece of driftwood,
or someone's left-behind jumper. "Dammit," Kahu would mutter when we arrived, and then, ever hopeful, we would run off in

some other direction, oblivious to how far we'd travelled from where we first started.

Whenever I lost something, my father got mad, and sometimes insisted on dragging me back to the beach to find whatever was missing. Thanks to him, I did manage to retrieve a book and my orange sun visor, which had been a present from Father Christmas, but the towels and the T-shirt refused to be found, and on those occasions my father and I walked home empty-handed.

Then came something different. A loss I couldn't even tell my father about. A day or two after the game of hide-and-seek—a loss so great it hit me hard between the ribs, in the soft part of my chest where breathing happened.

That day, I carried my beloved fire-engine red Walkman all the way to the beach with me. I wanted to play a Split Enz song to Kahu—I believed that to be a true friend of mine, you had to love the band as I did. At home, at school in Wellington, I had extracted from my friends a general grudging acceptance of Split Enz—that they were "the best band in New Zealand," or even "the best in Australasia." Kahu was fast becoming a true friend, so it was important to me that he complete this ritual of initiation. As well, I wanted to impress him with how thoroughly I knew my lyrics. Every morning at the holiday house, while I waited for my family to wake up, I would choose a song and listen to it over and over until I got every word completely right. If I made a mistake, I had to stop, re-wind, and start again. In this way I believed I could control things like the weather, or my sister's mood, or how long my mother would let me swim at the beach. Of course, it was a dumb idea to take my Walkman with me that day. Knowing my parents would strongly disapprove, I hid it in the folds of my towel, tucking it up under my arm. The headphones were uncooperative and kept threatening to slip out, into the open. Then, the instant we got to the beach, I forgot about Split Enz. For one thing, Kahu was already in the water—he'd arrived at the beach well before us, and had got bored waiting at the cross. For another thing, it was a wave day—the ocean heaving and crashing with waves five feet high. We heard Kahu squealing and hooting before we saw him. I dropped my towel in the sand and ran to the water with barely a backward glance. Then, when we finally emerged from the waves hours later, I thought nothing of my towel being empty. I had forgotten about my Walkman. Kahu grabbed his towel, I grabbed mine, and we ran home—my mother trailing behind, absent-minded, after a longer-than-usual walk at the southern end of the beach. (Vanessa had already returned home hours ago, having achieved the desired amount of sunburn on her arms, to match the sunburn she already had on her legs.) At home my father had bought lamb chops for dinner, but Kahu couldn't stay, he said, because his uncle was taking the whole family to one of the restaurants that lined the highway, close to the turn-off to the beach. Crystal wasn't there either that night, so the four of us spent a quiet evening in front of the television, no one saying much, but each of us quite happy in our own world. I think I was more exhausted than usual, having spent the day being battered about by waves. It wasn't until much later, around bedtime, that I realized. My Walkman wasn't with me. I had left it at the beach. I was brushing my teeth in the bathroom mirror—I lowered my toothbrush and stared dumbly at my own reflection. The awful knowledge coming to me suddenly and all at once, so that there could be no question, not even a sliver of hope. I could look all I liked— I wasn't going to find it. Not tucked under my pillow, not slipped down between the bed and the wall, not anywhere. It was gone, and I felt sick and dizzy. Worst of all, I couldn't ask for anyone's help, or even cry about it, because if my father found out that I had taken my Walkman to the beach and left it there, I would have been in more trouble than I could imagine. My father didn't get angry often, but when he did it was explosive, a thing you didn't want to be around. He'd bought the Walkman on the way back from a business trip to America— I could still remember how he'd knelt, crying, in the arrivals hall. (I was shocked—and more than a little embarrassed—to see my father on his knees in public, crying.) Then he'd stuck his hand into a giant duty-free bag, pulling out a bottle of perfume for my mother, and two sturdy Sony boxes for my sister and me.

The only conclusion I could reach, lying in bed that night, was that my Walkman had been stolen. There'd been a brisk wind on the beach that day, but not enough to blow a Walkman across sand. Besides, could wind unfold a towel, extract a beloved thing from within it, and then carefully re-fold the towel? No. Someone had crept out of the dunes while my mother was away. Someone who knew where to find my Walkman. Often on that beach I had the feeling I was being watched—I had put it down to my imagination, and my mother's patchy chaperoning. Now I knew it wasn't imagined, it was true.

(I pictured a small child—an urchin, bronzed by the sun, with missing teeth and wild hair.)

Along with my Walkman, I had lost my only cassette tape—*True Colours* by Split Enz. All the songs I knew so well, gone. All the lyrics I had learned. How could I expect anything now but bad luck? The cassette tape had cost me fourteen dollars, I had paid for it with a term's worth of pocket money, and I had loved it. I had loved it. Twice, its ribbon had been chewed by my Walkman, and both times, I had painstakingly extracted and re-spooled it with a bobby pin, flattening out its creases to minimize the damage.

Who was I, without my music? I didn't know. I couldn't imagine.

It was as if a part of me had died.

~~~

I didn't sleep well that night. I kept waking, reaching for my Walkman, realizing it was lost, and crying myself into a fitful sleep, only to wake, and begin the whole process again.

Then, after hours of this, I woke and before I could reach for my Walkman or even think about it, I heard, coming from somewhere close by, a hollow moaning.

I recognized the moaning as Vanessa's.

"Vanessa," I whispered. "Shush."

Sometimes Vanessa talked and muttered in her sleep and sometimes I did, I'd been told. The moaning seemed to pause for a while but then started back up again, so I threw off my covers and got out of bed, thinking that I would give my sister a poke in the backside to make her shut up.

"*Vanessa*," I said, crossing the room, but Vanessa's bed was empty.

I stared at the bed for a few moments, not quite comprehending. The moaning was there, but Vanessa wasn't. I climbed up on top of the bed and peered out the open casement window. My sister, unbelievably, was outside. She was crouched down in the grass where I had crouched, eavesdropping, a few nights before. I saw that she was wearing clothes—not her nightie—and that her hair was loose and tumbling down over her face. Even more unbelievably, I saw that Crystal was there. She was crouched down beside Vanessa, rubbing her back, and tutting into her hair.

I blinked several times to check that I wasn't dreaming. But the air was cold against my face, and my Walkman was still lost—I looked behind me and saw that it wasn't lying on the floor by my bed or folded into my covers. Those two facts convinced me that I was awake, and that what was happening was real.

"What's wrong with her?" I said, through the open window. "Why is she moaning?"

Crystal snapped her head back to look at me. Her eyes were white and round, and circled with thick black eyeliner, like a racoon's. I thought she looked awful. "Shit, you gave me a fright," she said. "Keep your voice down. She's not feeling well."

"Did she . . . fall?"

"Huh?"

I knew it was a dumb question even as I asked it. But I couldn't think of any other explanation for my sister being outside her window, and for all the moaning she was doing. "Did she . . . fall out the window?"

Crystal sniggered. "Yeah, sure. Something like that. Hey, help me, would you?"

"How?"

"Let us in the front door. She's never going to be able to get back in the window now."

My sister let out one long low moan and tipped forward. Her feet were tucked under her, and both hands were flat in the dirt, like a runner waiting for the starter's gun.

"Shhh!" Crystal told her, rubbing her back again, but more roughly this time. "Quit your groaning, you'll wake your parents."

Vanessa mumbled something neither of us could catch.

"What?" Crystal said, leaning closer.

"Stop rubbing. Makes it worse."

Crystal gave a huffing sound and straightened up, rolling her eyes. "Someone can't handle her liquor," she said, under her breath, or as an aside to me. I knew what liquor was. It was something you needed a licence for, like driving. I was pretty sure my sister had no such licence.

"Are you going to meet us at the door or what?"

I looked into Crystal's racoon eyes, and nodded.

"Okay, good," she said. "I'll see you there in a minute."

She put her hand under Vanessa's arm and pulled her upwards, making an *oof* sound as she did. Vanessa rose a few inches before letting out another moan and collapsing back down to the ground. "Crap," Crystal muttered. I jumped down off the bed and ran across the room, through our door and into the empty lounge.

In the lounge I paused. My first instinct was to turn left, to my parents' room. *Vanessa fell out the window*, I would say. My parents would handle the rest—the moaning, my sister fully clothed in the middle of the night, the liquor she couldn't handle, Crystal. I would not be needed for any of it—I would be allowed to crawl back to bed.

But Crystal and Vanessa would know that I had told—that I had known this was no window-fall, and that I had told our parents anyway.

I wasn't a snitch. Not any more, not now that I was ten going on eleven.

Kahu *loathed* snitches—two of his cousins snitched on him routinely, he said, and he had a special kind of snake bite he liked to give them when they did.

I padded across the lounge to the front door. Opening it without a sound was tricky, and then I had to leave it open, letting all the cold, dark air rush in, because Crystal wasn't there yet—she still hadn't made her way around the house with my sister, despite the time I'd taken deciding what to do. Realizing there was nothing else for it, I ran through the damp grass to our bedroom window, where I found Crystal struggling to lift Vanessa from her crouching position.

"Take her other arm," Crystal said. She didn't thank me for having come all the way around the house barefoot in the dark, instead of just waiting at the door like we'd talked about. I grabbed Vanessa by the arm and we lifted her to her feet on the count of three. It took an age to get my sister's legs moving, and then she groaned all the way around the outside of the house, and twice said "Stop!," clutching her stomach, so that we had to stop and wait, until she indicated she was okay to be moved again.

At the front door I noticed Crystal trying to get her hand out from under my sister's arm.

"What are you doing?"

"I have to get back, it's nearly morning."

I knew there was no way I could get Vanessa all the way across the lounge on my own. Also, she was scaring me—the way she kept moaning, and clutching at her stomach. On television, I'd once seen a movie in which a teenage girl had given birth to a baby on the kitchen floor, while her father worked the fields outside. Was my sister about to push a baby out right there, on the front doorstep of the holiday house, in the middle of the night?

Crystal must have seen my panic because she sighed and relented. "Okay," she whispered, "but we've got to hurry up."

The lounge floor was smoother than the ground outside and we managed to half-drag Vanessa across it quite quickly. But as soon as we reached the safety of our bedroom, Vanessa sank to the floor to resume her runner's position at the starting line. This seemed to be where she felt most comfortable, with her face close to the ground, and her mouth partially open, as if air was in scarce supply higher up.

"Okay, thanks kiddo," Crystal whispered. She flicked her hair back and rubbed her face with her hands. "God, what a night."

I was very close to asking her where they'd been. And to asking her if she could please not go there again and not let my sister drink liquor without a licence. But then I heard a noise coming from my parents' bedroom next door. It was the soft, cautious sound of someone creeping about, trying not to wake others in their beds.

"Mum," I said, to no one in particular.

Lightning quick, Crystal ducked into the corner behind the door.

I kicked Vanessa. "Vanessa," I said, "Mum's up."

To my absolute horror, instead of jumping into bed and pulling the covers up as I'd expected, Vanessa began to hiccup—only not in a normal way. The sound she made was a bit like the sound a frog might make. A really big, fat frog—a toad. I watched her, barely able to believe what I was seeing. From her corner behind the door, Crystal whispered, "Here we go," and then I saw why Vanessa had wanted her face close to the ground, and her mouth partially open like that. She was vomiting. The vomit was thick and hot and it stank really bad. "Oh yuck, gross, way out," said Crystal. The vomit didn't flow like blood or spilt milk but sat in a thick glutinous glob more or less right where it landed.

As soon as Vanessa had stopped vomiting she stood, pushed her hair out of her face, and stumbled into bed, rolling over to face the wall as if none of us existed and none of this had happened. I was left standing, a puddle of greyish vomit at my feet, while behind the door, Crystal had her hand over her mouth. Her black-ringed eyes were wide and laughing.

Behind me, floorboards creaked.

"Darling? Darling heart? I heard noises, can't you sleep?"

I turned to see my mother, small and strangely girlish in her light summer nightgown. I watched her take in the scene—my sister lying with her face to the wall, my covers pushed back, my blank, shocked face, and hot, stinking vomit at my feet.

"Oh, my darling! Your poor thing, you're sick. Here, sit down, oh my God, how awful. Awful." She took me by the shoulders and steered me back to my bed. "Oh! You're so cold! You're shivering. You must have a fever. Sit down, I'll get a bowl, sit down."

From the bed my sister groaned.

"It's all right, Vanessa," my mother said, "your sister's been sick, that's all. Stay where you are, don't get up."

Once I was lying down my mother pressed her warm hand against my forehead. "Not too bad, thank goodness. Let me grab a bowl."

She ran to the kitchen and clattered in the cupboards for a bowl, which she brought back and placed on the floor beside my bed. All the while, Crystal hid in the corner behind the open door. "Now I'll clean up and get you a towel." My mother hurried away again, toward the bathroom, which was along a short passage leading off the kitchen. As soon as we heard her in the bathroom, running water from the tap, Crystal stepped out from behind the door and made a dash across the lounge. I was so sure she'd get caught that I had to hide my face under my covers. There was a horrible second in which I heard Crystal fumbling with the lock on the front door, and at the same time, heard my mother returning from the bathroom, but when I opened my eyes the front door was closed, my mother was in my room, and Crystal was gone.

My mother placed a towel under the bowl and smoothed out its edges. Then she knelt on the floorboards to clean away my sister's vomit with some rags she'd found under the bathroom sink. "Gosh," she said, wrinkling up her nose, "it smells almost . . . What did you eat?" I watched her as she frowned at the ceiling, trying to remember what we'd had for dinner. "How odd," she said.

"I'm feeling better now," I said.

"That's how it works, immediately after you vomit. You feel better for a bit, but then, if you're not careful, the sick feeling comes back. I want you to lie still and take it easy today. We don't want this thing to drag on, whatever it is. I'd hate for Kahu or your sister to get it."

No matter how many times I told my mother, that day, that I was feeling better, she insisted I stay in bed. It was a beautiful, sunny day, and I spent it confined to our room, which still smelled faintly of sick. My sister got up around ten, refused to look me in the eye, ate a large breakfast, and was off to meet Crystal at the beach by eleven. I was sure that when Crystal heard about my confinement, they'd come back together with an ice-block for me, and hugs, and many grateful apologies. But the two of them stayed out all day, and later, when I asked my sister whether she'd kept an eye out for Kahu, to explain my absence and to save him a lot of waiting around, she only shrugged. I cried intermittently at the injustice of it all, but I never once came close to snitching. Meanwhile, all the crying I was doing made my eyes red and my pillow damp, which only served to convince my mother that she was doing the right thing by keeping me in bed. It was the longest, most boring day of my life, and it would have been entirely forgettable, except for something that happened around four in the afternoon.

I was lying on my side, facing the wall. I was running my finger over bumps in the wallpaper, memorizing its swirly pattern, staring at it until I could close my eyes and see it pulsing behind my eyelids. I remember I ran my finger further down, beneath the level of the bedclothes, and felt something different there—a series of hollows and ridges that had nothing to do with the swirls in the wallpaper. Back and forth, my finger went over this patch, trying to make sense of it, until finally I sat up, pulled the bedding back from the wall, and peered at it.

It was a word, etched into the wall by a previous occupant of the room, using a nail, or a sharp stick. Nine letters long; it started tentatively, but ended strongly, as if the author had gained confidence along the way. The letters were large and clumsy, and in places, where the etching was particularly deep, the wallpaper had snagged and ripped around them. For several minutes I sat on my bed, examining each letter carefully, making sure I wasn't mistaken. I wasn't. The word, hidden from view, close to where my pillow lay, was *Charlotte*.

TWELVE

My father went out early most mornings, walking to the shop to get a newspaper, bread, coffee, and anything else we might need. Sometimes I went with him, striding to keep up, trying to match the slap of my jandals to his. Other times he went alone. The day after I was kept in bed all day by my mother, I was so keen to see Kahu that I told my father I didn't want to go with him—I would eat a quick breakfast instead, and get to the beach as early as possible. My mother was taking Vanessa to the mall for "feminine supplies," but she'd given me permission to go to the beach alone, so long as I swam further up the beach between the flags, and stayed with Kahu. If Kahu wasn't there to meet me, she said, I needed to come straight home. I was heading for the front door with my towel tucked up under my arm when my father returned, whistling, newspaper in hand. He was wearing his very short shorts, his red jandals and his denim shirt, which was unbuttoned and flapping open with its sleeves rolled up.

"Shame you didn't come," he said when he saw me. "Could have done with you today."

I wished then that I'd gone with him—it wasn't very often my father needed me for anything. "What happened?" I asked.

"I ran into someone. Bit embarrassing actually—he knew my name, but I couldn't for the life of me remember his. And I forgot your friend's name too."

I said the first name that came to mind. "Kahu?"

My father shook his head. "No, no, your friend from school. Little Asian girl."

I hesitated. "Lucy?"

"That's it! I knew it was something normal. I mean, not Asian. I ran into her father."

I didn't know Lucy's father's name either. He was "Lucy's father."

"He was at the shop?"

"He was jogging. He's a fitness freak, I think. Nearly bowled me over on a tight bend." My father said "jogging" as if it was an indulgent thing to do, outlandish. "Anyway," he went on, "I invited them over for dinner tonight. They're staying down the beach a bit, somewhere south, not far from here."

I stood with my towel tucked under my arm, saying nothing.

"What is it?" my father asked. "Have you and Lucy had a falling-out?"

"No," I said. "It's just . . ."

"What?"

"Mum told me that Lucy was visiting family this summer. She said they don't have any relatives in New Zealand, so they must have gone overseas."

My father had dropped his newspaper on the counter. He was pottering about the lounge, straightening cushions and stacking magazines. "Well," he said, brushing crumbs from the coffee table into his cupped palm, "your mother isn't always right about everything. It was definitely Lucy's father I saw, and I invited him to dinner and he said yes, so that's that. It's a done deal, it's happening." He straightened up and looked at me. "It'll be fun."

I stood and watched as he resumed his tidying. I didn't know what to say. We were not *allowed* to see Lucy—that's what I wanted him to know. My mother had ruled it out. She had made it impossible that day, when she'd held her hand over the lines of her type and shrugged her shoulders and said to me in that very steady way, *I don't know what to tell you.*

I walked slowly to the door, pausing twice to turn and look at my father. I need to warn him, I thought. But warn him of what? I had no idea. As soon as the door was closed behind me, I took off running to the beach.

~~~~

When I got to the wooden cross Kahu was already waiting, arms folded. I noticed that there were fresh flowers pushed into the wire that looped the cross, and the grasses that grew around it had been cut back, so that the cross was more visible. Kahu was wearing jeans and a T-shirt, instead of the shorts he usually swam in, and he wasn't carrying a towel. "I didn't know if you'd be here," he said, jutting his chin a little as he spoke. I apologized profusely, and told him in great detail about my sister, and the vomit on our bedroom floor, and how I'd had to spend the day confined to my bed, or else be labelled a snitch. Then, almost as an afterthought, I told him I'd found the word "Charlotte" written on the wall beside my bed.

He immediately became very excited, pacing around in the sand, and punching the air with his hands. "You know what this means, right?"

"Um . . ."

I thought that I did know what it meant—that Charlotte had slept in the very same bed as me. That she had stayed in the holiday house that looked like a public toilet. That she had felt the tough, springy grass under her feet and maybe even trailed her fingers along the fence, as I had.

I had thought about this a lot, and every time I did so it made the hairs on the back of my neck stand up.

But then Kahu said something that was much, much worse— something I hadn't even considered.

"It's a message," he said, "from the other side."

"The other side?"

"Yes. She's trying to make contact with us because she knows we're looking for her."

"Make . . . contact?"

"Yes, you know, from the grave. Or from wherever she is." He glanced out at the ocean. I looked down at my feet. I had begun to feel a little sick. "What you have to do," he said, "is this. You have to go all around the whole house looking for other messages. They could be anywhere—even on the ceiling. And they might be . . . in code. Or, you know, a bit weird. Did you ever see *The Exorcist?*"

I shook my head hard—no. My father had watched that film late one night after we'd all gone to bed, and the next day he'd looked pale and worn, and had said, over breakfast, that under no circumstances should any of us girls watch a thing like that, *ever.*

"Well, yeah, me neither," Kahu said. "But my cousin saw it and told me about it, and from what she said I think the messages might be in some other language—like, Greek or something? So look out for weird words that don't make any sense. And shapes, like triangles. And also things moved around. Look out for things in places they weren't before, or shouldn't be. Okay?"

I thought then of the mascara—the way it had come back into our house from outside, as if by magic. "Sure," I mumbled, wishing I'd kept my mouth shut about *Charlotte*. After that I felt strangely cold, even though the sun was shining, and we did a lot of running around. As the morning wore on I caught a sunburn on my shoulders, which I used as an excuse to go home early. Kahu examined each of my shoulders, declaring them quite red, and said that if I wanted, he'd come home with me to help me find more messages. I said no, he couldn't come, because we were expecting guests for dinner—which was true—but really it was all just an excuse. The truth was that I didn't want to think any more about *Charlotte*, or to look for ghost messages in the house where I was staying. Already, I was wondering how I was going to sleep another wink in that bed, knowing that the writing on my wall might have come from the other side.

~~~

Back at the holiday house, it was almost a relief to find my parents arguing in the lounge. "I don't even know if the vacuum cleaner works," my mother was saying. I figured my father had told her about his plans for the evening, and guessed, too, that she wasn't pleased. She stomped her foot to show my father the extent of the problem with the carpet—a thick puff of sand rose up to swallow her ankle. "I'll sweep," my father replied. He already had the broom out; he was shoving aside one of the armchairs, pushing it with his foot. I hurried across the lounge with my head down—under the armchair was where I tended to hide my chocolate wrappers, when I couldn't be bothered walking to the bin in the kitchen. In our bedroom, Vanessa was sitting on her bed with her hands tucked under her thighs. "Mum's on the warpath," she said. I nodded, pleased. All the way home I'd been worrying about ghost messages, but none of that seemed likely now. Ghosts didn't exist alongside vacuum cleaners and boring adult arguments about dinner parties. I pushed my pillow up against the wall so that I could lean comfortably against it, but also so that it hid the word *Charlotte*. Charlotte wasn't an unusual name anyway—there were at least two in the year above me at school. If Kahu asked me about further messages, I would say that I had searched thoroughly and found nothing. "Maybe we'll get something yummy for dinner," I said to Vanessa, because I was feeling optimistic. "Wouldn't count on it," she grumbled.

My parents spent the rest of the day fighting about every aspect of the evening—whether to have lamb chops and sau-

sages or lamb patties and chicken drumsticks, whether my
father needed to go to the shop for more beer, whether we
should try to move the table and chairs outside onto the concrete slab by the front door, whether Kahu and Crystal should
be included (they were not). I felt sure that it was going to be a
terrible night—we would all sit, in silence, counting the minutes
until it was over—but then, ten minutes before our guests were
due to arrive, I found my mother in the bathroom, doing her
make-up. The air was filled with her favourite perfume, and she
had brought a little black transistor radio into the bathroom so
that she could listen to pop music while she worked. My mother
only ever did that when she was feeling happy, or excited about
something.

I was confused. At home in Wellington her rules about
make-up were clear—she didn't leave the house without it. "Just
putting my face on," she would call from the bathroom, as we
three waited impatiently by the front door. On holiday, though,
she hardly wore make-up at all—the last time I'd spotted her
polka-dot bag full of cosmetics, it had been in the boot of our
car, tucked into a corner with the spare towels and pillowcases.
My mother had been tetchy and cross all afternoon, and now
she was leaning into the mirror, humming along to the music,
brushing colour across her cheeks. "What are you doing that
for?" I asked. "Not for you, that's for sure," she replied. Her
words were harsh but there was a giggle in her voice. I said,
"Who then? Daddy?" She pulled back from the mirror and
snorted. "Your father wouldn't notice if I came to dinner with
one green eye and one purple." I thought this was unfortunate,
but true. I said, again, "Who then? Why?" because I was newly

interested in make-up, and why girls bothered with it—why my sister would risk everything for a tube of mascara that lay under her bed, unopened, and why, sometimes, Crystal would want to make herself up to look like a racoon. My mother had moved on to her lips. "I think we fool ourselves that we do it for men," she murmured, one hand half-covering her mouth, "or that we do it for ourselves." She was leaning all the way over the bathroom sink so that her face was inches from the mirror, and her breath was fogging the glass. I saw that she was wearing a knee-length dress and high-heeled sandals. "But really," she went on, "I think we do it for other women. That's what I think."

I thought my mother's comment about make-up was very interesting, but Lucy's mother, when she arrived, was wearing none at all. I felt sorry then for my mother, who had gone to a lot of trouble, and had not had the favour returned. My mother seemed pleased, though, when she saw Lucy's mother—in fact she appeared to relax for the first time that day. I saw her draw her shoulders back before she moved forward almost as if gliding. Lucy's mother was tiny, barely as tall as Vanessa. The effect, when my mother stooped toward her, was of a queen greeting her subject. I watched as Lucy's mother gazed up, an expression of what looked like wonder on her face, but maybe it wasn't wonder, maybe she was horrified. Back in Wellington, my mother liked to say that only "raging feminists" went about with no make-up at all. I didn't really know what "raging feminists" were, but I understood from my parents that they were undesirable females—laughable. Still, I couldn't help thinking that I preferred Lucy's mother's clean face. Next to her, my mother looked dark and interesting—unpredictable.

I wasn't sure I wanted a mother who was unpredictable.

The commotion when our guests arrived was like a gust of fresh air sweeping through the house. My parents, who had been at each other's throats all afternoon, suddenly couldn't stop touching each other, making little jokes that only they understood, and laughing louder than necessary. Vanessa hung back, rolling her eyes. I guess my father was just relieved that my mother was no longer on the warpath, or maybe he *had* taken in her appearance—maybe my mother was wrong about that. I had noticed that he'd drunk two glasses of wine before our guests arrived—the first to "test the vintage," and the second "for luck." I was glad he'd had all that wine to drink because it made him chatty, and his chatter filled the gaps that might have been awkward otherwise. For example, there was a big gap when Lucy's father first saw my mother—his smile faltered, and his mouth, which had been open to speak, simply closed again. My own father said, "Breathtaking, isn't she," and my mother slapped him playfully on the shoulder, telling him to shush. Vanessa rolled her eyes about three times for that one, and briefly stuck her finger down her throat as if she was going to puke.

"What a lovely place this is," Lucy's mother said, turning to let my father take her coat.

My father shrugged. "Your typical bach, nothing flash. Where are you staying?"

"A little further south, on the ridge above the beach."

My father looked surprised. He'd folded the coat over the back of a kitchen chair. "On the beach?"

"On the ridge above."

"The ridge above the beach *is* the beach."

My father was smiling. Lucy's mother blushed. "Yes, I suppose," she said. "A big ugly place. Huge. I prefer this, it's—how do you say? When something is small and comfortable?"

"Cosy?"

"Yes, cosy. How did you find it?"

"It was advertised in the *Evening Post*," my father said. " 'Quintessential New Zealand bach, ideal for a young family.' " He looked at my mother. "Well, we're still young, aren't we?" My mother laughed. He grinned, spreading his hands. "Some of us are anyway. Now, what would everybody like to drink?"

Once drinks had been poured, and I had been made to hand around a bowl of chippies (only my father took a handful, everyone else politely declined), Lucy and I went outside. We ran to the back fence, where we practised our handstands, cartwheels and splits. Lucy was better at all of these things than I was—her movements had a sureness about them that must have come with many hours of practice. I, too, had practised these things, but I had to pretend that I hadn't, to account for my lack of form. I showed Lucy my sunburn from earlier, which was coming up a deep, crimson red, and pointed out to her the little aluminium boat, and a crab shell complete with legs, which Kahu and I had found at the beach and took it in turns to keep. Then, as the darkness deepened, and we both got bitten by insects, I showed Lucy how to slap, rather than scratch, itchy bites to calm them down. Lucy was always polite, but seemed somehow above it all, as if she was touring a museum and I was a curious exhibit. She had a delicate, thoughtful way of doing things—sweeping her hair out of her face, checking her Mickey

Mouse wristwatch, adjusting her dress—that made me feel clumsy and awkward. I found myself missing Kahu, who was always into everything, no questions asked. I wondered then if I would ever have another friend who would make me feel as comfortable as he did, and thought I probably wouldn't.

Just as it was starting to get dark, my father came out to cook on the barbecue, which he'd lit hours earlier. It was a calm night, still enough for us to hear the sausages spitting from where we were playing. Lucy's father joined my father at the barbecue, while Lucy's mother stayed inside with my mother and Vanessa. I felt happy then, because the adults seemed to be getting along, and because I saw myself as responsible for the entire evening, having been the original link between our two families.

After a while, there was a swap. Lucy's father went inside, and Lucy's mother came out. She stood at the barbecue, smiling, with a cardigan wrapped loosely around her shoulders and a glass of wine in one hand. I saw that she had long, black hair that fell almost to her waist, and that her legs were as thin as a girl's. I hoped my father wouldn't say silly things, or talk incessantly about cricket. Lucy's parents spoke English perfectly well, without pauses or mistakes, but while Lucy sounded like a Kiwi, they did not, and while she knew all the appropriate shortcuts, they would often take the long way around a sentence, leaving you hanging for a time, wondering if it would all work out in the end. I couldn't imagine what it must be like for Lucy, knowing two languages, one even better than her parents.

Having spent a little bit of time at the barbecue, laughing politely at my father's jokes, Lucy's mother began to move toward us. I watched her making her way across the grass in

careful steps, trying not to spill her wine, which she'd hardly
touched. She was smiling, but I sensed the smile didn't go very
deep, and I thought for a moment that she was going to tell us
off for getting our clothes dirty, or for letting so many insects
bite us. It was my greatest horror to be told off by an adult I
didn't know very well, but Lucy's mother, when she got to us,
only said, "Who is that?"

She didn't point or gesture. In fact, she smiled the whole
time, a quizzical smile—a serious one.

"Who is what?" I asked. We were almost out of light.

"That man."

With the smallest jut of her chin she indicated—*up*. I
looked, and saw that our neighbour was in his usual spot. The
whiteness of his hair and the plastic chair made it possible to
see him in the near-dark. "Oh, don't worry about him," I said,
bravely, with a flick of my hair. My attitude toward our neighbour was mostly defiant now, teasing. I liked to stare angrily at
him, to show I wasn't scared. But Lucy's mother put a hand on
each of our shoulders. "I think you should come in now," she
said, turning us around in the grass. Her grip was surprisingly
powerful for such a small woman. I forget whether she was
still smiling at this point—I think not. She moved us across the
grass, toward the barbecue, which was spitting, and smelling
wonderful. "Does your father know about this man?" she asked.
"No," I replied, "I don't think so." She nodded and said nothing
further. As we approached the patio, I slipped out of her grasp,
running toward the door. I was afraid that I might be in trouble,
because I viewed the neighbour, and his watching, as being my
fault somehow. As I neared the door, I saw Lucy's mother turn

quickly back to the fence, as if checking something. I checked too. He was gone, our neighbour. The white plastic chair was empty, the sliding door closed. My father, who was prodding at the barbecue with his tongs, said, "Won't be much longer now." I waited, but Lucy's mother, after a brief pause, only replied, "How delicious. Doesn't that look delicious, Lucy?"

Relieved, I burst into the house, alone.

Our bedroom door was closed. I guessed that Vanessa was in there, probably listening to music on her Walkman, and sulking that she had not been allowed to invite Crystal. My parents' door was open, and their room empty. "Mum?" I called. The lounge felt hot after the cooler air outside, and seemed glaringly yellow, bathed in artificial light. I saw rumpled cushions, an empty chippie bowl on the floor, and a beer can on the coffee table. In the kitchen, a salad was sitting ready on the bench, and a French stick was partially cut into slices. I headed across the lounge, toward the passage that led to the bathroom, until whispering, and a muffled giggle, stopped me in my tracks. Whispering meant a game, or secrets. I listened for a moment, but couldn't make out any words. Outside, I heard the clunk of the barbecue lid, and my father clapping his hands together, as he always did when he'd completed a job to his satisfaction. I stayed where I was, standing in the lounge near the passage to the bathroom, hardly daring to breathe. Something told me that what I had stumbled on was not a game, but secrets. "The sausages are ready," I said loudly to the empty room. Immediately the whispering stopped. I turned toward the front door, closing my eyes because I didn't want to see. There was a rustling behind me—a skirmish—and then I heard a rattle at the front door. Opening my eyes, I saw my father ushering Lucy and her mother inside, a plate of half-burnt sausages in his hands. I turned, worried about what I would see, but there was nothing behind me that suggested secrets. Only my mother, standing at the kitchen bench, cutting bread neatly into slices.

THIRTEEN

The next morning I slept in, and woke to find that my sunburn
had got much worse. My parents were in the kitchen, making
a lot of noise at the sink. They'd been too tired to tidy up after
the dinner party, and were doing it now instead. I sat up and
tested my shoulders with my fingertips. They hurt—a lot. Vanessa was in bed too. I asked her if I could borrow some of her
after-sun cream. She pursed her lips as if to say no, but then
she caught sight of my shoulders and gasped. That's when my
mother got involved. My mother dropped what she was doing
in the kitchen and inspected my shoulders carefully. "I can feel
blisters coming up," she said, shaking her head. "No sun today.
None at all." I nodded, promising I would wear sunblock, not
swim, and keep my T-shirt on all day. This seemed to satisfy
her for a while, but then, just as we were preparing to go to the

beach as usual, my mother put her towel and notebook down on the kitchen table and said, "I'm just not happy about this."

She inspected my shoulders again. Already a blister or two was coming up. "Do we bandage them?" she asked my father. "What's the protocol?"

I didn't know what "protocol" was, but I sensed that my day was about to get ruined. My mother said she wasn't happy about me running around in the harsh sun with those blisters on my shoulders. My father tried to help, saying salt water might be "just the ticket," but she dismissed that suggestion. The blisters would tear and get infected, she said, and sand would get trapped in the wounds. A day out of the sun would do me good.

"You'll thank me when you're older and your skin isn't covered in moles and wrinkled like leather."

I didn't care if my skin turned to leather, I wanted to see Kahu.

I tried everything. I said, couldn't I stay in the shade under the pines? My mother appeared at first to consider it but then said that the way Kahu and I tore around "from pillar to post," we'd soon find ourselves back in the sun. Instead, she said, the three of us would have a nice quiet morning at the mall— Vanessa was going to the beach.

I sent anguished looks at my father but all he did was shrug— *Mum's the boss*, the shrug said. I went to find Vanessa, who was moisturizing her legs in the bathroom. "If you see Kahu can you tell him I'm with Mum," I said.

"I guess," she replied.

"He'll be at the cross."

She looked up from her legs, blinking slowly. "The what?"

"The cross," I said. "In the little clearing, off the path, in the pines."

She stared at me as if waiting for some punchline. I shrugged. "Please," I said. She sighed, reaching for her moisturizer, which was behind her on the vanity. "Sure," she said, "whatever."

I had no idea what that meant.

~~~

At the mall, we split up. My father went to get charcoal and some cleaning fluid for the barbecue, while my mother and I went to the supermarket, where my mother walked quickly from aisle to aisle, saying, "nearly there," and "only a few more things." I got the feeling she felt bad for forcing me to go to the mall with her. When we got to the checkout, she squeezed my hand and said, "Only two more things I need." I nodded. I was beginning to feel hopeful, because we were getting through the list fast. My mother had found a tube of high-strength sunscreen at the supermarket—maybe with that on my shoulders, I'd be allowed to go to the beach and catch up with Kahu. My mother paid the checkout lady and said, "Okay. Antihistamines, and some kind of cream for your shoulders."

That's when I knew that my day was about to get a whole lot worse, because we were going to the chemist.

I had not been back to the chemist since the first time, when Vanessa and I had run into Crystal, and Vanessa had done what she'd done with the mascara, and I'd said the stupid thing I'd said, which was *Palmer Street*.

"I might go wait for Dad at the car," I said, but my mother said the car was too far away, it wasn't safe for me to go all that way on my own, and besides, the people at the chemist might need to look at my sunburn. If I was good and patient, she said, maybe we could grab a couple of custard squares from the bakery afterwards. "You can give one to Kahu," she said. I nodded, but then when we got to the chemist, I pulled my hand out of hers and said, "Can I wait here?" She thought that was very odd, because generally I loved to visit chemists with my mother—loved to run my hand along the perfume bottles, with their colourful labels with fancy French words on them, and to look at the different kinds of hairclips and nail polish colours. But my mother said all right, I could wait outside, so long as I stayed right where she could see me, at the entrance to the shop, next to the sun hats.

Which was tricky, because standing there at the entrance to the shop, I could be seen by the ladies at the counter too.

I stood there for the longest time, crossing my fingers that no one would ask to see my sunburn, and listening to the same tinkly piano music I remembered from last time, which had made me want to pee. Meanwhile my mother went up and down the aisles, collecting various items and putting them in a little plastic shopping basket she'd picked up at the door. Every now and then I would glance over my shoulder to see how she was doing, and every time I did that, I thought I caught the lady at the counter—the blonde one from last time—frowning at me.

I tried to duck down behind the sun hats, to make myself invisible, but I think that only made the lady at the counter frown harder, and as well, my mother looked over and couldn't see me, which made her call out my name, and say in a really loud voice that drew further attention, "Stand where I can see you."

That's when the blonde lady ducked to get something from beneath the till, lifted a section of the counter, and stepped through to the shop side. I heard her say, "Mind the counter would you, please," to another lady who was working that day, and I heard the other lady reply, "Sure thing, Cheryl."

Then the blonde lady began to walk toward me.

I didn't know what to do. My heart began to beat really fast and hard, so that I couldn't even hear the tinkly piano music any more—couldn't hear what the lady was saying as she walked toward me, skirting the sun hats. I watched her lips move and heard her words as if they were coming to me through water. She spoke again, more loudly this time, but I still couldn't make out what she was saying. Behind her, my mother saw what was happening, and began to walk toward us as well. I felt sweaty and shaky, and thought for sure that I would faint, right there on the polished floor next to the sun hats. The lady gave up trying to talk to me and turned to my mother instead. "I've figured it out," she said. "Why your daughter is so familiar."

My mother smiled. "Yes?" she said. "Why's that?"

I wasn't sure if I could talk because I sure couldn't breathe. But next thing I knew I was saying in a very high voice that I could hear very clearly over the top of the weird swooshing noise that had started up in my ears, "It wasn't us, it was Crystal."

Both women looked at me and frowned.

"I beg your pardon, dear?" said the blonde lady.

I looked from her to my mother and back again. Of the two women, my mother was the one who was frowning the hardest. The blonde lady was already smiling, laughing even, saying, "It's nothing to worry about, I was just saying to your daughter that I recognize her from the photos."

My mother nodded. "The photos," she murmured. But I could see she wasn't interested in them.

She was interested in, *It wasn't us. It was Crystal.*

I didn't care about the photos either—I wanted to run. Run and run and run and never see the blonde lady or the horrible bad-luck chemist ever again. The blonde lady, however, was insistent. She had in her hand a green-and-yellow packet, and she was opening it, saying to my mother, "Are you the photographer in your family? Or your husband?"

My mother said, "Um, I . . . those aren't ours. Excuse me, I need to—could I give you this?" She thrust the plastic basket she'd been carrying into the woman's arms, even though the blonde lady had her hands full already with "the photos," and even though there were things in the basket that I knew my mother wanted to buy, like antihistamines and cream for my sunburn.

"Well, no, but I'm sure it's your daughter," the blonde lady was saying. "That's how I recognized her—I do all the printing here." She smiled a wide, glittering smile, a smudge of lipstick across her two front teeth. In her hand the photo packet flapped open—I caught a glimpse of a sun-drenched lawn, a corner of glaring corrugated-iron roof, and in the centre of the frame, a child I recognized, but at the same time didn't recognize, because it wasn't possible—it couldn't be me. My mother was still frowning, pushing her basket into the blonde lady's arms. "You might want to adjust your settings," the blonde lady was saying. "The light could be handled better—and what you really need is a zoom lens. There's a camera shop here in the mall, I can point it out to you if you like."

My mother gave up trying to get the blonde lady to take her basket and put it down on the floor instead. "I'm sorry, you're mistaken."

My father had bought himself a Polaroid camera in America, at the same time as he'd bought my Walkman.

That was how my mother knew for sure that the photo packet wasn't ours, without having to look at a single photo.

"But—"

"If you'll excuse us, we need to get going," my mother said. She stepped around the blonde lady and grabbed my arm, pulling me out, across the polished floor of the mall. I looked back, over my shoulder, and saw the blonde lady staring after us, the open photo packet in her hand.

My mother pulled me a little further away from the chemist, and then crouched down in front of me so that we were eye to eye. Her hands were on my shoulders, pressing down. It hurt a lot because of the sunburn, and as well, my wrist was aching from where she'd grabbed and pulled.

"Now," she said in her firmest voice. "You are going to tell me what you meant back there, about Crystal."

I shook my head.

"Young lady," my mother said.

I was shaking my head, and I was close to tears but also I was mad, because my wrist and shoulders hurt, and because I had never wanted to be here at the bad-luck chemist—not the first time, and definitely not now. None of this was my fault—*none of it*—and yet I was the one being punished.

I pressed my lips together and shook my head again. *I will not tell.*

My mother was squeezing my shoulders now, her fingers were digging into my flesh. People kept sweeping past us, carrying bags that bumped my head or swished past my ears. I could hear the tinkly piano music coming from the chemist and at the same time, I could hear the music that was playing in the main part of the mall—a song by Paul Young that was everywhere that summer. It was a good song but the two different types of music playing at once were making my head hurt, and as well, I was worried about what I'd seen in the bad-luck chemist— photographs of me that I couldn't explain.

"Young lady," my mother said again—she didn't seem to mind the two tunes playing at once or the shopping bags that kept almost colliding with our heads. "We don't keep secrets in this family," she said. "We don't tell lies, and we don't keep secrets. Now, tell me what it was that Crystal did."

And suddenly all the noise seemed to go away, along with the swishing shopping bags and the pain in my shoulders where my mother's fingers were pressing too hard. It all went away and I felt very calm and strong, because of that word my mother had used—*secrets*.

I didn't say anything. I didn't need to. My mother knew straight away that she'd made a mistake—as soon as the words were out of her mouth, I saw that she knew. Still, I kept right on looking at her. I was thinking about the night before, when I'd had to say loudly into the empty room, *The sausages are ready.* And I was thinking about the beach walks, and the time on the stormwater pipe when the figures in the sand had pressed their faces together until there was no light left between them.

I kept looking at my mother, thinking about these things, until eventually I saw something in her eyes flicker, and felt her grip on my shoulders loosen.

I knew then that I wasn't going to have to tell her what Crystal and my sister had done at the chemist.

My mother took her hands off my shoulders and stood up. She patted her skirt down three or four times, even though there was nothing in her pockets and nothing about her skirt that needed patting. Then she said, "I wonder where your father's got to."

"We said we'd meet him at the car," I said.

And she said yes, so we did, clever you, and we walked to the car in silence.

~~~~

When we got back to the holiday house my father climbed out of the car first and went around the back to unload the groceries and the big bag of charcoal he'd bought. My mother stayed where she was for a moment, sitting very still and silent in the front passenger seat, while I fiddled with my seat belt, and with the door, which was stiff and heavy, and always difficult for me to manage.

When I was almost out of the car my mother said, "Vanessa's lucky to have such a loyal little sister."

I said nothing. My hand was on the door handle, and one foot was out of the car.

"I'm proud of you, Ally-pally," she said, "for being so loyal."

I nodded, and then I slid out of the car.

FOURTEEN

Some days, all Kahu and I wanted to do together was swim. A few days after the dinner party, we were heading home from the beach in the middle of the afternoon, very hungry because we'd been swimming all morning. It was a wave day, and we hadn't wanted to come out of the water, not even when my mother had told us she was heading home to make lunch. (After what had happened at the chemist, my mother seemed less inclined to tell me what to do—she had relaxed some of her rules, and was careful around me, I noticed, watching me as she spoke.) "Give us ten more minutes," we'd said, but we'd taken longer than that, and now we were shivering, dressed only in our wet togs, with nothing but a damp towel each for protection. Our stomachs were growling, and we were talking longingly of all the food there might be at my house—pink icing buns from the bakery at the mall, corn on the cob, and maybe a bag of chippies still left over from the dinner party.

We got to the intersection close to our house, and I saw, standing on a wide, grassy verge at the top of Palmer Street, a group of people milling about.

All the people in the group had grey or white hair, except for a few of the men, who had no hair at all. They were all wearing walk shorts with long socks and sneakers or sandals—even the women—and some of them wore sun hats that flopped down over their eyes, or caps with a flap at the back to protect their necks. They had large packs on their backs, and one was holding a big metal stick that looked like a cross between a weed-eater and a vacuum cleaner. I spotted some of those pairs of walking sticks that people in Wellington sometimes carried when they went on long hikes into the hills.

Beachcombers, I thought.

"What do you call them?" my mother had said, the night she'd shared a cask of wine with my father beside the barbecue. "People who wander along, looking for stuff on beaches?"

Beachcombers, my father had replied.

"It's them," I said, grabbing Kahu's arm.

"Huh? Who—those nerds?"

"Yes, it's them, the beachcombers."

Kahu's eyes widened. He sucked air in through his teeth. "The last people to see her alive," he breathed.

"Yes," I said. "Them."

I had told him, of course, what I had overheard my mother saying to my father that night. That the last people to see Charlotte alive were the beachcombers. That they had spotted her running into the pines on the ridge above the beach, alone, on the day she drowned.

That they wished they had done something to stop her.

We stared at the group for a while. I think we'd imagined they would look more interesting than they did, but in fact they were very ordinary. If they were consumed by guilt over what had happened to Charlotte, they weren't showing it. "I'm cold," Kahu said eventually, "shall we cross?" I nodded. We stepped out, onto the road. As we headed for the other side, I spotted something in that huddle of people—a flash of something I recognized.

"Wait," I said to Kahu, holding up one hand. "Don't cross."

He was there—my neighbour. At the centre of the group. He was holding a small black-and-silver camera. His hair was brushed neatly across his head, and he had on the same yellow shirt he'd been wearing on New Year's Eve.

~~~

"We can't go that way," I said to Kahu, grabbing his arm, and pulling him back to the other side.

"What do you mean?" he said. "What other way are we supposed to go?"

He was right—there was no other way. The beachcombers were standing at the entrance to Palmer Street. To get to the holiday house, we'd need to walk right past them.

"We'll have to go to your place," I said.

Kahu was annoyed with me. I'd got him really excited about the pink icing buns. Also, his house was a longer walk from the beach than mine. "I can't explain right now," I said, "we just have to go." I knew I was being stubborn, and a bit stupid. Nothing would have happened to us if we'd crossed the road and passed right under the noses of the beachcombers— nothing. But I couldn't bear it—the thought of my neighbour's eyes on me. My feet were bare, my hair was wet, I was dressed only in togs. What if one of the group acknowledged us? My shoulders, since the sunburn, had blistered all over and then begun to itch and peel. The new, exposed skin was tender and pink. I just knew one of those beachcombers would stop me and say, "Ooh, ouch, look at those shoulders," and I'd be obliged to stop and reply politely, "They're getting better, thank you," and "Yes, I have sunblock on." At school, I was in the habit of taking the long way to class every morning because there was a group of senior boys who sat outside the art room with their legs sticking out and their bags lying about. To get past them you had to pick your way through this obstacle course of legs and bags. Every now and then someone would trip, or be tripped, and always— *always*—the boys snickered and muttered as you went by. This was no different. I refused to pass under my neighbour's gaze, shivering and wet.

I pulled Kahu along. "There'll be food at your place," I said. He rolled his eyes, his cousins would be there too, he said. I ignored him, pulling him on. Up ahead there was a bend in the road—once we got around that bend, we would be out of sight of the beachcombers.

"We'll go to my place tomorrow," I said.

When we got to the bend in the road I turned back for one last look. On the grass verge, the little group had opened up, and my neighbour had moved forward. He was leaning out over the kerb, looking up and down the street, and glancing at his watch. A few moments later, when we were nearly at the top of Kahu's street, I saw a van whistling past. It had rows of seats in the back and words printed along the side, KĀPITI COAST DAYTRIPPER, or something like that. I wondered if the van was going to scoop my neighbour up and take him away—if it would be safe now, to return to Palmer Street. But we were nearly at our destination, and I didn't have the heart to tell Kahu to turn back.

~~~

When we got to Kahu's house, I sat down on the lawn outside to dry off. The sun had come out, and was warm on my skin. Kahu ran inside to see what food was available, leaving the front door open behind him. I waited a few moments, and then I lay back in the grass to think.

My mother had made it sound as if the beachcombers were nice, helpful people who kept the beaches clean, and felt bad for letting Charlotte run off alone that day.

But my father had used a different word for the beachcombers. *Scavengers*, he'd said.

Drifters, hobos, bums.

Scavengers were dirty creatures, I knew. They hung around in shadow, or circled the sky, waiting to swoop in and take things that didn't belong to them.

I was lying in the grass, thinking about the beachcombers, when I heard a lot of energetic clicking and squeaking coming from the street. I sat up, squinting into the sun to see. It was Kahu's girl-cousins, or a collection of them, and they were on bikes. One or two of the bikes looked brand new, white, with neon-green seats and handles—Christmas bikes—while some were more like the ones my sister and I had at home—rusted and old, bought from the second-hand section of the newspaper. As a group these girls mounted the pavement, cleared the letter-box, and came skidding to a halt on the lawn, enveloping me in crashing, creaking bikes. I could do nothing but roll myself into a ball in the grass and hope not to be run over. Meanwhile, out of the open front door, Kahu's uncle's dogs, Dotty and Scottie, came rushing over to join in the fun. The cousins, who were used to the dogs, lay around laughing, or began to playfight with them, making growling noises, encouraging them. By now I had jumped up and was standing with my feet together and my towel wrapped tightly around me, but it was no good—one of the dogs stuck its nose into my crotch and wouldn't back off, no matter what I did. No matter how many backward steps I took, or how I tried to twist and turn, it pushed its hot snout into the gap between my legs, nudging me there, while one or two of Kahu's cousins watched with wry smiles. In my efforts to escape, I tripped over a bike, landed on my bum in a tangle of metal and wheel grease, and was immediately mounted by the dog—I think it was Dotty.

"Off," I kept saying, pointlessly. "Off. Off."

That's when Kahu's uncle finally emerged from the house. Walking at first, and then moving quickly, crossing the lawn in a couple of giant steps. "Oi, you two!" he shouted. I think he meant the dogs. With a click of his fingers the dogs were off; called to heel, tails wagging. I scrambled up, pulling my towel around me. "Hey," Kahu's uncle said, grinning. "It's Starsky! I didn't recognize you under all that dog." He winked at me. I tried to smile but my face wouldn't budge; it felt hot and at the same time frozen, like a mask.

The uncle turned away from me—I think he guessed I was having trouble with my face. "What have I told you girls?" he growled at the cousins. "No riding bikes on the lawn." Then, with the dogs trotting meekly behind, he turned and went back inside, shutting the door this time, and leaving me alone with the cousins.

"Hello," one of them said. I said nothing. Kahu had appeared on the lawn looking sheepish—I think his uncle had chewed his ear off about leaving the front door open. I was just relieved he hadn't seen me flailing around in the grass with the dog on top of me. Picking my way through the bikes, I headed for the road. Kahu could catch me up, or not—in that moment I didn't care. I didn't care if I was alone for the rest of the day. I just wanted to shake, for good, the feeling of that dog's snout in my crotch. Between the beachcombers blocking the entrance to Palmer Street, and the cousins mounting the pavement on their bikes, I felt small and stupid, like one of my trapped grasshoppers. "Where're you going?" one of the cousins called. Again, I said nothing. As I neared the letterbox, I passed the oldest girl. She must have been Kahu's age, or a little older. She had managed to stay out of all that mess, straddling her bike by the letterbox. She was tall, and not as scruffy as the younger ones—in fact she was quite beautiful, with auburn hair that tumbled over her shoulders in loose, shiny curls. Her bike had a basket on the back of it—I saw in there a blue sweater with grubby sleeves, a crumpled ice-block wrapper, a pair of black swimming goggles, and at the bottom, something red. As I got closer, the girl reached back to adjust her sweater, pulling it out toward the corners of the basket like a blanket, as if she didn't want me to see.

That's when I thought of my missing Walkman.

By the skin of my teeth, I had managed to prevent my parents from finding out that my Walkman was gone. Whenever we went anywhere in the car, my father would tell me to get it, and I would have to lie, saying that I wanted to read my book instead, or play I-Spy. Sometimes that would prompt my mother to say, "I wish you wouldn't read in the car, you'll get carsick," or "I think we're all too tired for I-Spy." Once, to bring a quick end to the conversation, I'd said my batteries were running low, but that only made my father cross, saying, "I only just replaced them, what are you doing with that thing?" I knew I was walking a very fine line. My best option, of course, would have been to tell my parents straight away that my Walkman had been stolen. The telling-off I would have received then, for taking it to the beach with me, would have been nothing compared to the one I'd get now, for lying to them about batteries and I-Spy.

I could think of no reason for Kahu's cousin to hide what was in her basket—the only reason she could possibly have was guilt. I walked to the corner of the street, and then I stopped and waited for Kahu. When he finally caught me up, I saw that he had a sandwich in each hand, but I shook my head. My appetite was gone.

"What's the matter? The dogs? Uncle said they—"

"Your cousin," I said.

"Which one? Kiri? The little one with freckles? I'll beat her up for you tonight."

"No, not that one. The one by the letterbox."

He swung around to look. "Oh—April, she's all right. What'd she do?"

I swallowed. "I think she's got my Walkman," I said.

Kahu was eating one of the sandwiches, carefully pulling on a slice of tomato with his teeth. Tomato juice dribbled down his chin. He stopped chewing, and lowered the sandwich. "She what?"

"It's in her basket."

He turned to take another look at April, who was standing by the letterbox with one leg swung over her bike, staring back at us.

"You mean she found it?"

I shrugged.

Kahu had never professed much love for his cousins. He had called them stupid, useless and annoying. We had laughed together at the childish things they said—I knew which ones farted in their sleep, and which ones were still afraid of the dark. Until that moment, it had never occurred to me that he cared for them. At least not as much as he cared for me.

"You're wrong," he said.

"I'm not, I saw it. It's at the bottom of her basket."

Kahu pressed his lips together, shaking his head. "No way."

"She tried to cover it up."

"It's not, she didn't—take that back."

"No. You need to get it back for me, it was expensive." Tears were blurring my vision. The more I argued with Kahu, the more certain I became of what I'd seen. "My dad brought it all the way from America, you need to look in her basket."

"No," he said, shaking his head. "April's okay, she wouldn't do that, trust me, you're wrong."

We were making some noise now. Over at the letterbox, April and all the other cousins must have heard. I folded my arms. I was too far in to back out now. "You have to at least ask her," I said. "You have to look inside her basket."

Kahu's shoulders slumped. "April wouldn't do that," he said, one last time. Then he walked slowly back toward April. From the corner of the street I watched, trembling. Now was the time to call out to him—to tell him I'd only been teasing. But I was still angry about what had happened on the lawn, and I knew I was going to enjoy being right. I was going to relish it. Soon, Kahu would be full of apologies for doubting me, and for siding with his cousin.

I watched as Kahu paused to throw both sandwiches into the bushes by the side of the road, and then watched him wipe his hands on the back of his shorts. When that was done, he moved over to April, saying a few short words to her, and leaning over, into her basket. She said nothing, as far as I could tell, and did nothing to stop him. She only looked over his shoulder at me, holding my eye. I tried not to blink. My heart was pounding so loud in my ears that I thought I'd come away deaf. I saw Kahu pull out the grubby blue sweater and hand it calmly to April. I held myself still, even though I had begun to feel, all down my spine, a creeping doubt. Kahu ignored the goggles and ice-block wrapper, and reached into the bottom of the basket. What he pulled out was definitely red, but it was too large to be

a Walkman. Holding it higher, he waved it slightly for emphasis, and briefly flapped open its lid. That's when I saw that it
was a box of Cadbury Continental chocolates, just like the
ones Vanessa and I had been given on Christmas morning, and
empty inside, except for the wrappers.

FIFTEEN

The next day, when I went to the wooden cross at the usual time, Kahu wasn't there. I looked for him in the water, and down at the stormwater pipe, but he wasn't in any of the usual places. "I'm sure he'll be along soon," my mother said, settling herself into the sand. I couldn't tell her about the fight we'd had, because she didn't know my Walkman was missing. I hung about at Charlotte's cross for as long as I could bear, but I was wary of that place, and didn't much like being there without Kahu for company. Strange winds whipped through that little clearing, filling the air with plaintive sighs and long, drifting moans. Also, the flowers at the base of the cross were faded and dry, and because they were never left like that for long, I knew I ran the risk of running into Charlotte's mother again.

Back in the beige sand, my mother began to get very impa-

tient with me. "He'll be here soon," she kept saying. "For goodness' sake, it's like you never knew life before him." I think she
felt she couldn't go for a walk until I was properly occupied in
some way. Finally, to please her, I went into the water to do some
dolphin-diving, but my heart wasn't in it—it seemed pointless and childish. I couldn't believe this was how I'd spent my
days, before Kahu had come along. As soon as I saw my mother
heading south, beyond the stormwater pipe, I came out of the
water, grabbed my towel, and began to wander up the beach,
toward the surf lifesaving club. It was mid-morning by now—
a hot, windy day, not very pleasant. I knew that if I wandered
far enough north I would eventually bump into my sister, who
would be hanging out with Crystal and Stuart close to where
Josh was working.

The water that day was rough. Sand kept whipping into my
eyes. I couldn't find Vanessa anywhere on the beach or spot her
in the waves, and in the end it was Josh who helped me—he at
least stood out, in his bright red surf lifesaving shorts and yellow T-shirt, with two stripes of yellow zinc across his cheekbones. "She's there," he said, pointing. When I still couldn't see
her, he squatted down beside me and guided my eyes with his
finger. "*There*," he said, tapping my nose and then pointing at a
spot on the horizon.

Vanessa was standing a long way out, in waist-deep water,
her arms folded across her body. She was being buffeted by
waves, and she looked cold and reluctant. I thought nothing
of it. My sister was a perfectly capable swimmer, just not an
enthusiastic one. Crystal and Stuart were in the shallows, talk-

ing with their heads down, kicking their feet through the foam. I began to walk into the water. There were quite a few people about, but none as far out as Vanessa. I wondered why she'd gone all that way. I knew that she was being thrown together with Stuart a lot—was he getting on her nerves? Or Crystal? I saw a wave coming and turned my back on it, bracing myself, digging my toes into the sand. The wave slapped me hard on the backs of my legs, almost toppling me. I heard Crystal shriek and then laugh—she'd felt it too. My legs were stinging, and when I looked down I saw that they were pink and streaked lightly with blood. Pieces of driftwood were floating in the water, which was thick with sand, and the foam that was forming at the water's edge was yellowy brown. When I turned to face the horizon again, I couldn't see Vanessa. I searched for her, telling myself not to panic, and eventually I did spot her, further out than I'd ever seen her before—now just a head and shoulders, bobbing on the water and occasionally disappearing completely. I knew this was not a place she'd normally want to be. My father and I sometimes swam out that far, but never Vanessa. What was she doing out there? I turned to Crystal and Stuart, who were crouched down at the water's edge, inspecting the yellowish foam. "Hey!" I yelled. They didn't hear me. I looked out to Vanessa again. Was I looking at her face, or the back of her head? I swept my arm through the air: "Hey!" There was no reaction. I thought for sure that if she was really drowning, she would signal. She would shout and wave her arms.

That's when I thought of Josh. On previous occasions we'd seen Josh swim to people far out on the horizon, sometimes just to ask if they were okay. Vanessa wasn't drowning, she was trying to get Josh's attention. She was hoping that he would come jogging through the foam; that he'd swim out to her, and ask if she was okay. Maybe when he got there, Vanessa could fake a spell of dizziness, so that Josh would have to lock an arm around her waist and pull her back in.

When they got back to the shallows, he might even lift her off her feet and carry her.

It was a brilliant plan. I smiled, just thinking about it. Another wave came, and this time I decided I would face it head on, diving under and letting it swirl around me until I couldn't hold my breath a moment longer.

When I came up there was shouting. Without my knowing it, the wave had turned me, so that now I was facing the shore. I saw Crystal and Stuart looking at the horizon, but they were not the ones shouting. Another wave hit me on the back of the head—I had to dig my fingers hard into the sand, so as not to be bowled over. When it was safe to open my eyes again, I saw a commotion on the beach—in the beige sand, several people were getting to their feet, pointing out to sea. I felt excited, exhilarated—Vanessa's plan was working. I turned and thought I saw a figure, swimming in her direction. Josh, rescuing Vanessa! I walked over to Crystal and Stuart, preparing my face to look surprised and afraid. Crystal's hands were over her mouth— all I could see was her eyes, shocked and round. "What's happening?" I said. "Who's out there?" Neither Crystal nor Stuart could bring themselves to answer me—I had to turn away from them to hide another smile. Out in the ocean, the swimmer by now was barely visible. "Has he got her?" I heard someone ask—a stranger, further up the beach. "Oh my God, has he got her yet?"

We waited a long time in the shallows. To me, it felt like the elaborate games my friends and I invented at morning recess—as if at any minute a bell would ring, and we would be called inside to work on our decimals. I was embarrassed that strangers had become involved, and were gathering in numbers on the dank sand behind Crystal and Stuart. I wanted to wave them away, to tell them, "It's just a game we're playing, you wouldn't understand." But the game was going on too long. Soon, my mother would come walking back up the beach. She'd want to know if I'd found Kahu, and why I'd drifted so far north. She'd be mad, too, because she'd told us many times not to play at drowning, not to scream or wave our arms, unless it was absolutely necessary. I was frowning hard at the horizon, biting my lip. What was Josh doing out there? What was taking him so long? I thought of Kahu's uncle—the things he'd said about Tangaroa. *Sometimes he takes back.* Behind me I heard a familiar voice calling, "You should have come and got me." Impossibly, I turned and saw that it was Josh. He passed me, running into the water in high, hopping steps. I stared at his naked back—he had stripped his shirt off, just as Vanessa would have wanted. He waded out a way, and then stopped, turned, and said to me with pleading eyes, "She wasn't between the flags." I nodded, speechless. From the gathered crowd there came a hopeful murmur, and then sporadic, muted clapping, because out of the water, two figures were emerging. Vanessa, ashen-faced and hobbling. One arm folded across her chest, the other slung over the shoulders of a man with thick calves and a swollen belly, a man barely recognizable in shorts not meant for swimming, his usually fluffy white hair plastered thinly against his skull. The crowd, cheering, closed around them, and I was pushed back, to its edges. That's when I saw my mother approaching from the south, moving slowly at first, and then, after a brief, stunned pause, dropping her notebook and running.

SIXTEEN

The hospital was decorated with diagonally striped brown-and-gold wallpaper that at first made my eyes zing and then, as the hours dragged, made me feel giddy and sick. Vanessa lay on a narrow bed, dressed only in her togs, which had been stripped down to the waist, and a pale hospital gown, tied in three places at the back.

I had never seen my mother look so old. I had never seen her cry so much. At one stage the nurses debated putting us into a double room, so that my mother could be treated on a bed alongside Vanessa. "You'll have to be the strong one," a nurse winked at me, but then my father arrived, and I was allowed to be ten and invisible again.

My father only got halfway to my sister's bed before my mother grabbed him and clutched at him, burying her face in his chest, darkening the breast pocket of his T-shirt with her tears. Her behaviour seemed out of kilter with what had happened, even taking into account the shock. Vanessa was sitting up in bed with a cup of orange cordial and some colour in her cheeks. She had been rescued, she had never lost consciousness, she remembered the whole thing. "I tried to swim," she said, "but every time I looked up, the beach was further away. I kept swimming, and it kept getting further away." The nurses nodded and tutted—they had heard it all before, just last week they had heard it, and they would hear it again, they knew, maybe even before the day was out. "It can happen to the strongest swimmers," they said. Everyone nodded, and told Vanessa not to worry, it wasn't her fault. "Were you between the flags?" one of them pondered, and when it was revealed that we weren't, "Well, maybe they need to extend their reach." Quietly, in the corner, I had my doubts. I was the one watching Vanessa out there—the only one, barring her rescuer—and what I saw was not swimming. Was my sister drowning? Or was it a failed attempt to get Josh's attention?

On and on my mother cried. I became annoyed by her, and felt guilty for it, but then I caught the nurses glancing at each other, and I knew that they were irritated too. My father was patient, but wanted to know the details. First of all, was it a rip? And did Vanessa remember what he'd taught us about rips—to never swim against them, to let yourself be carried out, to swim to the side? Vanessa shook her head blankly—it wasn't a rip, it was a wave. "If it was just a wave you would have been able to swim back in," he countered, leaning forward. "It must have been a rip."

"I was there," I said. "I didn't see a rip."

He sighed—my answer frustrated him. Clearly we hadn't paid attention to his lessons about rips. "You can't see rips when you're in the water," he said. "That's what makes them so dangerous."

"Dad, I don't think it was a rip," Vanessa said.

"Well then—cramp? Did you get cramp?"

"I don't remember."

"You'd remember cramp."

My mother lifted her face from her hands. "Maybe it was an undercurrent?"

My father didn't know what to say then—we'd exhausted everything we knew about the ocean. I watched his shoulders sag a little, and thought I understood—if it wasn't a rip or a cramp that nearly took my sister, then it was something unknowable, something we were powerless to avoid or prevent.

My father took my chair and I sat on his knee. It was warm in his arms and for a while we were quiet. A nurse came in, saw my father for the first time, and said, "Well, hello there, Dad." She listened to Vanessa's chest with a stethoscope. "Good as gold," she said. "You'll be able to go home soon." "Is there anything we need to watch out for?" my father asked. "We'll give you an information sheet," the nurse replied. Then she turned to my mother. "How's Mum doing?" My mother smiled wanly. I had never spent time in a hospital before and had never heard anyone talk to my parents in this way—as though they were children. Before she left, the nurse said to my father, "Be sure to ask for a sheet." After that, we all fell silent again. Vanessa shuffled down the bed a bit and closed her eyes. My father's knee was drumming under my thigh. It had been good while the nurse was in the room, but now we were all too aware of the hum of the tube light behind Vanessa's bed. I sensed that my father had more he wanted to say, and realized I was holding my breath.

"Where were you when it happened?"

I think I knew that he was talking to my mother, but it was easy enough to misunderstand. "In the water," I said. "I got knocked over by the same wave."

"No, you didn't," Vanessa said.

"Yes, I did. It took me under and I went round and round, but I just held my breath, and when it stopped, I came up again." I turned to my father. "It was only knee deep."

"I was further out than you," Vanessa said.

"A bit further, not much."

"What would you know? The water was up to my chest."

"Actually, it was up to your waist."

"Chest."

"Waist."

"Chest."

"Girls!" my father barked.

Our little quarrel had set my mother off crying again. "We'll have to thank that man," she said, dabbing her eyes with the balled-up fragments of a tissue the nurses had given her hours ago. "We'll have to find him and thank him."

"Where were you though, when it happened?"

Under my thigh, my father's knee had stopped drumming. This was what he'd been building to, all along, and he wasn't going to be diverted this time. *Where were you? How could you let this happen?* My mother swiped at the swollen tip of her nose with the tissue-ball. I thought she hadn't heard, and that we would have to endure the question for a third time, but then she shrugged, and said, "I was on a walk."

"On a walk?"

"Yes, on a beach walk. I do it every day."

"Every day."

My mother rolled her eyes. "Yes, dear, every day."

My father cleared his throat, shifting back a little in his chair so that his knees came up, tipping me off balance. "How far do you go? I mean, how long are these beach walks?"

I wriggled out of my father's grasp, sliding to the floor. To remain on his knee was to choose a side.

"I don't know—twenty minutes, half an hour?"

I glanced at Vanessa, who glanced back at me. My mother's walks always took her away from us for at least forty minutes. I climbed onto the high bed, next to Vanessa's feet, and pulled my knees up to my chin. Vanessa moved her feet a little, so that they were resting against my back.

"You were only gone twenty minutes, and this all happened?"

"It only takes a few minutes for things to go wrong in the water."

My father made an exasperated, puffing sound with his lips, as if to say, *My point exactly*. My mother replied, "I don't know why you're huffing and puffing. You were the one rolling your eyes when I suggested the girls needed watching at the beach."

"Well, I'm just not sure why you'd make such a fuss about going with them to the beach every day, only to wander off and leave them alone in the water. I mean, I thought you were watching them—that's what I thought. If I'd known . . ."

"If you'd known—what? You would have done what?"

"Come down to the beach and helped out."

"Really? You would have torn yourself away from the cricket?"

"Yes."

My father's voice was mild, reasonable. My mother pressed her lips tightly together, as if holding back a torrent of words—clever words that would win the argument. She held her face like that for a long time, sitting stiffly on her chair with her arms folded and her legs crossed, thrusting her foot back and forth in time with the hum of the tube light. I watched the wallpaper zing until my eyes throbbed, and then I watched the door handle, praying for a nurse with an information sheet. Finally, Vanessa yawned, and it seemed to break the spell—we were reminded of why we were there. My mother brought her swinging foot to a halt. "I could have become that woman," she said.

"What woman?" we asked.

"That poor woman, the one who lost her daughter a couple of years ago. That could have been me." She looked at my father. "Remember I told you? The one who keeps that shrine on the beach. I saw her the other day. I'm sure it was her. I saw her and I thought . . . oh, it was awful. I thought, There but for the grace of God. I mean, I tend to think . . . because our girls are such strong swimmers, you know?" She unfolded her arms and began to hunt around for her tissue-ball, which had dropped down beside her on the chair. "They say she wears a coat—well, she wasn't wearing a coat. But she wasn't dressed right—that's what drew my attention. She wasn't dressed right for the beach. She was wearing this long-sleeved, shapeless shirt—a man's shirt, is what I thought—and she was standing, just looking at the water, sort of hugging herself. I was . . . walking, and I passed by quite close to her, and I could have sworn she was crying. Her eyes were closed and she was sort of . . . My God, my heart went out to her, mother to mother. I could hardly bear it." She held the tissue-ball to the end of her nose and closed her eyes.

"When did this happen?" my father asked.

Her eyes opened. "The other day. I meant to tell you but by the time I got home . . . well, anyway, it's not kind to gossip. Plus, there were children and teenagers around and I didn't want to upset anyone. But the point is, you never think it can happen to you, do you?"

"It hasn't happened," my father said gently. "Vanessa is okay."

My mother nodded. I thought it was a good thing she'd found the ball of tissue because her eyes were welling up again. "Yes, yes, but it *could* have happened," she said. "I mean, it might have, if it wasn't for that man. We must thank him. We must find him and give him all our thanks."

"Of course we must," my father agreed, gesturing for me to come back to his knee. I slid off the bed, relieved. They wouldn't argue while I was sitting on his knee, between them.

"Do we have his details? Was he just a passer-by?"

My mother looked at Vanessa, who shrugged. I held my tongue for as long as I could, but it seemed a hopeless situation—they were bound to find out, one way or another.

"I know who he is," I said, pressing my face to my father's chest. "He lives in the big house next to ours. He's our neighbour."

In the end, a doctor came and said my sister couldn't go home just yet. There was a thing called secondary drowning, he said, and my sister was at risk of it. I had never seen my mother's eyes get so large and scared as they did then. "I've never heard of secondary drowning," she said, and I could tell that she couldn't wait to get on the phone and tell our grandmother about it. My mother loved to swap horror stories with her mother, and to shudder and tut down the phone.

After the doctor had gone the nurse came back and said, "No need for Mum *and* Dad to wait." I got the feeling she had her doubts about secondary drowning. My father stood up and slapped the pockets of his pants, checking for his wallet and keys. "I'll take this one home," he said, tilting his head toward me. The nurse nodded approvingly. I was so desperate to get out of that striped room that I forgot to say goodbye to Vanessa on my way out. Later it occurred to me that she could drown secondarily, and the last memory she would have of me was my walking out of that room without a backward glance. But then I realized that dead people don't have memories—only the living do. I was thinking about this in the car driving back to the holiday house, when my father pulled up at a fruit-and-veg shop I didn't recognize, on the outskirts of town. The shop had FRESH BERRIES and FANCY LETTUCE painted in huge blue letters above the door, which was in fact a large, corrugated-iron door like the one on our garage at home. I closed my eyes and rested my head against the window, hoping for corn on the cob and watermelon—not asparagus and grapefruit. But when my father came back he was holding a big bunch of yellow-and-white flowers, wrapped in waxy green tissue paper, which he held out to me. "Take these, would you?" I sat up straight, taking the flowers, which were heavy enough to make my wrist ache. I knew very little about flowers but knew that these were the kind that would stain your clothes if you brushed against them. "Watch the stamens," my father said. I was very tired, and couldn't be bothered talking. If I could have been bothered, I would have said, "Are these for Vanessa?"

The drive home was just long enough to send me into a half-sleep. Twice I nearly dropped the flowers, with their bright orange stamens, into my lap. When we pulled up outside the holiday house, I was relieved to pass them back to my father so that I could climb out of the car. "Just a quick stop here to freshen up," he said, "and then we'll deliver the flowers."

I paused, one foot out of the car. "We're going back to the hospital?"

"No. The flowers are for our neighbour. You said you knew which house he lived in, right? Is it that one?" He pointed to a dark wooden house on a large, leafy section directly next to ours, on Palmer Street—not to the one at the back, where the neighbour lived. "We'll pop over there in a minute."

"We're going there?"

"Yes," my father said, unlocking the front door. "We have to thank him for what he did."

Inside, he pulled a large glass bowl out of a cupboard and put it in the sink, filling it with water. He balanced the flowers in the bowl and went to the bathroom. "Get into some dry clothes—we're leaving in ten minutes," he called. I went to my bedroom and sat heavily on my bed. I had the feeling I was caught in a surprise wave—one of those ones that hid itself, churning just beneath the surface, until it was right beneath your feet. I didn't want to visit the neighbour or have my father visit him. I wanted nothing to do with him.

If I had kept my mouth shut at the hospital my parents still wouldn't know the identity of my sister's rescuer. Perhaps I could have come up with an elaborate lie: *I thanked him then and there—he said he didn't want any fuss.* Now, my only hope was that my father thought my sister's rescuer lived in the dark wooden house next to ours. If I chose to say nothing, our mission to deliver the flowers would fail. A woman might answer the door of that house, or a younger man, or nobody at all. My father would grow irritated with me, but I could live with that. "Sorry," I'd mutter. "I thought I'd seen him before, but maybe I was confused." The flowers would be returned to the sink. But what if the man came out on his deck tomorrow, or the next day, as he almost always did? My father would be bound to notice him now. "Why didn't you tell me it was that house?" He might be really angry then—especially if, in the meantime, his expensive flowers had died in the sink. I felt hot just thinking about it. Already, that summer, my lies were stacked up around me—the lost Walkman, the vomit that wasn't mine, my fight with Kahu.

I decided to tell the truth. Tell my father that the man who rescued my sister lived in the house directly behind ours. As soon as the decision was made, I felt better—I was out of the churning wave, standing on my own two feet. Delivering the flowers with my father, I would be sure to keep my eyes down—hang behind him, tuck into his leg like a much younger child. How many times had I made myself invisible? With any luck, the neighbour would hardly notice I was there.

I changed into dry clothes and went straight to my parents' bedroom, full of resolve. Ten minutes had gone by already. I expected to find my father patting his pockets for his keys, ready to go. My parents' room was smaller and less light-filled than ours—it housed one queen-sized bed, a small bedside table with a single drawer and a cupboard underneath, and along the wall, a low bookcase. My father was sitting on the bed with his back to me. His shoulders were hunched, his head down. Beside him, the single drawer in the bedside table had been pulled all the way open. It was empty. I knew this drawer—it was where my mother kept the pages of the book she was writing. I knew because one evening, when I was looking for a pencil to do some drawing with, I had wandered absent-mindedly toward this bedside drawer to open it, and my mother had said sharply, from the lounge where she was watching the television with one eye on me, *Out!* She meant out of the drawer, not out of the room, but her shouting gave me such a fright that I whirled right out of their bedroom and had hardly dared to go back since. "Sorry," she said to me later, when no one was around. "It's where I keep my book."

My father was sitting on the bed reading my mother's book. Or not exactly reading it, but searching through it—scanning it. He would turn a page and run his finger in a loose zigzag all the way down it, for five or six seconds, and then he would flip the page over and move on to the next one. Every now and then he would pause and appear to read more closely for a while. He was so absorbed in his work that he didn't notice me until I was standing right at his shoulder. "That's Mum's," I said. He nodded, clearing his throat, and tucking the pages of the book back together. "Yes, I was just . . . Your mother mentioned something about losing her notebook today. So I thought I'd have a look for it."

"She lost the notebook at the beach. Not here."

"Ah yes, of course, that would make sense," he said, putting the pages back in the drawer. I frowned—he hadn't put the book back together properly, some of the pages were turned the wrong way or partially folded. If my mother saw her pages like that, she would know immediately that someone had been looking at them.

My father put his hands on my shoulders and propelled me out of the room, into the lounge. I saw the dreaded flowers poking out of the sink and knew the time had come to tell my father the truth about the house next door. But my father started tidying up the lounge, straightening cushions and putting away magazines, as if we had nothing pressing to do, and nowhere to be. I stood, watching him. It was on the tip of my tongue to tell him that he needed to go back and straighten the pages of my mother's book. "Don't we get ourselves in a mess," he said, sweeping crumbs from the seat of an armchair. I didn't know if he meant the crumbs, or something else. He pottered about a bit more, and then, without looking at me, he said in the same light, half-hearted manner, "Don't you want to listen to your music? Or read a comic?" I headed back to my room, relieved. We wouldn't be delivering the flowers after all. A few minutes later I heard, coming through the wall, a low scraping sound, a kind of gentle rumbling. It was the sound of the bedside drawer opening—the one where my mother kept her book.

SEVENTEEN

My mother was thoroughly rattled by the term *secondary drowning*. She brought Vanessa home in a taxi around dinner time, with fish and chips they had picked up on the way. The evening had a mildly celebratory feel, helped along by the flowers in the sink. My parents sat close to Vanessa, and kept touching her, stroking her hair or patting her arm, as if to check she was there. My mother was obsessed with her colour. Was she a little pale? Was that a touch of purple around her nose? Did her cheeks look waxy to anyone else? We were allowed extra helpings of ice cream for dessert because my mother said the sugar would do Vanessa good. Then, at bedtime, my mother gave Vanessa paracetamol and a hot-water bottle, even though it was usually too warm inside our room, and we always kicked off our sheets. "Fresh air will be the thing," she said next, opening the window above Vanessa's bed.

I thought it was odd—the hot-water bottle and the open window—and found the whole thing ridiculous. My sister had been under the water for no time at all, brought down by a wave I had outlasted. I couldn't help but resent the fuss that was being made of her. "Personally," I sniped at her while we were brushing our teeth, "I'd rather drown than be rescued by *him*."

I guess she must have been feeling pretty wiped out, because instead of flying at me, or yelling for our mother, all she did was give me a frown and a nod. Feeling brave, I added, "I know what you were trying to do, by the way. I know you were trying to get Josh's attention." She looked at me so blankly then—toothpaste foaming at the corners of her mouth, eyes all heavy and bloodshot—that I wondered if I'd been wrong about what happened on the beach that day.

That night, my mother checked on Vanessa three times, each time leaning all the way over my sister's face almost as if to kiss her; laying the flat of her hand against her brow, and then the back of her hand against her cheek, adjusting her sheets and pillows, tweaking the curtains, and then standing still and silent next to the bed for a few moments with her elbows bent and her hands drawn up to her face. I couldn't see well, in the dark, with only one eye open, but I think what she was doing was praying, and I was really surprised, because my mother generally scoffed at people who prayed. I stayed very still, and tried to look sweet, in the hope that she would stop at my bed on the way out—tweak my sheets, touch my brow, and pray for me too. (A part of me thought it would be nice to have a mother who wore hats to church and said grace at the table, like the mothers I saw on American television shows.) I have to say that she didn't pray for me at all, in fact she swept past my bed without the slightest hesitation, but I felt safer anyway, sleeping well between checks, and waking the next morning with a hopeful feeling inside me, that things were going to go back to normal.

~~~~~

But the first thing I saw when I emerged, early, from our bedroom, was the tips of those yellow-and-white flowers, rising out of the sink. Their stain-spreading stamens, lit up in the morning sun like candles on a cake. I had forgotten about them, and about my father's promise to deliver them, and now it all came flooding back, and the hopeful feeling evaporated. The thought of knocking on our neighbour's door—coming face to face with him—made me sick to my stomach. I thought about pouring boiling water on those flowers to prematurely shrivel them. I thought about dropping them out the kitchen window, running around to where they lay in the grass, shredding them with my fingers, and scattering their remains under the bushes by the fence. I *did* carefully tip all their water down the sink, leaving the bottom of the bowl dry, but when I checked a few hours later, the bowl had been refilled. Prolonging my agony, all of that day passed, and still we didn't deliver the flowers—my parents slept late into the morning, as did Vanessa, and then it was discovered that we had left Vanessa's bag of lotions at the hospital. We drove back to the hospital to collect the bag, and there, my mother got talking to a couple of nurses about Vanessa's poor colour, her lack of appetite (she had refused breakfast), and her mood, which was flat.

After the hospital we got petrol for the car, and cream

doughnuts for lunch, which we ate sitting by the side of the road with the car doors open and our legs in the sun. It was a hot day, and I was dying to go to the beach, but I was also afraid to open my mouth—afraid to disturb in any way the course of the day, which I believed was slowly bending in my favour. With every hour that passed, it became less likely that we would deliver the flowers, or it became more likely that Vanessa would have to do it—the nurses had said that in a day or so, she would be completely back to normal, and could swim, walk and sunbathe as usual. Arriving home from our excursion that day I held my breath, fearful that our neighbour would be sitting in his white plastic chair, watching for our car, but he was not there, although his chair was out, his sliding glass door wide open, and music was coming from inside his house.

By four p.m. I had begun to think the flowers might never be delivered. Their stamens, to my eye, looked a little less bright, and had begun to shed orange powder into the sink. At a quarter past four my mother announced that she was going for a walk. She announced this only to me, because I was the only one awake. My sister was curled up on her bed with a magazine partially covering her face, and my father was in my parents' bedroom, napping. My mother said she was only popping out for a short time to see if she could find her notebook, which she'd dropped in the sand the day before, but I noticed that she'd changed into a pretty pair of white shorts, a woven leather belt and a navy singlet top. She then went to wet her hair a little in the bathroom, shaking it out, and saying, "That'll do." I thought it was a lot of trouble to go to, for a notebook she'd probably never find.

"Will you be able to finish, if you don't find it?" I asked.

She looked confused. "Finish what?"

"Your book," I said. It felt strange to say it, because the book was a secret. I wondered if, following Vanessa's accident, we would no longer have secrets from each other. But my mother shrugged. "I'll manage," she said.

She'd only been gone a few minutes when my father emerged from the bedroom. "No Mum?" he said. He looked surprisingly alert for someone who had been asleep for almost an hour. I told him that she'd gone for one of her walks. Maybe I shouldn't have put it like that—*one of her walks*. My father went back into their bedroom and re-emerged with sneakers on his feet. "Time to pay a visit to our neighbour," he said. After all my fretting, I almost felt glad. At least it would be over soon. I began to rouse myself from the couch, but my father shook his head. "You stay here and look after your sister. I'll go."

I sat quickly back down, swallowing my surprise—at home in Wellington, we were never left alone in the house, and, being the youngest, I'd never been tasked with looking after anyone, ever, in my life.

My father dithered for a moment, looking for his house keys, and then realized he wouldn't need them, because both of us girls would be at home. I watched him, hardly able to believe my luck. I would no longer have to worry about the flowers, and with both my parents out of the house, I'd even be able to sneak a couple of biscuits from the tin under the sink. My father went quickly through a list of instructions: don't open the door to anyone, don't touch anything, and don't wake your sister, she needs to rest. I nodded, trying hard to look serious, and keep the excitement from my eyes. "I won't be long at all," he said. "I'm just going to deliver the flowers and then I'll be straight back." He seemed in a hurry to go—he kept glancing out the kitchen window as he was talking. It wasn't until after he'd gone that I realized I'd forgotten to tell him to go to the white house, not the brown wooden one. But it hardly mattered anyway, because when I went to the kitchen to steal biscuits, I saw that my father had left without taking the flowers.

EIGHTEEN

I'm not sure why my mother decided to check on Vanessa that second night—more than thirty-six hours after what had happened at the beach. Secondary drowning was playing on her mind, I guess, and Vanessa had been so quiet and sullen all day, eating only a small dinner, and taking herself off to bed early.

It was well past midnight when my mother came to our room. I slept through her entrance, and woke to find her fussing with the open window. High winds were forecast that night, and my mother had opted to keep our window closed. Now it was open, and the curtains were whipping wildly in the air above Vanessa's bed. My mother was so thrown by this, that at first she didn't notice the bed was empty. I did—I knew what the open window meant. I came to my senses very quickly, sitting straight up in my bed and saying in a clear voice, "She must have gone to the toilet." I think I gave my mother a terrible fright, because she gasped and froze, her fingers on the window latch. Maybe she thought I was sleep-talking, because at first she didn't answer. I said again, "She's on the toilet. She always takes ages on the toilet."

My mother said sharply, "Go back to sleep." She was still confused I think—by the open window, the whipping curtains and my too-clear voice. I heard her patting the sheets where Vanessa's sleeping body should have been. Then she crossed the room and switched on the light, revealing what I already knew—that Vanessa's bed was empty.

"What . . . ?"

I began to utter my toilet excuse again, but my mother cut me off. "She's not in the toilet, I just came from there." There was nothing I could say then. I could only watch as my mother's panic grew. It was almost comical—the way she checked the kitchen floor, as if Vanessa might have decided to take a nap on the linoleum, and checked the couches—even lifting cushions—and then the bath, behind the curtain, and the laundry, where there was nothing but a washing machine, a stainless-steel tub and a peg basket. All the while, her movements becoming more frenzied, her voice rising—she turned on every light, and turned nothing off. By the time my father emerged from his bed, bleary-eyed, the house was lit like a stage.

"She's gone!" my mother wailed. I had never heard her wail like that before. I felt as though I left my body then—I felt myself rising to the ceiling. To calm down I would usually have reached for my Walkman—not even to listen to it, just to feel the soft foam ear cushions under my fingers—but my Walkman was gone and I had nothing. "She'll come back," I said to my mother. My voice sounded foreign and distant. "She always does." My mother flew at me—grabbing me by the shoulders. I was glad to be up there on the ceiling, and not really in my body. "What do you mean, *She always does?*"

I tried to take back what I had said, claiming confusion, but it was too late. My parents sat me down on an armchair and fired questions at me, taking turns to pace the house—my father must have checked our bedroom four or five times, hoping to find it was all a mistake. My mother kept going to the kitchen sink, wailing at the windows, and coming back. I think my calm annoyed them—I was up on the ceiling, that's why. I was seeing them for the first time as if they were strangers. My father's face was old and crumpled, my mother's hair was streaked with grey. "How often does she do this?" my mother wailed. "How many times?"

"Not every night," I said calmly.

"*Not every night?*"

They repeated a lot of the things I said, and looked at each other, incredulous. I just kept saying that she would be back. "Where?" my mother said. "When?"

"She'll come back to the window, with Crystal. She'll climb in."

I felt very disloyal saying this about my sister—I felt I had broken some kind of sister-code, and was becoming a snitch. But I knew that if I had said nothing the problem would only have got bigger—my parents would have called the police, they would have woken the entire neighbourhood. My father walked to the other side of the room and back again with his fists clenched. "That *bitch*," he said. "That little *bitch*." I thought he was talking about Vanessa, and it seemed like the end of the world, the end of everything I knew—my father talking about my sister like that. But then I realized he meant Crystal. My mother told him to shut up, and watch his language. I sat in the chair and closed my eyes, willing it to be over. The next time my mother stationed herself at the kitchen window, I said to my father, very quietly, "Don't tell Vanessa that I told you." My father nodded sharply, as if it was a given that he wouldn't tell—but also to show me that my concerns were childish and silly, the least of our worries. Still, I *was* worried. Vanessa would never, ever forget that I told—that's what I was thinking. When we were old ladies together, with white hair and grandchildren, she would still remember. I shook my head and said again to my father, "*Please* don't tell."

He nodded again, but less sharply this time.

I felt myself move back inside my body then, and after that, no matter how bad things got, I stayed there—I never went back to the ceiling again. I'm not sure I could have if I'd tried. Eventually I was put to bed in my parents' room. It was the first time I'd ever slept in a double bed—not that I slept. I had a bad feeling in my tummy—a ball that fizzed and bubbled. I lay in the very middle of the bed, in the dip between the pillows, so that my ears were shielded, but I still heard most of what happened when Vanessa tried to come back in through the window.

My parents, by then, were waiting in the dark in our bedroom. They had decided to spring a trap on my sister, rather than rush out to meet her at the gate, or leave all the lights on in the house as a warning to her. The first sign that Vanessa was back was a crunching outside the window. A low thud against the wall. I heard a voice that might have been Crystal's. The ball in my stomach began to spin. There was a loud click, which I took for a light switch, hit hard, in anger. A moment of stunned silence and then a gasp—*Holy shit!*—followed by running footsteps. Crystal. I was surprised my parents let her get away. Next came a strange, scuffling silence—a pause, as my parents helped Vanessa back in through the window. A jangle of curtain rings and my father's muted grunt. The silence confused me—had my parents' anger burned itself out already? Was Vanessa going to be let off with a warning?

But of course, it was only the calm before the storm.

My parents took it in turns to shout at Vanessa, and even though I was on the other side of the wall, lying alone in the dark, I cringed as though I was in Vanessa's place. I tried to invent responses that might lessen the trouble she was in, and when I thought I had a good one, I tried to send it to her by telepathy, through the wall. But Vanessa didn't say much. I hardly heard her voice. My parents' voices wore away at what remained of the night. *You are forbidden to see that girl. You are forbidden from going to the beach. The cheek! Do you understand the danger you put yourself in, you stupid, stupid girl? You are not to leave this house. No, not at all!* I wondered how my mother could be praying over Vanessa's bed one night, and shouting at her with such venom the next. I gathered that they took away Vanessa's magazines—I heard rustling, and soft protests from Vanessa, and then I heard our bedroom door being thrown open, and a series of dull thuds. My father was throwing Vanessa's beloved magazines across the lounge, one by one. He was aiming them at the far wall above the couch, where they smacked and tore.

I can smell it on your breath!, he was shouting. At that point I knew our family would never recover from this—not completely. The words that had been shouted would die on the air, but in the morning the ruined magazines would still be there, lying on the floor behind the couch. No amount of time would fix their broken spines or straighten their crumpled pages.

I rolled onto my stomach, pulled the two pillows over my head, and willed myself to sleep.

NINETEEN

The flowers my father bought for the neighbour died in the sink. My mother tutted every time she walked past them, and occasionally batted them with the back of her hand. They began to smell. The smell reminded me of the gym at school after PE class. Meanwhile, our neighbour kept a low profile, only occasionally coming out to sit in his usual spot on the deck behind our house, and never once coming forward to enquire after my sister. *How are you doing, since you nearly drowned that day?* To me, this felt wrong. A *real* good Samaritan would not have concealed himself in the shadows. A man with nothing to hide— a man like my father—would have introduced himself, smiling and waving, and resting his elbows on the glass balustrade to chat. *Oh*, he would have said modestly, *it was nothing. Right place at the right time, she was light as a feather, anyone would have done it.*

Vanessa, who had been banned from seeing her friends and

banned from the beach, had nothing to do but sunbathe on the lawn. My parents were at a loss for what to do with her. She did not speak. She had not spoken a word to any of us since that night. She blamed me for the way my parents had ambushed her as she'd tried to climb back through the window, as if I should have invented some warning system to let her know her cover was blown. The fact that I was tucked up in my parents' bed when she got home suggested to her that I had ratted her out, without my father ever having to say a thing.

She was so *good* at not talking. It was fascinating to watch her get through breakfast with nothing but a series of shrugs and blinks, and from breakfast, how she negotiated her way through the complicated morning routine of showering, bed-making and laundry-sorting without a single word. She walked a fine line between contrite and rude, but my parents' voices too were worn out, their anger well and truly spent. They had nothing left. My mother was obviously missing her beach walks, and spent the mornings repeatedly wiping the kitchen bench, hardly eating, and pacing the lounge, gazing at the windows. Her pacing made us all nervous—my father's hands shook. I was the only "normal" one, and I played my part the best I could, filling Vanessa's silences when we were indoors with nonsense gabble about anything I could think of—Split Enz, the weather, the number of days 'til school, 'til Easter, 'til *next* Christmas. When we were outdoors, I threw myself around the lawn, counting the number of cartwheels I could do in a row, or the number of grasshoppers I could scatter with one sweep of my leg. Anything to make us seem like a family again.

After a couple of days of this, my parents decided we should go to the local swimming pool together. The beach was ruled out indefinitely because Josh worked there, and wherever Josh was, Crystal was too. The mall was also thought unsuitable for a grounded teenaged girl—too much like fun. (I was pleased, at least, about that.) My mother and father conferred quietly in their bedroom and decided the local swimming pool was just right, with its three toddler pools, one ancient water slide, one large lane pool with diving board, a "family spa," and everywhere, primitive murals of leaping dolphins, swooping seagulls and sunbathing turtles. It was uncool, wholesome, cheap, vast and loud—the perfect place for all of us to be together, without actually having to *be together*.

I think we were all pretty desperate by then to get out of the house. My father barely had to utter the word "pool" before we were all rushing around, helping each other get ready. We ran back and forth from the car, packing towels, goggles, sun hats and books. We slathered our legs in sunblock and put our togs on under our clothes. My mother threw four cushions in the back seat, and then, at the last minute, decided the cushions belonged to the holiday house and we shouldn't take them. In the confusion, we forgot to bring the picnic she had hastily prepared—it was left sitting on the bench in the sun and all the food inside, the ham and cheese and lettuce, went limp and sweaty and had to be thrown out when we got back. We also forgot to check what time the pool opened, and had to wait fifteen minutes in our car in the near-empty parking lot. The air, at that time in the morning, was too cool for swimming—there was a breeze that skidded through the tops of trees and threatened to spoil everything. But the pool, when at last we were allowed to enter (we were first-equal with a tired-faced woman and what looked like her two elderly aunts), was pristine. The morning sun, where it touched the water, sent out tendrils of light that danced across the yellow-painted wooden seats and licked the bellies of the leaping dolphins. We had no idea where to sit—we were spoilt for choice. In the end my parents headed for the blue plastic sunloungers over by the family spa, while Vanessa and I took a yellow seat each. (I lost mine later, to a family of red-headed children, and ended up perching on the end of my father's lounger on my wet towel.)

When my mother realized about the forgotten picnic, I thought the day might be ruined. We would be allowed to stay until our stomachs grumbled, and then we would be forced to go home. But my mother and father held another of their urgent little conferences—heads down, voices low, huddled together on the blue loungers. It was decided we could carry on without the food from home. Instead we ate junk food from the canteen at the pool—deliciously over-salted hot chips, sugary dough-nuts, sausage rolls, soft ice cream and warm fizzy drinks. The weather gave us something to talk about whenever our paths crossed—*Did the breeze pick up? Do you think it changed direction? Is it just me, or did it get warmer?*—and being first-equal into the pool gave us a sense of ownership. It was *our* pool, especially when the tired-faced woman and her aunts left about half an hour after they'd arrived. Vanessa didn't talk, but she didn't scowl either, or fake-sleep, or cry into her towel, as she'd done a number of times at home on the lawn; her shoulder blades jerking under a blanket of her sun-bleached hair. She climbed in and out of the pool enough to suggest that she wanted to be there, and when I asked her to watch me do stunts on the diving board, she turned herself in my general direction, shielded her eyes from the sun, gave the slightest nod when my turn came, and was still there when I resurfaced.

When I wasn't performing stunts off the diving board, I patrolled the deep end of the pool like a shark. Watching my parents on the loungers. Studying them. Did they look normal sitting there, or was there something unusual in the distance between them? Some couples had tried to make a little island of themselves—they'd pulled their loungers together until they touched, or they'd angled them inward to make a triangle. My parents' loungers were as they'd found them. My father was reading the same newspaper he'd bought from the corner shop on the way to the pool. My father was dedicated to his newspapers but to make one last all day was a feat even for him. He was wearing his swimming shorts, which were small and black—not the smallest kind of swimsuit a man could wear but not far from it. His legs, protruding from the newspaper, were too long for the lounger, darkly tanned, covered in a fine downward sweep of nearly black hair, and as lean as horse's legs—skinny but with the promise of power. He might have been the happiest man in the world, hidden behind his newspaper, or he might have been brooding. His ankles were neatly crossed and his right foot, jandal-clad, tapped out some unknown rhythm. My mother, sitting next to him on her lounger that pointed straight ahead—not toward him—was reading a book, while across her lap, a new notebook lay open. She hadn't been able to find the one she'd dropped on the beach the day Vanessa had nearly drowned, and once the shock of that day had worn off, the loss of the notebook had affected her badly—for a few hours we'd all thought she might give up her book-writing altogether. The notebook had everything in it, she said, all her forward and backward planning, her plot alternatives, the little fixes she thought of in the middle of the night and meant to get to later. My father, meaning well, had taken a detour from buying petrol to track down a beautiful new notebook, slightly larger than pocket-sized, with a black leather cover and a slim grey ribbon. I thought it was an excellent choice, but my mother frowned when she saw it, calling it "too pretty to touch."

Now, the new notebook was lying open on my mother's lap, and I was hoping like anything that she'd write in it. Her acceptance of the notebook was critical, I believed, to the future of our family. While my parents had been taking it in turns to shout at Vanessa, they had at least been united, on the same team. Once the shouting was over, they'd seemed to drift in opposite directions. I thought that if my mother picked up that notebook and started scribbling in it, my father might lower his newspaper, look her way, and smile. He might even reach out and squeeze her knee.

I hung about in the greasy water for a long time, willing this to happen, but my mother never picked up the notebook, and my father's hands never left his newspaper. Then, just as I was growing hopeful (my mother had put the book she was reading down, and was gazing into space), my father got up from his lounger. He folded his newspaper quite carefully and placed it squarely on the seat to save his spot. Then he stretched his long arms, yawned, and dug his car keys out of the pocket of his shorts. I watched from the deep end with my breath held.

If my father walks away from my mother without a word, I said to myself, we're doomed. Never mind that my father had probably walked away from my mother without a word many times before—on this day I decided his doing so would doom us. *Smile at her*, I silently pleaded. *Say something nice.* My father was performing the most elaborate stretches with his arms—was he trying to get her attention?

Look at him. Smile.

My mother glanced up at my father, a slightly peevish expression on her face—my father's stretches were casting her legs into shade. I almost ducked under the water—it was too hard to watch. But then my father dropped his arms, and my mother gave a tight little smile, nodding her head. My father had said something to her. Not, I love you, let's be friends, but something like, I'm going to the car to get my book. We were not doomed then, but not exactly saved yet either. At the pool they played music over a crackly sound system and the song that came on just then was "Sweet Dreams" by Eurythmics. It was a very catchy song, very popular, but from the moment I'd first heard it, I'd felt that it was evil—a bad omen. To sing along to it, or tap my foot to its rhythm, would bring very, very bad luck. My father was walking around the side of the pool, jiggling his car keys, and in my distraction I accidentally, absent-mindedly sang a few words of "Sweet Dreams" while treading water in the pool.

I slapped my hand over my mouth. Had it been possible, I might have quickly jumped out of the pool, run to the loungers, and played some Split Enz songs on my Walkman to counter the bad luck. Without my Walkman, all I could do was watch the bad luck play out.

My father had jandals on his feet and his towel was nicely twisted and wrapped around his neck. Out here, dressed like that, he could have gone anywhere. He could have gone to a restaurant and ordered a three-course meal. I felt suddenly afraid that our father was going to leave us. I believed it even more strongly than I had at the bend in the river. I'd heard about men leaving in broad daylight—going off to the shop for cigarettes or to walk the dog and never coming home. I'd thought that could never apply to us, because my father wasn't a smoker and we didn't own a dog. Now I understood that a family wasn't a particularly solid thing—it was a bubble purely of our own making and just like a bubble, it could burst. "Sweet Dreams" was still playing over the sound system, loudly enough that I could hear it under water. It was such a hit song that every face I looked at was singing along, every mouth moving to the words, wrapping me in bad luck, drowning me in it.

I swam to the end of the pool closest to the exit. My father was saying something to the teenager on the door. She nodded, and he kept going, through the turnstile, into the car park. I climbed out of the pool and scampered to where the teenager sat. Water dripped from between my legs. The teenager was singing along too. I tried not to look at her mouth, or breathe the air she was breathing, which was full of bad luck. She had blue eyeliner right around the edges of her small brown eyes. I pointed at the turnstile. She shook her head once. "I can't let you out on your own."

I had to step aside then, to let a young couple through with a baby that was fussing. Then I pointed to where my father was loping across the car park in long strides. "That's my dad,"

I said. I was shivering now and there was a crack in my voice. The teenager frowned at me. She unfolded her legs, stood, and leaned out over the counter to see. "Okay," she said. She pressed a button that released the turnstile. I ducked through. My plan was to catch up with my father at the car; tell him there was something I wanted from the glovebox. He wouldn't be able to leave us for ever with me standing there, shivering in my wet togs.

I trotted after him in my bare feet—the tarmac was very hot, meaning that now I had blue lips, a chattering jaw and burning feet. I thought there might be a half-eaten packet of sweets in the glovebox that I could use as my excuse. Failing that, I was sure there was a dot-to-dot book. My father was almost at our car when I saw him stop. Abruptly he came to a standstill like something had occurred to him, or he'd spotted a big fat bug in his path. I stopped too. My father was looking across the car park at a family that was moving around a small red car. They were going from the boot to the front seats, collecting towels and floatation devices and small foldable chairs. They were fully clothed, and their dark hair was dry and tidy-looking. They'd clearly just arrived for the afternoon. I ducked behind a car so that I could watch my father watching this family. My father stood completely still. The family with the red car started closing doors—*thud, thud, thud.* I heard a high-pitched laugh that I thought I recognized. I raised my head a few inches and saw Lucy's mother, frowning, rooting through a big flowery bag. She was talking to Lucy's father in a quick-fire way that made me think she was impatient to get into the pool. My father began to move then—slowly toward our car. He unlocked the front passenger door, leaned in, lifted a book from the seat, and closed the door, and all the while he kept his head up and his eyes on Lucy's family. Lucy's mother by now had gone back to the red car to find whatever it was that wasn't in her big flowery bag. Lucy was pulling on her father's hand. I didn't need to speak their language to know that she was urging him to hurry up. But Lucy's father wasn't listening to her, because he'd finally noticed that he was being watched. Not watched exactly—*stared at*. The two fathers were standing stock still, staring at each other across the tops of the cars. My father had his towel wrapped around his neck, his car keys in one hand and his book in the other. Lucy's father held towels and books and cushions, and he had Lucy dancing at the end of one arm, but his head was still, and his face was like stone. I had once read that in a stand-off with a dangerous dog you must hold eye contact and force the dog to look away first. I thought of that now.

Then Lucy's father's eyes dropped. Just like that, they dropped, and I knew my father had won. Lucy's father turned back toward the red car—he jerked his hand away from Lucy, whose shoulders sagged. Lucy's mother, finally ready, her flowery bag stuffed full of gear, looked up, confused, as Lucy began to wail. I looked at my father. Calmly he began to walk back, toward the pool. His stride was long and measured, and there was steel in his eyes. I stayed where I was, crouched down behind a car, and he walked right past without spotting me.

I reached the turnstile just as it clicked shut behind my father. Over the sound system, Annie Lennox was still singing. The teenager saw me, rolled her eyes, and reached for the button to release the turnstile. My father was walking back to his lounger, which my mother was holding for him with the toe of her left foot. I jumped into the deep end of the pool and stayed under until I felt warm again and needed air. When I came up, a different song was playing. I hung there, treading water and watching the turnstile, but Lucy's family never came through.

~~~~

On the way home from the pool we stopped at the local shop for a jar of instant coffee. My mother and Vanessa stayed in the car, but I got out, partly because I was still watching my father closely, expecting bad luck, and partly because I found the silence between Vanessa and my mother unbearable.

As soon as we stepped into the shop I saw Kahu. He was standing alone at the counter in front of an enormous bag of potatoes, sorting coins in his palm while the shopkeeper stood frowning down at him. I turned instantly to the left because my heart was thudding and my mouth had gone dry. I had planned that if I saw Kahu—glimpsed him, even from a distance— I would run to him and say sorry. I had gone over it in my mind as I was trying to get to sleep; I had daydreamed about it while eating my breakfast. *Sorry, sorry, sorry.* But I had not counted on seeing him with my father standing there, looking exhausted, impatient to get home. I ran down the narrow aisle toward the jars of instant coffee and the dusty boxes of teabags. My father watched me from the doorway. He had not said much since the incident at the pool. He had fallen asleep on his sun lounger, only jerking awake when my mother announced it was time to go home.

I walked slowly back up the aisle. My father took the coffee from my hand and propelled me toward the counter—I guessed that he hadn't recognized the boy standing there with his head down and his back to us. My heart was thudding harder now. The shopkeeper, seeing us, gestured toward us, as if to serve my father first, but my father pointed at Kahu's back and said, "It's no trouble, we'll wait for the lad."

Kahu turned to look at us and went red, under his tan.

"Oh, hello," my father said. "That's an awful lot of potatoes."

Kahu mumbled yeah.

My father looked at me. I was red too. I looked away. I hoped he'd think it was just that the shopkeeper was frowning at us, making everything awful and awkward. Kahu went back to sorting his coins—I think he'd lost his place because we'd interrupted him. Another woman stepped up behind us, holding a bag of bread rolls. I heard her mutter something under her breath that I couldn't catch.

"That's it," my father said, "you've got it right there."

He must have been counting Kahu's coins over his shoulder.

Kahu nodded, his face a little redder now. He dropped the coins on the counter and heaved the bag of potatoes high up onto his chest. "You want a hand with those?" my father said. He had reached past Kahu and put the money for the instant coffee on the counter with nothing more than a nod.

"Nah, it's all right," Kahu replied.

We walked out of the shop, into the sunshine. My father looked left and right, but the only car parked out there was ours. My mother was looking down at her lap, and Vanessa had her head back, dozing.

"We could give you a lift, if you're walking?"

"Nah, it's okay. Thanks."

I looked at the ground. I knew that Kahu would want to walk all the way home with the bag of potatoes to prove to his uncle that he was strong enough, but I knew also that even without the potatoes, he wouldn't have wanted to ride anywhere with me.

"Okay, well . . ." My father seemed doubtful. He glanced at me. I knew I had to say something, to make it less weird.

"Are they for dinner?" I asked.

It was just about the dumbest thing I could have said. Kahu nodded, shifting his feet. "It's my uncle's birthday. We're having a hāngī."

"Oh," my father said, "a hāngī!" He looked at his watch and then at the potatoes. "You'd better get those things back. Sure you don't want a lift?"

Kahu said no, and thank you, again.

We climbed into the car and in less than a minute we were driving past him, walking with a slight stagger, the bag of potatoes clutched high in his arms and his chin resting on top.

My mother sat up a little straighter. "Isn't that . . . ?"

"Yes," my father said, "and before you ask, he insisted on walking."

I sank as low as I could in my seat. My mother was watching me in the rear-view mirror. A hāngī took hours, I knew. The potatoes would go into a pit in the ground where they would cook on hot rocks, alongside meat and yams and kūmara, all of it covered over with wet sacks and a mound of earth. I wondered if Kahu had helped dig the pit. I wondered if he remembered that he'd invited me already, way back, when the hāngī was just an idea his uncle was tossing around.

It'll be fun, he'd said. *You don't have to eat any vegetables if you don't want to, and we always get to stay up really late.*

Now it was happening just the way he'd said it would, only I wasn't invited.

I waited until I felt my mother's eyes slide away from the rear-view mirror, and then I turned my face to the window and cried.

TWENTY

Looking back, she timed it perfectly. Stepping out of our bedroom dressed all in white, with her hair clean and brushed in that fluffy way my mother liked, and white leather sandals on her feet. My parents had been bickering quietly, tensely, over their coffee, but when they saw her, they stopped. I could tell that my mother wanted to say something about how beautiful she looked, that it was an almost involuntary reaction, from mother to daughter, but she stopped herself just in time, because Vanessa was supposed to be in trouble, and my mother was supposed to be angry.

My parents had been trying to figure out what to do with our day. They had both asked me, at separate times during the morning, if I would like to be taken to the beach to meet Kahu, and both times, I'd had to shake my head and pretend not to be interested. My mother had guessed, I think, that something was wrong, and would watch me closely as I answered, and then press her lips together afterwards.

With Kahu out of the picture, and Crystal off limits, I gathered that my father wanted to return to Wellington. There wasn't much left of our holiday anyway—it had been 1986 for a full three weeks now, and in just over a week's time, the surf lifesaving club would pack up its flags, and we would be driving home. My mother was appalled at the notion of leaving early—we had never, ever, cut a holiday short. We were the kind of people who stuck to a plan—my mother knew on Thursday what we'd eat for dinner on Sunday. She knew from looking at the forecast what days she'd be able to hang out the washing. She hadn't planned for an extra week in Wellington at the end of January. My father huffed and puffed, he said we should "cut our losses," but it was hard to argue with my mother, who kept stating bare facts. The cat was booked in at the cattery for another week. There was no way we'd get our money back, it'd been hard to book—the cattery was full. Pompom only got in by the skin of his teeth, excuse the pun, because of that expensive dental work he'd had earlier in the year. The rent on the holiday house was prepaid. My mother planted her forefinger on the table with every point she made. The neighbours' son was being paid to sweep the path and collect the mail. He was counting on the money for that cricket camp he wanted to attend. And, *and* (a double plant of the forefinger), we'd told everyone we were away until the end of January—what would we tell them if we returned now? What would they think? That we couldn't manage a five-week holiday without (my mother lowered her voice but my ears were locked on the conversation and I heard the word anyway) *imploding?*

This was the conversation into which Vanessa stepped, wearing her white dress.

The dress had never bothered me before. Like all Vanessa's clothes, one day it would be mine, a hand-me-down. White cotton, halter-neck, with a short, swinging skirt. For the first time it occurred to me that the only thing holding the dress up was a large, loosely tied bow at the back of my sister's neck. I wondered if every man my sister had ever walked past while wearing this dress had wanted to reach out and tug on that crumpled white bow. I noticed for the first time how the halter-neck emphasized her shiny, round shoulders. It was designed to do this, I realized, and to make a neat triangular envelope of her chest—my sister was a parcel to be unwrapped. Recently, Vanessa had begun to wear a bra. She had three, bought at a department store in Wellington. They were brightest white, with cotton cups that looked like sailor hats when they hung on the line, but the halter-neck must have looked bad with a bra, because I could see the whole of Vanessa's back and there was nothing there but a few freckles. Also, the skirt of the dress was very short. If she moved quickly in any direction, it flew up. A few weeks ago, wearing this dress, she had twirled, and we had all laughed that we could see her knickers. My mother, my father, and me, all laughing, and Vanessa twirling round and round in her pale blue knickers.

I thought surely, after everything that had happened, my parents would see the problem with this dress. They would look past the fluffy hair and childish sandals and see my sister the way I saw her. I waited for my father to say what I had heard so many fathers say on American television shows, *You are not leaving the house like that. Think again. Over my dead body.* But my father only sat looking wearily at her. I think he was still coming up with a response to my mother's argument about the neighbour's son and his cricket camp. I think he was halfway to Wellington already. In his head, he'd given up on us, the holiday house, and the rest of January. There were only a few days left of our holiday anyway. What more could go wrong?

"I thought it was about time I said thanks to that old guy next door."

This is what she said, casually, as if she hadn't just spent an hour preparing. I looked toward the sink and was surprised to see that the flowers had gone. Someone—my mother, most likely—had spirited them away. Come to think of it, I had noticed some orange staining around the lid of the plastic rubbish bin, in the cupboard under the sink. My father made a move to stand up—he pushed his chair a few inches away from the table, and rolled his shoulders back.

"Yes," he said, "quite right. Of course you're right. We don't have anything to give him . . . but we can't let it go any longer."

"I have something to give him," she said. She held up her hand, and I saw she was holding a small piece of folded grey card. It was the card that had been used to stiffen the notebook my father bought for my mother. Vanessa must have scooped it up before it could be thrown away. She held it out now as if she didn't really want us to see it, but I could see she had drawn her trademark flower on the front of it—a sunflower with a snaking stem and two small sprouting leaves. She drew this flower everywhere—on her exercise books at school, on the bathroom mirror. She'd even threatened to get a tattoo of it on her ankle. Inside the card, I saw tidy lines of black ink—I didn't want to think what they might say. *Thank you for saving my life. It wasn't you I wanted to rescue me, but thanks anyway.*

It was a brilliant move. Card-making was a highly prized activity in our house. I'd known my mother's eyes to fill with tears just because I'd taken ten minutes to fold a piece of paper in half, draw a heart on the front, and write a few kind words inside. My parents smiled at each other the way parents do when their child has done something that makes them look good. "Okay, great," my father said. "I'll just change my shirt."

She'd thought about this too. She didn't protest, or roll her eyes, or beg to go alone. She just shrugged, and said sure, but then added, a half-beat later, "Might look better if I go by myself."

"Look better?"

"I dunno. More sincere. Like I'm not being dragged over there by my *father.*"

She said "father" with a shrug, and then she looked off to the left as though it didn't matter either way to her, she was just thinking about the old dude, trying to get it right for him. My father, whose bottom had just left his seat, paused. My mother looked at him and tilted her head to one side as if to say, *Maybe?* My father's bottom went back down onto his seat.

"What will you say to him?" he asked.

"Dunno," she shrugged, bored already with this conversation. "Thanks, I guess."

"Well, Vanessa, you might have to be a bit more forthcoming than that."

This time she did roll her eyes. "I'll say, that was pretty awesome, what you did the other day."

My father nodded.

"And, I hope it didn't wear you out too much."

My parents looked at each other again—this was the most they'd heard Vanessa talk for a while, and I could see they were impressed, and frankly relieved, at what they were hearing. Maybe my sister wasn't such a horrible person after all. Maybe they'd done something right. I mean, she even had me fooled— the sunflower on the front of the little card, the fact that she'd scooped that piece of cardboard up off the floor and folded it neatly in half. Where had she found the felt-tip pens she'd have needed to draw it? I didn't know we had any.

"Well, that would certainly be a good start," my father said.

She tossed her head. "So. Should I go?"

Not, *Can I go?* or *Am I allowed?* just *Should I go?* As if it was a decision we were all making together. As if my sister didn't have a whole lot riding on this. My parents looked at each other across the little kitchen table for the longest time, while I pictured my sister standing on our neighbour's doorstep with that bow at the back of her neck. I pictured his smile widening when he saw her, his hand ushering her in. Maybe he would touch her lightly on her bare back as she moved through his door. I thought surely he would—he wouldn't be able to help himself. Her shoulders were so shiny, and her tan was deep and even. I closed my eyes and tried not to think about it—my sister alone in that man's house.

"I think it would be good for her," I heard my father say.

"It's only next door after all," my mother added.

"I'll tell you what," my father said, standing suddenly. "I'll walk you over there, but I won't come in. How about that?"

"Yeah, sure," Vanessa said, "that'd work."

"I'll see you into his house, and then I'll leave you to it."

"You'll come to the door? Like I'm a kid trick-or-treating or something?"

My father glanced at my mother, who tilted her head slightly, as if to say, *She has a point.* "Okay," my father said, "I won't come to the door. I'll just walk you to the gate."

My parents weren't thinking of the danger that might or might not exist inside the man's house. They were thinking of the danger outside it—they were thinking of Crystal, and the other teenagers who hung around the northern end of the beach. I opened my mouth to speak, but I didn't know where to start. I didn't have the words for what I feared.

Would it be the beachcomber who would greet my sister at the door?

Or the scavenger?

My father went to his room and changed into a short-sleeved shirt with buttons. My sister walked over to the window and peered out. "It's the white house, right?" She was speaking to me. Reluctantly, I nodded. "You're wearing that?"

"Obviously."

"It's not a special occasion."

"It's not a special dress."

"It doesn't fit you—it's too short."

"Oh my God, shut up, you're being weird. It's supposed to be this length."

My father came out of his room whistling a tune. If I was going to say anything, I needed to say it now. My sister scooped her hair up and swept it back, over her shoulders. "Stop gawking at me," she said. I turned away from her. Was I wrong to be afraid? Our neighbour had saved my sister's life. Why would he do that if he was a bad man—if he meant her harm? My father opened the front door and said, "Ready to roll?" I watched them step out, into the sunlight. It was a stupid feeling I had—that I would never see my sister again. I went over to the kitchen window to watch them go. My sister's dress was see-through, but it was too late to tell her that, and she wouldn't have listened anyway.

~~~

I waited until my father returned, still whistling his tune. Then I stepped outside. It was a day without clouds or wind. Next door, our neighbour's white plastic chair was empty, and behind it, the sliding glass doors were open. I could hear music coming from inside—something dimly familiar. I walked all the way to the back of the section, until I was in the shadow of the fence. The song that was playing was one I was sure I knew, but I kept catching a beat and then losing it before I could put a name to it. On our side of the fence, my mother was working on her book, and that noise—the typewriter—was competing with the music, muddling everything. On top of that, the cicadas were going full tilt. I looked for a crack in the fence that I could put my face to. My sister had been gone now for ten, maybe fifteen minutes.

I walked the length of the fence at the back, but there were no cracks wider than my little finger, and nothing to see. My father stepped outside, briefly stooping to lay a wet tea towel on the concrete to dry. He spotted me, waved, and went back inside. He was used to me hanging around the yard like a stray cat. I turned and began to move back along the fence the other way, running my fingers across the rough timber, avoiding cicadas and their empty skins. That's when one of the boards moved.

From a distance it had looked perfectly straight, like all the others, but now I saw that this board was fixed with only one nail—the one nearest the top. The bottom nail had rusted out. I pushed the board a little harder and it swung to the side, creating a triangular gap about four inches wide at the bottom. Crouching down, I put my face to this gap and saw our neighbour's yard for the first time. It was patchy—grass as high as my knees in places, and in other places, bare dirt. A concrete patio looked half-completed—some of the pavers were laid neatly, some were jutting out of the earth at angles, and in the middle of the yard, a pile sat in the long grass, waiting to be laid. I stuck my ear to the gap and listened, but I couldn't hear my sister's voice, or make out the song that was playing.

I stepped back. Behind me, steam was rising from the tea towel my father had laid out on the concrete to dry. If I listened hard, I could just make out the *tack-tack-tack* of my mother's typewriter over the chorus of cicadas. My father would lie down on the couch, fold his hands over his stomach, and take a nap in the sun. It was what he did most days, before lunch. I reached out and pulled the loose board, until it overlapped the one next to it. Then I swung it sideways. Without anything to stop it, it swung until it was almost horizontal to the ground. The gap was no longer a triangle. It was a rectangle as wide as a fence board, all the way up to my chest. A gap wide enough to step through, if you were ten and a girl, and small for your age.

I took one last look at the tea towel steaming on the patio, and then I slipped sideways, through the fence.

~~~

On the other side of the fence I felt calm—small and safe in the tall grass. I was a stray cat that nobody cared about or noticed. I made my way toward the house, being careful not to trip, or stub my toe on a loose paver. On my way I found a spade, lying rusted in the earth, and areas that looked recently dug over. I wondered if the man was trying to grow vegetables. My grandfather was an expert vegetable-grower, and would never have tolerated such a messy yard.

The washing line was slack and spotted with mildew, poorly positioned in the shade of the pōhutukawa tree. Clothes hung limp and forgotten—an orange T-shirt, a pair of jeans. I stumbled on a plastic watering can, briefly losing my calm, which I regained by standing very still and listening to the sound of my own heart. I began to move forward again. The house, on the ground floor, was shut-up and dark. Curtains pulled. If one of those curtains had moved I would have jumped, but nothing moved—only me. I was coming around now, toward the front of the property. I was a long way from the gap in the fence. Best not to look back, at all that ground between me and safety. Best to keep going forward. I could always say I was sent to get my sister. *It's lunchtime*, I could say. *Mum wants her back.*

But I couldn't hear my sister's voice, and it didn't seem possible that she was there. My sister hardly spoke to us but when she did she had a clear voice, strident, far-reaching. The opposite of my voice, which was soft and hesitant, no matter how strongly I believed in the things I said.

At the front of the house, I saw a porch with a solid wooden door and tall tinted windows either side. There was a wind chime, a doormat slightly askew, and several pairs of shoes, scuffed and flattened. None of these shoes belonged to my sister. I saw that the gate was closed, and the letterbox full. If I had not heard music earlier, and seen the sliding glass doors open, I would have believed that the house was abandoned.

I doubled back, into the messy yard. I thought that if I returned to where I had slipped through the fence, and circled the house in the other direction, I might find a way in, or a window without the curtains pulled, through which I might be able to see my sister.

He was standing near to where the spade lay in the bare earth. He was wearing shorts and his legs were very tanned and very thin. His belly on the other hand was big, it escaped the white polo shirt he was wearing, the hem of which was tattered and wavy, as if worn out with the effort of keeping him contained. He was smiling, but I got nothing from that smile—no warmth. I did not smile back. I was not a cat any more but a trespasser, with no way to get to the gap in the fence. At school we played bullrush on the sports field but I wasn't as good as I thought I should be—I could run fast, but I often collided with people, or tripped. Something told me that if I tried to get past this man his long arm would shoot out and stop me dead.

"Enjoying my garden?"

I hesitated—my heart was making such a racket in my ears that I almost missed the question. "I'm looking for my sister."

"I haven't seen her. Not here. How is she anyway? Fully recovered?"

His voice was even and smooth. I couldn't detect sarcasm or malice, no matter how hard I tried. I squinted at him, nodding along to my own thoughts. "She's fine," I said, even-voiced like him. "Thanks. If she isn't here, I'll go."

But I made no move to go and he made no move either.

"She most certainly isn't here, but there's no need for you to go running off. Come in and I'll give you a glass of lemonade."

As he spoke, he swept his arm out to the side. I saw that a ranch slider on the ground floor was open and the curtain swept back, revealing a room with a bed, an armchair, and something further back that looked like a piece of gym equipment. "Spare room," he said. "The kitchen's upstairs."

I stared at the darkness in that room and knew I didn't want to go in there. But his arm was blocking my path to the fence. A third possibility flitted through my head—that I could turn on my heels and make a run for the gate. I'd never been much good with gates. The one at home tended to bite my fingers, and the one at school was high and stiff. I was sure that the latch on this man's gate would confound me, and that his hands would come down on my shoulders as I fumbled with it. He would be angry then. I did not want to make him angry—I wanted to keep him like he was, even and smooth.

As long as he was even and smooth, I thought, nothing bad would happen.

I walked toward the ranch slider, into his spare room. Without hesitation, he closed it behind me and yanked the curtains across. I didn't like that. With the curtains pulled, it was as if he'd erased me from his yard. From existence. No one in the world knew that I was here. A few footprints in the tall grass were all I'd left behind. As I moved forward, I could hear his steady breathing at my back, the squelch of his feet on the wooden floor. He said nothing, but now and then he would touch my elbow to steer me in the right direction. I could smell him. He smelled of sunblock, which was comforting, but also, faintly, of beer. I was pretty sure it was wrong to smell of beer in the morning, especially if you were alone at home. The hallway was dim, and narrower than it should have been, lined with stacks of old magazines and newspapers. The smell of damp newsprint was overpowering in places. "Here we are," he said, when we got to the bottom of the stairs. I was relieved—I had begun to think we would never go up to the light. From the deck upstairs, I would be able to see our holiday house. I would be able to wave, and holler, if my father came out to check on the progress of his tea towel. On the staircase, every step was home to some item—an old transistor radio, a stack of official-looking documents, an open shoebox full of padlocks, two toasters with their cords wrapped neatly around them, a stained set of kitchen scales. "Junk," he said, from the step behind me. "Junk and clutter."

I reached the top of the stairs and saw a doorway flooded with light. He touched my elbow to move me forward. "Through there," he said. I was disorientated, blinded momentarily by the explosion of light, and confused by what I heard.

He was playing music—not as loudly as before, but it greeted us on the landing as if carried by the light. *My* music, as familiar to me as the blood flowing through my veins. A song I knew inside out and back to front, but in that moment, I couldn't have told you the name of it, or given you the next lyric. The neighbour, seeing my hesitation, slid past me, moving to a corner of his lounge. He stooped, and the music went away.

"Better?"

I nodded. I could have turned then—run down the stairs, torn back the curtain, stumbled out across the yard, found the gap in the fence, and been home. But it was hard to imagine— I saw myself falling down the stairs, getting tangled in the curtains, fumbling with the lock on the ranch slider, tripping on a paver, getting stuck in the fence. Besides, I was distracted, momentarily, by something on the wall. A wooden panel with small hooks sunk into it, and on those hooks, various keys, all with labels attached: SHED. BACK DOOR. The very last set, on the last hook, had its own red plastic key chain and a label that said 32 PALMER STREET.

The holiday house.

Our house.

"Coming in?" he said.

I stumbled on, away from the keys. Neighbours shared keys sometimes, didn't they? My mother had given a set of keys to our elderly neighbours in Wellington, "in case of emergency." Now I was in his lounge, and he was saying, "Sit," and gesturing to a couch that was long and low and stained in places. I shook my head just slightly, no.

He shrugged. "Lemonade?"

I nodded. Despite the stained couch, his lounge was better than anything I'd seen on the lower floor. Here the clutter was more attractive—there were things among it that you wanted to examine and touch. Stretching along the far wall there was a built-in bookcase, with shelves of varying heights. The shelves were full of books, framed photographs, chipped enamel jugs, an old typewriter, a stereo system, an enormous pair of binoculars, an assortment of cameras, and a number of bowls filled to overflowing with shells and sea-glass. Hanging from the ceiling there were model aircraft, a strange assortment of lanterns and lights, an old fishing net, and in the corner, the jaws of a small shark, polished to a high shine. His floor was covered in overlapping rugs. "Mind your step," he said, as I inched my way forward.

The drink he gave me wasn't lemonade at all—at least not as I knew it—and I thought that was a pretty sneaky trick. To promise lemonade when all you had to offer was this thick, syrupy cordial with bits floating in it. I hated it at first but found it tasted better as I got through it—sipping it prevented me from having to say anything and gave me something to do with my hands. He made a drink for himself and sat on one of the stools at the kitchen island, one foot on the crossbar of the stool beside him. "So your sister's recovered?"

I said that she was.

"No headaches? Blurred vision?"

I shook my head. "Nothing like that."

"Good for her. Mum recovered too? From the shock?"

I nodded.

"Quiet little thing, aren't you? What do you think of my shark? I call him Ray."

"Quite small," I said.

He laughed. "You've been watching too many films. That fella could take your arm off clean. Want to feel the teeth?"

I shook my head.

"Know why I call him Ray?"

I shook my head again.

He sighed, worn out by my silences, or annoyed by them. "Well, it's short for Razor. Know what a razor is?"

"Sharp," I said. Did he think I was an idiot?

"That's right, sharp." He looked at his fingers, which were wet from the condensation on his glass. "Take your arm clean off," he muttered again, as if comforted by the thought.

My drink was almost finished. I glanced toward the open ranch sliders, where thin net curtains billowed lazily in the heat.

"Go on out there," he said. "Have a look. See what I see."

I caught a wink in his voice. *See what I see.* I was torn. On the deck I'd be able to see the holiday house, perhaps shout to my father, but I'd be further from the top of the stairs, and my path to the stairs would be blocked by the long, low couch.

"Go on," he said. "It's a picture out there."

Because I could hear irritation in his voice, and because I was having trouble stomaching the last dregs of the lemon sludge he'd given me, I walked out onto his deck. It felt good to be outside, in the dappled shade of the pōhutukawa tree. I saw the white plastic chair, angled toward our back yard, and I saw our little house, a perfect square, a corner of the concrete patio jutting out, and our car, parked on the grass, windscreen glaring white.

32 Palmer Street.

I thought again of the keys.

"Take a seat," he called, but I wasn't going to sit in that chair. I moved toward the edge of the deck and leaned out over the balustrade. It was too far to jump. At school there was a rock wall I regularly jumped from, but this was twice as high, and besides, there was the balustrade to navigate, with its slippery glass, and cold metal handrail at chest height. I turned and saw that he was still sitting at the kitchen island. He was wiping condensation from his glass and applying it to his brow. Carefully, I poured the remainder of my sludge onto the grass below. The sound was swallowed up, instantly, by the cicadas.

"I've finished my drink," I said.

"Want a refill?"

Now he was right behind me, on the threshold between the house and the deck. He'd left his drink behind.

"No, thank you," I said. "I think I'd better go home."

I tried to say it strongly. *Home.* It was not a question. My shoulders were back, my jaw was set. *Home.*

He smiled. "Of course," he said, stepping out. "In a minute."

~~~~

He moved toward me, keeping his body between me and the open doors. I pressed myself hard against the glass barrier.

"Your father's no doubt asleep on that couch. Under the window." His brow was wet—sweat, or condensation from his glass. "That's what he likes to do most days before lunch, isn't it?"

I narrowed my eyes at him. The window he was talking about, and the couch that my father slept on, were not visible from the deck.

"Yes, asleep I'll bet, and no wonder. He's a busy man, your father. Three women to look after. I don't envy him. Not one bit. I bet he wanted a son, eh? Don't feel bad about it—every man wants a son, it's only natural." He moved forward, picking something out of his teeth. I could not have pressed myself harder against that glass. "Well, you're tomboyish I suppose, but it's not the same. And as for your mother. What's she doing on that typewriter every day? She a journalist or something?" He shook his head. "Not much to write about around here. Nothing ever happens. The odd burglary, the occasional boat-wreck, that's about it." He glanced at me, flicking something off the ends of his fingers. It landed wetly on my foot—a glob of lemon pulp that had probably come from his teeth. "Had my fill of journalists, let me tell you. Bloodthirsty creatures, they are. Worse than that shark over there." He chuckled, and then shook his head again. "Then there's your sister, running around like a wild animal." He pointed at me. "You'll go the same way. Mark my words. You'll be there in two years' time if you're not careful. What about that little brown kid you run around with, the one that wears a necklace?"

"It's not a necklace," I said suddenly, with force. "It's a pounamu."

"Yeah, that little Māori kid. Seen you running around with him. Your parents should put a stop to that, unless they want little brown grandbabies, and a daughter on the DPB."

I stared at him, one arm flung over the balustrade, gripping the glass. "I'd like to go home," I said. "Now."

He nodded. "There's something I have to do first." He turned and walked back through the open doors. I saw that his shirt was clinging to his back. I took one last look at our holiday house, squat and tidy in the sun, and at the grass below—still too far down, too hard a landing. "Come here," he called. "You'll like this." I doubted it very much. With a sickening weight in my stomach, I pushed off the glass and followed him inside.

At first, all I could see was black. I thought he'd played a trick on me, slipping something in my drink to blind me, until I realized it was just my eyes adjusting to the light. He was kneeling in front of a sideboard that stood against the wall beside the dining table. He'd flung the low doors open and he was rifling through piles of stuff—the sideboard was full to overflowing. Mostly it contained coloured envelopes that slid over one another, refusing to stack nicely, or keep their lids closed, so that their contents kept spilling to the floor. They were photo packets, and they were all different colours, as if he was in the habit of visiting a different chemist every time he needed to process a film. One packet I saw was yellow and green. I remembered the woman at the bad-luck chemist holding an identical packet in her hands. *I've figured it out. Why your daughter is so familiar.* As quickly as the photo packets tumbled forward, our neighbour pushed them back, swearing under his breath. I managed to catch a glimpse of one or two, face up, before he could tidy them away. They weren't very interesting, or even very good. One was of a beach—I saw a stretch of over-exposed sand, mostly blurred. The other seemed to show a large expanse of grass, with a tiny figure standing off-centre in the distance.

What you really need is a zoom lens. There's a camera shop here in the mall.

"Bloody mess in here," he muttered. "About bloody time I got around to it. Just wait. Wait 'til you see what I've got."

He shoved the photos aside and grabbed at something underneath—a small metal ring, a handle. He pulled the handle upwards and I saw a section of the sideboard lift—in the bottom, he'd made a kind of trapdoor or a hatch. Hidden beneath the hatch, in the hollow base of the sideboard, were more photo packets, as well as a small wooden box that had once been used to transport apples. It had in-built handles and no lid. The box was stuffed full, jammed tightly into the space beneath, so that it was only with a grunt and a slight backward stagger that he managed to lift it out, onto the top of the sideboard.

"There," he said. The sweat was in his hair now, revealing areas of bare, pink scalp. He kicked the sideboard door closed with his foot, trapping a couple of photo packets in the process, and began to rifle through the box. "Just wait, just wait 'til you see," he was saying, but I didn't care. While he'd been kneeling at the sideboard, I'd been inching my way across the lounge, toward the landing. Another step or two, and I'd be able to make it all the way down the stairs and out through the spare room, even if I lost my footing, or fumbled with the lock on the ranch slider. He was old and sweaty and I was young and strong. A few more inches, I decided, and I would do it. "What's that?" I said, seeing something in his hand, and stalling for time.

"What's what—that? Oh, I don't know, just something I found. You'd be amazed what I find on the beach. People are careless. If it wasn't for me, that beach would be a rubbish tip." He puffed his chest out, warming to his subject. "I was once given a commendation by the mayor—did you know that? Of course you didn't." He waved a hand. "Why would you know a thing like that. Services to the community. That's what they said—I was serving the community, keeping the beach so pristine. People should remember that. People who talk about me— they'd do well to remember that."

The thing he was holding didn't look like rubbish to me—it looked like the top half of a small bikini; new, hardly worn. I made another move, toward the door, and turned my body slightly that way, to prepare myself.

"Why do you ask?" he chuckled, swinging the bikini. "You think it would fit you?" He turned toward me. "Hey, where do you think you're going? I'm not done yet. Stay where you are." He held one hand out toward me. "Wait. Stay."

But I wasn't staying. I had pushed my weight onto my toes, ready to spring. All it would take now was one great lunge for the door. He saw my intention, and was torn, momentarily, between the contents of the box, and my imminent escape. "Dammit, girl, just wait!" he shouted. I lunged. Didn't slip. Made it through the door. Skidded slightly on a rug at the top of the stairs, caught myself, and headed down. He was not behind me. I felt a rush of adrenaline so pure I might already have been out of the house, in the fresh air. But I wasn't. I was at the bottom of the stairs, and now I had a problem. I couldn't remember the way. I had thought it would be obvious—which was the door to the spare room. But the ground floor was a maze, and all the doors leading off the hall were closed. I flung one door open and found a toilet, covered in dust and filth. Rearing back, I knocked over a stack of magazines as high as my head. The magazines tumbled forward, their pages flapping like birds. I batted them away and ran in the other direction, to where I saw light coming from the panels of glass either side of the front door. He was on the stairs now; I could hear his footfalls and his heavy breathing. He did not appear to be in a hurry to get to me—I soon understood why. The front door was locked. I jiggled the handle, pulled it toward me, kicked the door, wrestled it, but it was hopeless. In a calm part of my mind I could see that the door had been fitted with at least four different locks, all of them secure. I wasn't going anywhere, but I wasn't ready to accept my fate. He had reached the bottom of the stairs, but I still thought I had a chance. I tried to dart past him, back in the direction of the spare room, but it was never going to work. He flung an arm out and I collided with it—I was surprised by his strength. Even with me barrelling forward, desperate, he could stop me with one stringy arm, slick with sweat. I was bitterly disappointed and very, very tired.

"There, there," he said, pulling me toward him. Toward his hot chest. I began to cry, quietly. "There, there," he kept saying. I thought of Kahu, who would not have let me go through the gap in the fence alone—he would have come with me, and together we might have been safe. The neighbour was moving his free hand through my hair, his breathing was ragged.

Then a sound came from the outside. Very close by, a cough, and the scuff of a shoe on concrete. I heard a metallic clink, and another shoe-scuff. The hand in my hair went still, and then dropped. A shadow flickered across the tinted windows either side of the front door. I felt his arm around my waist slacken. On the other side of the front door, the shadow dropped to the ground. There was another light cough, a sliding sound, and through the bottom of the door, a card appeared. Small and neatly folded, it was decorated with a sunflower. We stared at it, the two of us, as if it was a thing from outer space. The shadow at the door was fragmenting, becoming smaller. In a moment we would hear the clink of the gate and it would be gone. I stepped toward the door, out of his grasp. He made no move to stop me. "Vanessa," I said, quietly at first. And then, as loud as I could, "Vanessa!"

Outside, the shadow held. "Vanessa!" I said again, banging on the door.

"There, there," he said, moving forward. I thought he was going to clamp a hand over my mouth and drag me back, into the darkened hall, but instead he reached past my head and began to release each of the four locks on the door, one by one.

TWENTY-ONE

"Why does it look like you've been crying?"

We were walking back, toward the holiday house. Vanessa a few steps ahead, walking slightly too fast for me, forcing me to trot, her white dress bouncing at her hips.

"I was scared."

"God. I wasn't gone *that* long. Why did you even go over there? You're not my mother, or my, like, nanny or whatever." She wasn't looking at me—she was speaking into the air, hoping her words would carry back to me. Or perhaps she didn't care. A passer-by might not have been able to tell that we were together. "You know, you think you're clever, but you're actually kind of creepy," she went on, "always hanging around, eavesdropping, sticking your nose in where it's not wanted, staring at me. You need to chill. Get a life of your own."

"It wasn't you I was scared about."

"What then—him? The old dude?" She laughed—a derisive hoot, directed at the sky. "The guy that saved my life. *That* guy. What's scary about him? He gave you lemonade. And what about that?" She turned and pointed at my hands. "How long since you lost that?"

My Sony Walkman, returned to me. Its red plastic case slightly dulled, scratched in places it hadn't been. It wasn't the beautiful object it had been before I lost it, but it was mine—my name etched into the back—and I was glad to have it returned to me. *Found it on the beach*, he said. *A few days back.* This was what he'd been searching for, in the box he kept in his sideboard. Yes, I felt silly now. I had panicked. I had watched him work his way through the four locks on his front door, hardly able to believe my luck. If Vanessa hadn't chosen that moment to deliver her card! If I had not been standing where I was, within earshot! But then—when the door finally opened, and I slithered through, into the light, to grab Vanessa's hand (she withdrew it, and I had to settle for a corner of her skirt)—I looked back and saw that he was small and old. Not much taller than Vanessa, with grey circles under his eyes that no amount of tanning could hide. *There, there,* he'd said to me, like a mother to a child. I looked at his shorts and saw that there was nothing in his pocket—no gun or knife. All he had in his hands was my Sony Walkman, and this he held out immediately, like a peace offering.

Remembered I'd seen you with it in the garden. Thought it might be yours.

Vanessa was whistling through her teeth. "Wow, if Mum and Dad found out you took your Walkman to the beach. That guy saved your bacon. You should write him a card!" She laughed at this, and swung her hair back, over her shoulder. I noticed that the bow on her dress was clumsily tied, not at all like it had been when she'd left the house, and that there were blades of grass, flattened and dry, all over her back. "I think he's okay. Old and gross, but nice enough. I think we should invite him to dinner. I think it's the least we should do. If Mum and Dad weren't so wrapped up in themselves, we would have done it by now. I suppose *you* wouldn't want that though, because he might tell them about your Walkman. About how you left it at the beach."

"I didn't. Someone took it. I hid it under my towel, and someone took it."

"Whatever." She was losing interest in this conversation, and in me.

"He said you were like a wild animal."

She slowed her pace a little, giving me a chance to catch up. "He did?"

I nodded. She was smiling, turning it over in her head. *Wild animal*. "Hah! Funny. I kind of like that. I'll have to tell Crystal. She'll piss herself."

You're not allowed to see Crystal, I thought, but didn't say.

"He watches."

I had expected her to show confusion, or to ask me to explain, but instead she swung around to face me. "You noticed that too? Yeah, well, I guess he's lonely. Being ancient must be pretty boring."

"You knew he was watching?"

"Sure."

"And you still went out sunbathing?"

She shrugged. "It's not like there's much else to do. I mean, if

I worried about every old dude perving at me, I'd never leave the house." We were nearly home, and abruptly she stopped walking and grabbed my arm. "I was there the whole time, right?"

"Huh?"

She rolled her eyes. "At his house. I was there the whole time. You came to meet me because you're, like, obsessed with me, basically. Okay?"

I nodded.

"Cool." She swung back around and continued at an even brisker pace. I was running now, clutching my Walkman in both hands. "By the way," she said, "guess who I saw?"

"Who?"

"Your boyfriend. I forget his name."

"Kahu?"

"Yeah, him. Hanging around the entrance to the lagoon, all mysterious and shit. What a weirdo. What happened between you two anyway? Did he try to kiss you and you punched him in the face?"

"No!" I almost shouted. "Nothing like that. Nothing. I don't want to talk about it."

"Ah," she said, grinning. We had reached the place where our car was parked. "So something did happen. Poor Kahu, rejected by his first love."

I stopped walking. It pained me to give her the last word, especially when she was wrong, but I knew there was no point arguing with her. Anything I said would only be used as ammunition against me. I let her go ahead. She continued to laugh over her shoulder at me, saying, "Poor Kahu, poor you," as she skirted the car, sticking her bottom lip out like a baby. I gripped my Walkman in both hands and waited for her to go inside so that I could be alone. Something was bothering me. Something in the air. I looked toward the end of our section, where the neighbour's deck loomed over the fence. The sliding doors were still open, and the white chair was empty. It was the music he was playing—that's what was bothering me. He'd turned the volume up several notches since we'd left. In his house, in my panic, I hadn't been able to name the song, but now, when I closed my eyes and listened, it was obvious. I flicked the little plastic door of my Walkman open and found it empty. The song that was playing over the fence was from the *True Colours* album. It was "I Hope I Never."

~~~

Later that night I was lying in bed, unable to listen to my Walkman because it was empty, when I heard a low, persistent knocking at the front door. I guessed it was well past ten o'clock, because Vanessa, whose holiday bedtime was ten, had already spent time flicking through one of her crumpled magazines and had fallen asleep.

I sat up. In the lounge my father was watching television. My mother had gone to bed to read a book. I heard the squeak of my father's armchair as he rose. The knocking wasn't loud or frantic, but it was persistent. It told you the matter was urgent, but it told you politely. My father cleared his throat just before he opened the door. I waited to hear him say hello, or can I help you? But he didn't say either of these things. In fact, after

I heard the front door open, I heard nothing for a long time. Next door, my parents' bed creaked. My mother, too, was confused by what she heard.

Then my father finally said, "You."

It wasn't a friendly "you." Not at all.

I heard the door to my parents' bedroom open, and then my mother made a gasping noise. I pushed back my covers, planted my feet on the floor, and got ready to run. Maybe it was a monster at the door. An intruder in a black mask.

Or *him*. Him from next door.

Then I heard a soft male voice, hesitant, apologetic. I thought I heard "disturb you." *I'm sorry to disturb you.*

"What?" I heard my mother say. "What is it? Why are you here?" I heard her cross the lounge, even though I knew she had changed already into her nightgown, and she never let anyone see her in her nightgown—even on Christmas Day, she liked to get dressed before the presents were opened.

I jumped out of bed, pressing my ear to the door. When that didn't work—when I still couldn't make out clearly what was being said—I carefully opened the bedroom door, just a crack. Just enough to hear.

"I thought she might have come here," the voice at the door was saying.

It was Lucy's father's voice.

"Why would she come here?" my father said. "I would have thought this was the last place she'd come."

"I don't know. To talk, perhaps. Woman to woman."

"Oh great, just what I need, a cat-fight."

"Shut up," my mother said. "Shut up, let him speak."

Lucy's father made a sobbing sound. "If she comes here, please, tell her I want her home. Lucy wants her home. I've spent all day looking for her. I've looked everywhere."

"You've got a whole lotta cheek," my father muttered.

"Of course we'll tell her," my mother said, talking over my father. "Of course, if we see her, we'll send her straight home."

"I know it's a lot to ask, and I'm sorry, perhaps I shouldn't have come, but I'm worried. We don't know anyone else out here. I can't think where else she'd go."

My father's voice dropped to a low hiss. "She left you, mate. Face facts. She left you and you deserve it. Now how about you piss off and leave my family alone. You hear me? Piss off."

There was a scuffling sound, as if someone had been pushed, and was trying to regain their balance. "Wait, no, stop," my mother said, but the next thing I heard was the front door closing firmly. I jumped into bed, yanking the covers over my head. In the lounge, my mother had begun to cry. I didn't want to hear what happened next, but my door was still open a crack, so I heard anyway.

My father, hissing at my mother.

"Fucking bastard can fuck off. Fucking two-faced slanty-eyed prick."

Then a slap that rang out, bouncing off the linoleum, off the windows. As if it wasn't one slap but two, or three.

And after that, silence.

TWENTY-TWO ·

The next morning I woke early, with a bad feeling in my stomach. I slid out of bed, thinking that if I opened my bedroom door and saw the lounge tidy, with the rugs straightened, and the sun slanting across the kitchen floor, I would feel better. My stomach would know that everything was all right.

But when I stepped into the lounge all I saw was my father, asleep on the couch.

He had not fallen asleep there by accident, as he sometimes did. I knew this because there was a pillow under his head—an actual pillow, not a cushion—and a blanket covering his legs.

I crept back into my room and sat on the floor by my bed. The couch-sleeping was a bad sign. It meant that what I'd heard the night before was real, and furthermore, it was something that could not be contained to *last night*—it had leaked and spread, into *today*.

I was sitting on the floor, wondering if I dared wake my father, when I heard, coming from the window, a scratching noise like a bird, or like leaves, rubbing against glass. I glanced up but the curtains were pulled, and I couldn't see anything.

Then, another noise—a thud this time, and a shadow passing behind the curtain.

I crossed the room and climbed, gingerly, onto my sister's bed. She was curled up against the wall, her headphones still over her ears, her hair spread out across her pillow. I was careful where I put my feet. Reaching up, I pulled the curtain back and saw, to my complete surprise, a face flash by; blurred, eager. An *oof* when he landed. It was Kahu. I glanced at my sister again before gently opening the window.

"My sister's sleeping," I said.

He was standing in the grass, looking up at me, wearing a white T-shirt with a red circle on it and the words THE KARATE KID. "I thought you might have gone home by now," he said, "but then I saw Vanessa yesterday."

I nodded. "We go home on Sunday. The day after the surf lifesaving party."

"Me too," he said. "I mean, Friday. We go home on Friday."

I frowned. He seemed nervous—distracted. He was chewing his lip, cracking a twig into pieces in his hand. I wanted to open the front door for him, but I knew that in doing so I would wake my father, and Kahu would see he'd been sleeping on the couch. Still, it was Kahu, and I'd missed him. I decided I would. "Come around to the front," I said. I leaned out to pull the window in, but he stuck a hand up and held it open.

"I found it," he said.

I paused. My shoulders sagged. I'd hoped we wouldn't have to talk about what had happened between us—that we could just go back to the way things were before.

"No," I said quietly. "*I* found it."

"What?"

"My Walkman. I found it. So, sorry about that. I should never have said that dumb stuff about your cousin. She's actually really pretty. You can tell her I said that."

He shook his head. "No, I found *it*. The thing we were looking for. I found it, last night, at the lagoon. Except . . . it was late . . . getting dark . . . I *think* I found it. You have to come with me. You have to come see."

I blinked several times, with my hand on the window, and his hand on it too. The thing we'd been looking for. It took a while for the words to settle into place—to assume their correct meaning. *The thing we'd been looking for.* A chill lifted the hairs on my arm. Beneath my feet Vanessa stirred, shifting her legs so that briefly they butted up against my feet. I waited until she was still again.

"It's not possible," I said. "You can't have."

"I did . . . I think. I think I did."

"You're wrong. You probably saw something else. A jersey, or, I don't know, a lost shoe."

"It's not like that. You have to see. You'll see and then you'll know."

"The police looked for her, there were search parties—how could you have found her, all on your own, at the lagoon?"

He was shaking his head energetically, left to right. Eyes

closed, lips bunched together. "I don't know, but I did. You have to come see. You have to come now."

I looked at him for a long moment. "My parents aren't even up yet," I said.

He shook his head once more, with emphasis. "*Now.*"

~~~~

It was good to be back with Kahu again, falling into step with him, as if nothing bad had ever happened between us. His hair was longer, bouncing around his head in choppy waves. I felt he'd lengthened out, grown stronger and leaner, since that day I'd first seen him on the lagoon. It stung me to think that soon he would be going back to his home somewhere near Auckland, while I would be heading south, to Wellington.

"Vanessa almost drowned," I told him.

"I know, I heard."

"The old guy from next door rescued her. The creepy one—the one I don't like."

He hadn't heard that. His eyebrows went up.

"Also, Mum and Dad caught her sneaking back in our bedroom window one night."

His eyebrows went *way* up. It seemed important, suddenly, that he know everything.

"She's grounded, but she got out the other day. She lied about going to the old guy's house to say thank you to him for rescuing her. She made a fake card and everything. I mean, the card was real, but she didn't care about thanking him. I went there, I snuck through the fence to look for her, and she wasn't there."

"You went to the old guy's house?"

"Yes, to look for her." I hesitated. I wanted to tell him everything—all about the shark's jaws, and the horrible lemonade, and the view from the neighbour's deck, and the keys I'd seen. But telling him everything would have meant admitting that this is where I had found my Walkman—that the neighbour had been looking after it all along. Also, I might have had to admit that I'd got myself trapped, and had cried, and been comforted by that man, and rescued by my sister. I hurried on. "Vanessa was wearing this gross dress and no bra. I think she went to see Stuart."

"Stuart?"

"Yeah, I think so. Afterwards she had grass all over her back."

The old Kahu would have giggled, but this one didn't. This one kept his eyes on the ground and gave two short nods to show he understood. I wondered if he'd entirely forgiven me for what I'd said about his cousin.

"I think she's decided she likes him," I went on, filling the air with words. "I think she wants to wear the dress to the surf lifesaving party on Saturday night."

"But you just said she's grounded."

"She is. But she has a ticket to the party. Crystal got one for her ages ago, from Josh. Mum and Dad haven't decided yet. They said it all depends on her behaviour. If I told them she lied about going next door, that'd be it. No surf lifesaving party."

"But you won't tell," he said, eyes on the ground.

"No, I won't."

But I *had* been thinking about telling, because I'd figured it out—what Crystal and my sister planned to do on Saturday night. For weeks, Vanessa had been hiding a magazine under her pillow. It was different from her other magazines—thicker, glossier, more serious somehow. It had escaped my father's wrath the night she'd been caught climbing in the window. Possibly my father had seen it lying around and assumed it was one of my mother's. One day, while Vanessa was in the shower, I'd carefully slid it out from under her pillow and crouched down between the beds to see what it was about. Most of it was boring stuff, exercise routines and moisturizers. But one of the pages had its corner folded over, and when I turned to that page, I saw the heading, HOW TO KNOW WHEN YOU'RE READY. Three times I read the article, searching its words for meaning, but it was only when I turned the page and saw a second article called, HOW TO KNOW WHEN YOUR BOYFRIEND'S READY, that I truly understood. My sister was a virgin, like me, but she didn't want to keep her virginity a second longer. She wanted to get rid of it, and the person she'd decided to give it away to was Stuart.

"My parents aren't really paying attention at the moment anyway," I said. "They've been, like, arguing and stuff."

I thought of my father, sleeping on the couch. As I'd run through the lounge to join Kahu, he had opened one eye and said, "Where do you think you're going?"

I'd stopped in my tracks—mortified. Not that I'd been caught, but that he had been, sleeping on the couch.

"I'm going for a walk with Kahu," I'd said.

He'd nodded. "Don't be too long."

Kahu put a hand on my arm. I thought he was going to ask me to tell him more, and I felt a surge of relief, that finally I was going to be able to talk about my parents, tell him all the things I was muddled about, but then I saw he was staring straight ahead, not really listening to a word I'd said. We'd walked the entire length of the road that ran parallel to the beach, and we'd arrived at the main entrance to the lagoon, where there was a picnic table, a sign that looked like it had been carved out of driftwood, and a small gravel car park.

"You know there's a path to the lagoon right beside my house," I said.

"Oh yeah," he said. "I forgot."

I thought he must have been very distracted to forget a thing like that.

He shrugged. "Well, we're here now."

Something in his voice made my stomach hum and zing. Until then, I hadn't really believed in his "find." I'd thought it was just an excuse he'd made up, so that we could hang out one last time before our holidays were over. Now I saw that he didn't want to be here, with me or anyone else. He wanted to be anywhere else in the world.

"Okay," he said, swallowing hard. "Follow me."

We walked a short way across grass to where there was a bridge made of round logs. "We're going to have to cross over," he said. We had gone over that bridge many times, usually at a jog, giggling and jostling, one threatening to push the other off. The bridge had only a single rope for a handrail, and could be very slippery early in the morning, before the sun had burned away the morning dew. Today we crossed in silence, Kahu leading, head down. "You might want to take your shoes off," he said, when we got to the other side. I was wearing my white sandshoes with no laces and thin, smooth soles. But I shook my head, because I was beginning to feel sick, and didn't want to stoop to take them off. I just wanted to get this over with and go home. Soon, I hoped, we would be playing at the beach like we always had, laughing about what idiots we'd been.

The grass on the other side of the bank was damp and cool. The further we walked, snaking behind houses, back in the direction we'd come, the more difficult the ground became. We were well below the path, close to the water's edge. Mostly, it felt as if Kahu had forgotten I was there. He pressed ahead, eyes searching the banks of the lagoon, barely checking to see that I was behind him. Soon we were half-crouching, one hand always in contact with the ground, and the other in the air, for balance. "Are you sure about your shoes?" he said. I nodded, even though I'd hardly worn the shoes all summer, for fear of getting them dirty. Nothing else was said. We passed back yards filled with chatter—children preparing for a day at the beach, blowing up inflatables and squabbling over water guns. It was a beautiful morning—the few clouds that hung in the sky were fluffy and white. Grass gave way eventually to mud, moss and mulch. My white shoes were ruined. "We're nearly there," he said. Looking up, I saw that we weren't far from the holiday house—the lagoon and its banks were becoming more familiar. Another five minutes and we would be back where I had first spotted Kahu, hooking slime with that long, forked stick. I pictured my father and me, pushing our way through the flax on our hands and knees, and all I felt was a kind of fond pity, the way you feel about your classroom on the last day of school, after the teacher has taken down all the art, and the desks have been shoved against the wall with all the chairs stacked upside down on top of them.

"Here," Kahu said.

He stopped and I stopped too, keeping my distance, in case it was some kind of trick—a prank, a bad joke. "Where?" I said. There was glare coming off the glassy surface of the lagoon, and patches of deep shade too, where trees and flaxes grew out over the water, casting it into gloom. "There," he said, pointing. I followed his finger to a clump in the water. "That's just rubbish," I said, without really looking. *Yeah, rubbish*, I hoped he would say. *Let's go.* There was a feeling in my legs like I wanted to run. "People dump stuff here all the time," I said. I didn't know if it was true. In the confusion of gloom and glare, I couldn't see what made this clump any different from all the others, dotted along the banks of the lagoon. Kahu felt my disbelief, and grabbed my hand. "You have to look properly," he said. "See that stick there? That's how I found it. I pushed it with that stick and it sort of . . . floated up."

I saw a stick, about two feet long, and quite thick, lying abandoned on the bank, directly above the clump in the water. So Kahu had been poking about, hooking slime, and he'd disturbed something that had reared up at him like a monster from a horror film. "Here," I said, stepping around him on the bank. The more I pretended to be brave, the more brave I felt. Keeping low to the ground, I made my way along the bank, to where Kahu had dropped his stick. Seeing skid marks in the mud, I guessed that he must have lost his footing, in a desperate scramble to get away. This made me feel braver still—*I* wasn't scrambling, *I* was calm. When I reached the stick, I picked it up and turned, planting my bottom down, facing the lagoon. My feet were a few inches from the water's edge, and now my bottom was cold and wet—my shorts would be ruined, along with my shoes. I glanced up, and saw that Kahu had moved back a few feet. "See?" I said, pointing at the water with the stick, but I hadn't looked at the clump yet—I was carefully ignoring it. At home, when a film I was watching became scary, I had learned to focus on a corner of the screen, or on one of the buttons on the side of the television. In this way, I could watch an entire horror film without flinching, while around me, others jumped and screamed.

"What do you see?" Kahu called.

"Nothing," I said. "Rubbish."

In fact I could see, at the bottom of my vision, just beneath the water line, suspect patches of pure white.

Kahu took a step toward me. "What sort of rubbish?"

"Household rubbish," I said, proud of this phrase I had remembered from a sign I passed on the way to school— DUMPING OF HOUSEHOLD RUBBISH IN THIS AREA IS STRICTLY PROHIBITED.

"Poke it," he said.

I swallowed. To poke the thing I would have to slide closer— my feet might touch the water. "I can't reach," I said. "This stick isn't long enough."

"You have to poke it like I did. It's the only way to be sure."

I nodded. I was inching my way closer to the water, allowing myself tiny, fleeting glances at the clump, trying to sort its various shapes and colours into something familiar that I could name. Behind me, on the bank, I saw a snaking vine, thick and rooted into the earth, which I grabbed to stop myself from sliding. Then I leaned out over the water with the stick in my hand, still not looking, or not really, my face tilted up toward the sky. Off to the side, I noticed Kahu moving back, retreating slowly. *Don't go—don't you dare leave me.* Underneath my bravery, I still couldn't shake the feeling in my legs that I wanted to run, and now there was a new feeling—that something behind me might give me a push. If that happened, I knew I would scream, and flail, and probably wet my pants too.

I shuffled forward another inch, gripping the vine with all my strength. The stick made contact with the clump, and I felt a watery, rubbery mass. With my eyes shut tight, I prodded. "What do you see?" Kahu called, thin-voiced. I had leaned out so far—my weight so high over the water—that there was no easy way back. If the vine broke, or its roots pulled out of the bank, I would be in the lagoon before I could gasp.

I prodded again. The thing at the end of the stick pushed back. I might have decided it wasn't worth it—turned and made my way back up the bank with my eyes firmly closed—but at that moment a bird swooped, fluttering its wings close to my head.

I opened my eyes.

"What is it?" Kahu called again, but he knew. He'd known all along.

It was a figure under the water, girlish and pale, only it wasn't Charlotte. Charlotte I had never seen before—I couldn't have described her face, or picked her out in a photograph. The face at the end of my stick had long black hair coiled around it like a nest of eels, and, impossibly, a small smile on its lips.

It was a face I recognized.

TWENTY-THREE

My father stood, coffee cup in hand, frowning at our bloodied knees, our mud-caked shoes, our ashen faces. Behind him the lounge looked neat and tidy, the pillow and blanket gone from the couch. "Tell me again," he said, and then he stuck a single finger up. "One at a time."

We told him, and when it looked as though he didn't believe us, we told him again. Finally he drained the last of his coffee, walked to the kitchen to put his cup in the sink, and wiped his hands carefully—both hands, both sides—on a tea towel that lay nearby.

Then he put the tea towel down on the bench.

"Show me," he said.

He was certain it would be a false alarm. A car tyre or bicycle seat. He was certain—I could see it in his face—but there were our bloodied knees, our trembling chins. We said nothing along the way. I wondered if we would be in trouble, if the thing in the lagoon turned out to be a false alarm.

I wondered if I wanted to be right, or wrong.

Going back, we took the path that ran beside the holiday house. It was much quicker—we got to the lagoon in a few minutes, following the flaxes until we found a clear spot, roughly opposite the point where our panicked feet had left skid marks in the mud. "Show me," my father said again. We stood between flaxes, desperately pointing at the other side. "There?" Kahu would say, and I would say, "No, it was further that way." We were hopelessly disorientated, shivering, and suddenly exhausted, as if we'd been awake for hours, when in fact it was only morning—the start of what should have been a beautiful day.

"There!" I was relieved to see the clump and at the same time I was not. It *did* exist. We had *not* imagined it. My father could not possibly be cross with me for making up stories.

"There," I said, more quietly this time.

My father saw what I saw and made a long, low noise like a hiss. The clump, from this side of the lagoon, was clearly not a car tyre, or part of an old bicycle, or any other thing you might throw away without a second thought.

"Holy God," my father said.

We stood there, the three of us, for several seconds, while sand flies danced around our ankles, and children laughed nearby. Then my father said, "Back." This time we didn't run; we walked quietly, either side of my father, who put a hand on the back of my neck and squeezed, and then did the same to Kahu.

We walked like that, with our heads down, all the way back to the holiday house.

~~~

I thought the police would make us kids go back again, but they did not. They took my father, and they went the long way round the lagoon, in two police cars. On the way they dropped Kahu home, and because I was shivery with shock and exhaustion, it didn't occur to me, as he climbed into the back of a black-and-white police car with my father, that I might never see him again. I didn't say goodbye, or wave, or even smile. I didn't tell him that I was sorry I'd wasted time with my stupid accusations, or that I'd had more fun with him than I'd ever had with anyone. I just looked at him, and he looked back at me, and then he left.

I had not told Kahu, or my father, that the face in the lagoon was familiar to me. I had not been able to summon the words. Walking back from the lagoon, the second time, I did try. A couple of times I glanced up at my father, at the underneath of his chin. His stubbly jawline and long, tanned neck. But a silence had fallen over us that seemed sacred, and I said nothing.

I planned to tell as soon as we got home. As soon as my father was done calling the police. As soon as Kahu moved away, out of earshot.

Dad, there's something else.

Something, I don't know, maybe bad, very bad.

But we had emerged from the path to the lagoon to find our car turning into the driveway. Indicator light flickering.

The graunch of the handbrake, and the tick of the ignition as it died. My mother was climbing out of the car with plastic bags full of groceries, Vanessa in the seat behind her. Before we could say a thing, she began to speak. "Last grocery shop of the holiday, done and dusted. Ran into the neighbour, actually, the one who rescued Vanessa." She locked the car, glancing quickly at us to check that we were listening—convinced that she was the one with important information to impart. "Vanessa recognized him. I invited him for dinner on Saturday. That's why I bought so much." She lifted the grocery bags high in the air. Then she noticed Kahu and her face lit up. "Kahu," she said, "how lovely to see you, I feel it's been ages." She frowned—she'd spotted my shoes and shorts, covered in mud. "What's happened, did someone have an accident? Oh my goodness, did someone *fall in*?" Vanessa, behind her, with a grocery bag in each hand, muttered angrily, "Can we get this show moving? These things are heavy."

Now my father was gone—headed to the lagoon in one of the two police cars—and my mother was fussing over me as if I was some kind of hero, and I felt bad about it, because I hadn't told them about the face in the lagoon, and the longer I left it to tell, the harder it became. My mother cleaned my knees with cotton wool soaked in stinging antiseptic solution. She washed my hands in a bowl of warm soapy water that she brought to the couch, rather than asking me to stand at the basin in the bathroom. "You're shaking," she said, "and no wonder, the shock you've had. My poor, poor darling. Water please, Vanessa." My sister didn't roll her eyes, or even hesitate, she just ran the glass of water over to me as quick as she could, placing it carefully on the floor beside my foot.

"What a terrible time you've had," my mother said, peeling plastic bandages away from their sterile backings. It was on the tip of my tongue to tell her about the face. "What a shock. Wait here and I'll go see what medicines we have in the car. I have a feeling there's paracetamol, but you might need something stronger than that to get to sleep tonight. Damn, I should have asked the police officer. Wasn't he kind?" she said, turning to Vanessa. "Didn't you think he was kind, the way he spoke to the kids?" Vanessa nodded—the police officer, who was also young and quite good-looking, was very kind. My mother hurried off to the car, but not before she touched my bandaged knee and gave it a gentle squeeze. "Brave girl," she murmured, smiling with her eyes, and then she was gone, and Vanessa, seizing her chance, moved closer to me and said, "What did it look like?"

I shrugged.

"Face up or face down?"

I closed my eyes. "Face up," I said.

"When you close your eyes, can you still see it?"

Yes, I nodded, opening my eyes.

"Bloody hell," she shuddered, hugging herself. "Bloody *hell*." She sat next to me, close enough for our thighs to touch. Then she began to rub my back. "Did you scream?"

I shook my head.

"Bloody *hell*," she whispered again, under her breath. "I would have screamed."

My mother came back into the house with a packet of paracetamol, squashed and half-empty from the glovebox. "These might do the trick. Two now and two before bed." She nodded approvingly when she saw Vanessa beside me. "That's right, keep her warm, keep her talking. We don't want her to go into shock."

My sister said quietly to me, "It's like something out of a movie. Wait 'til Mr. Peterson finds out." Mr. Peterson was the headmaster at my school. "I bet he says something in assembly. Or pulls you aside, for a chat, and then says something, with your permission. Or maybe not the assembly thing, but I bet he pulls you aside."

I buried my face in my hands and began to cry. My mother dropped the paracetamol and rushed to take Vanessa's place on the couch, wrapping me in her arms. "There, there," she said, just like the man next door. "There, there, it's all right. In the morning you'll begin to forget."

But I knew I would never forget, and I wanted to push my mother away; make her listen, tell her about the face in the lagoon.

"Vanessa," my mother said briskly. "Two pills please, for your sister. I never did like being so close to that damned lagoon," she said, under her breath, while we waited for Vanessa to pop the paracetamol out of their foil tray. "Your father thought it was a good idea, but I didn't, I found it spooky." She shuddered.

Vanessa put a white pill in the palm of my hand. Then she lifted the glass of water that was sitting by my foot. "Here," she said. "Take a big sip." I placed the pill on my tongue and swallowed. Vanessa held the second pill back. "Are you sure?" she asked my mother. "Usually you only give us one."

My mother nodded. "Special occasion," she said, with a wink.

I was put to bed shortly after that, even though it was only the middle of the day. "You don't have to sleep," my mother said, "just try to relax." I don't think she really knew what to do with me. Vanessa said she'd keep me company, and came into the darkened room to sit cross-legged on her bed, a magazine spread open across her lap. I was pleased to have her there, but the paracetamol seemed to do nothing; I couldn't relax, let alone sleep.

Finally I propped myself up on one elbow. "Vanessa," I said.

"Yes?"

"What if we knew her?"

Vanessa frowned. "Knew who?"

I swallowed. "The person . . . in the lagoon. What if it was someone we knew?"

Vanessa thought for a moment, then put aside her magazine and got up from her bed. Crossing the room, she leaned over me, touching my forehead, the same way my mother did when we asked if we could have a day home from school.

"We don't know anyone out here," she said, "so don't worry."

She gently pushed me back down, pulled the covers up to my chin, and then left the room. A moment later I heard her talking in a low voice to my mother, who said, "Yes, very likely in shock, poor thing."

I lay there for what seemed like hours, slipping in and out of an itchy, uncomfortable kind of sleep, until finally I heard the sound of a car pulling up outside, and a car door thudding shut. I had to sit up then, to stop the bile rising in my throat. Now my father would tell. I heard my mother move quickly across the lounge. Their murmured voices at the door. Footsteps coming back, toward my bedroom—but they passed, moving on to the kitchen. I heard Vanessa ask, "Will we wake her for dinner?" and then the kettle spitting into life. The drag of the instant coffee jar across the bench, the *pop* of the screw-top lid. I couldn't make out their words after that, but I knew from the yawn in my father's voice that the police hadn't figured out who it was in the lagoon yet, or if they had, they hadn't told him.

TWENTY-FOUR

My mother didn't blame me, when the news came. Didn't seem to care about what I had told, or had not told. Didn't look at me at all.

It was Friday morning. The second-to-last day of our holiday, and the last day of Kahu's. The day before the surf lifesaving party. I woke expecting chaos. Expecting to have slept for minutes, not hours. My visions were of cutlery drawers tipped out, suitcases emptied and flung on the lawn, torches pointed in our faces, Palmer Street filled with flashing sirens and blank white vans parked at all angles on grassy verges. My visions were of search warrants and interrogation rooms, but my little family had been left alone. Allowed to sleep in our beds all night long— to wake naturally, one by one, to cicada song, and sunlight filtering through our curtains. The handsome young police officer let us eat breakfast in peace, and then waited beyond that, giving our food time to settle, giving us time to think it was going to be a normal day. Laundry was put on and dishes were done. My mother spoke in a bright and cheery voice about what it would be like to get home, to Wellington. The lawns would need mowing, she said, and the cat, once we got him home from the cattery, might hide behind the washing machine again, like the last time we went away. He might take some coaxing to come back out, my mother said to me especially, because in our house, I was the one who knew the cat best, and the only one small enough to fit between the side of the tub and the washing machine. "I'm glad I defrosted the fridge before we left," she said, "but what do you think will have become of my garden? There's been hardly a drop of rain in Wellington. I'm worried it will all have died. The hydrangeas especially. I might as well say goodbye to them."

My father was tired from his afternoon on the lagoon, directing traffic. He nodded and grunted and half-closed his puffy eyes. I wondered if he had spent the night on the couch again, or back in the bedroom he shared with my mother. Vanessa stared at me still, jigging her knee in her chair. I think she was wondering if from now on, I would be her dorky little sister, or someone new and more impressive—someone she would have to take seriously.

I began to feel hopeful, almost happy.

Was it possible that I was wrong? About the face in the lagoon?

A different face, similar to the other.

Chinese people tend to look alike, my mother had said.

After breakfast I remembered that it was Kahu's last day. At home in Wellington I owned a letter-writing set, complete with stickers, envelopes and a smooth, very adult ballpoint pen. I had owned this set for more than a year, but I had never dared touch it, never peeled a single sticker away from its backing (I couldn't bear to put a gap in a row), never put a mark on a single sheet of paper (I couldn't think of anything important enough to say). Now, I planned to devote the set to keeping in touch with Kahu. I planned to ask him to be my pen-pal. I figured there must be at least fifty sheets of paper in the set, and so, if I wrote to Kahu once a month, and restricted myself to one sheet only (front and back, extra-small writing), I could keep in touch with him for four whole years, by which time I would be fourteen—old enough perhaps to make plans to see him. All I needed was his home address, and a promise from him that he would write back.

I dressed quickly in a rainbow T-shirt and a pair of navy-blue shorts, deciding not to wear my togs under my clothes because I wanted to stay clean and dry and warm—the thought of water touching my skin was suddenly repulsive to me. Folding my togs into a tiny bundle and pushing them into a corner of my suitcase, I felt as though I could go the rest of my life without ever dipping my toe in a sea or river again. Pools only, I said to myself, and then only on the hottest of days.

That's when he came. The handsome young police officer, who wasn't nearly so handsome in the light of day. Visibly uncomfortable, chewing over his words, eyes blank and closed off to us, notebook poised, police-issue trousers clinging tightly to his thighs, and finishing in a slight flare, a little too far above his solid black rubber-soled shoes. I heard the knock, but I was so absorbed in the contents of my little suitcase, and in my letter-writing plans, that I failed to recognize its significance. It was only when I heard his voice, clipped and formal, that a stone dropped into my stomach and I knew.

Not wrong. Not mistaken.

The face in the lagoon, known to me and to us.

"We have identified the female in the lagoon," the policeman said, as, in my bedroom, I lowered the lid of my suitcase and rose slowly to my feet.

Slipping through the bedroom door, into the lounge, to stand, unnoticed, behind my father.

"I'm here to check out a possible connection."

"Connection?" My mother had been cleaning the coffee table, readying the house for our departure the day after next. In her hands she held a bright orange sponge, fresh out of the packet.

"Yes. We're following up with everybody in the area who knew the deceased."

"Yes?"

"As a matter of fact, apart from her family, who are staying nearby," the policeman frowned into his notebook, "we understand that you are the only people who knew her. Out here."

I reached out to touch the edge of the kitchen bench. To anchor myself in the real world, where conversations like this didn't take place. From the bathroom, we heard Vanessa shut the water off and rip back the shower curtain. I knew it would be a while until she emerged, because she liked to shave her legs after she showered, one foot up on the side of the bath.

"No, I don't think so," my mother was saying, confused, polite, smiling. "We don't know anyone out here, do we, Colin?" My father had his hands on his hips. He was frowning hard at the policeman's rubbery black shoes. "No one. Just kids."

"Oh no!" my mother gasped, sinking into the chair behind her, clutching the bright orange kitchen sponge to her chest. "You're not telling us it was Crystal out there?"

The policeman shook his head. "No, no, we're not talking about any kid."

"Crystal is fifteen," my father said.

"No, the deceased was"—the policeman referred quickly to his notebook—"thirty-eight years of age."

"Oh. Well. Thank God." Irritation was creeping into my mother's voice. For an awful moment I wondered if she'd wished Crystal dead, for all the trouble she'd caused. But she had cleaning to do, and the wet sponge had left its imprint on her freshly laundered T-shirt. My father took his hands off his hips and folded them across his chest in a gesture of impatience. In the bathroom I heard a sharp intake of breath, a hiss. Vanessa, cutting herself with the razor. The policeman seemed to hear it too, pausing, his attention briefly diverted. But then he cleared his throat, lowered his notebook, and delivered his news—slowly, watchfully. Measuring its impact. I was confused, because the name he spoke was one I'd never heard. Almost not a name but a series of sounds. A Chinese name—I hadn't expected that. Lucy had been given a name we Kiwis understood. Her mother had not. I suppose I hadn't expected a name at all. I suppose in my self-centred, childish way, I had expected him to say, *Lucy's mother.*

~~~

I was sent to my room but not really. Barely. My mother had begun a process of folding in on herself, of shrinking. She stayed in that armchair, the one she'd sunk into when she'd thought, briefly, that the face in the lagoon was Crystal's. She stayed there, only the chair seemed to grow bigger, and my mother smaller, like something out of *Alice in Wonderland*. Watching her, I half expected the chair to spread and thicken like a tree, lifting my mother up, through the ceiling, into the open air.

But the chair stayed where it was, and the whole time the policeman spoke, my mother kept her eyes on him, her head dropping, so that in the end she looked like a dog that had been kicked.

It took time for them to notice me standing there, even though they looked right at me, and spoke about me. "So, to clarify, your daughter and the deceased's daughter are at the same school," the policeman said, gesturing toward me. "That's the connection? I mean, originally. In the first instance."

When my father finally *saw* me, standing with one hand on the bench to anchor myself, he ushered me back, into my room, where Vanessa was sitting on her bed with her freshly shaved legs crossed. "Put your headphones on," he said, and then he pulled the door shut behind him, but in his distraction he didn't notice that it hadn't latched—it was left open a fraction. "Fucking hell," Vanessa whispered. I had never heard this combination of words out of her mouth or anyone else's.

Fucking hell.

I nodded, yes. After that we sat together on my bed because it was closest to the door, and we left the door open, and our headphones on the floor.

Other words I'd never heard before:

Pending.

Intoxicated.

Toxicology.

Post-mortem.

Inquest.

I looked at my sister but each time she shrugged, or frowned, or held one finger up: *I'm listening, wait.* She was patient with me—we were a team.

Phrases:

Reasonable to assume.

Extreme emotional distress.

Most likely scenario.

(I knew this one, I'd heard it! When the cat disappeared, after the last holiday. My mother said, "Most likely scenario he's under the shed." But he wasn't. He was between the washing machine and the wall, and it was me that found him, with my extra good cat-instincts, and my extra skinny arm.)

And another word that entered my head like a knife blade. Instantly, when I heard it, I pictured it this way. Slippery, cold, shiny, and delivering pain. Maybe it was the way my mother cried when she heard it—a cry not human but like an animal wounded. And my father's words, same as the night before: "Holy God, holy God."

Suicide.

This word repeated so many times I had to know—I had to press my fingers into my sister's arm and raise my shoulders and eyebrows in unison: *What is it? Suicide? What?*

She shook her head at first—she knew but wasn't telling. *No, no, no, tell me!* I squeezed her arm so hard the skin began to tear under my fingers. She smacked my wrist and made a face with all her teeth showing like, *Piss off I will EAT you!* But then, reluctantly, she got off the bed and went to her magazine— the one she kept under her pillow that she thought I didn't know about, the adult one. With a frown of concentration and memory she flipped through the magazine while in the lounge the policeman droned, ". . . important for the family that we make a thorough investigation even in the circumstances, assumptions are nobody's friend, due diligence and so on, i's dotted, t's crossed. We don't want people thinking they can come out here to the beach and get away with things they wouldn't get away with in . . . where did you say you were from, sir?"

My father waited so long before replying that I thought he might have forgotten where we lived back home.

"Wellington."

"Wellington, exactly, sir. So, unpleasant as it may be, I'm going to take you back to that night, if you don't mind."

"The other night? When he came here looking for her? It was late."

"We'll get to that, sir. First, this dinner party. Take me back to that, please."

My sister found what she was looking for and evidently she needed clarification too, because she stood for a moment, reading the page she'd found. I watched her eyes scanning the words, the left-hand page all the way to the bottom and then the right, and I thought, You're my sister and I love you and we're in this together. But it was a fleeting thought and then she climbed clumsily back onto the bed, accidentally kicking me in the knee, setting me off-balance. When I had righted myself, she placed the magazine in my lap, open to the page.

Suicide.

A photograph that took up most of one page, of a teenaged girl with glossy brown hair and torn jeans, cool bangles, painted nails, sitting as we had been, with her knees pulled up to her chest, against a wall. An outside wall perhaps in a playground? Graffiti behind her and possibly rubbish. She had her head in her hands and her face was hidden.

Despair, I saw, in the first paragraph. *Emptiness. Hopelessness. Loss. Betrayal.*

Hard to focus on the words on the page and at the same time, listen to what was happening in the lounge. My father growing angry, exasperated. Vanessa now with her head in her hands exactly like the girl in the suicide picture.

My father: "I really don't see the relevance, I mean, raking over . . . this is old ground surely? And not . . . I don't see how this is even relevant."

"Anything that helps us gain a better understanding of the deceased woman's mental state in the weeks leading up—"

"Yes, yes, Christ! I swear, you've said that already. I swear you have a script somewhere. You're reading this bullshit from a script. Can't you see what this is doing to her?"

(My mother perhaps crying, wailing, this whole entire time—it was too much to take in as well as words-on-page, words-in-lounge, so I had partially tuned it out.)

"Sir, I am not reading from a script. I am trained to deal with . . . I am following protocol, sir. I mean if you want I can call for a WPC if you think your wife—"

"No, okay, okay, forget it, Christ, please, no more police." I pictured my father patting the air down with his big strong hands, beloved hands that had lifted the little rowboat through the flax bush that day.

Trying all the while to read the article and none of it making sense. Or sense being made but no comprehension. In school we were taught, it's not about how-many-pages-how-fast, or about counting chapters, or size-of-print or pictures/no-pictures, it's all about COMPREHENSION. And I did not COMPRE-HEND a single thing about SUICIDE.

I did not comprehend what it had to do with what Kahu and I had found in the lagoon. That white face, bloated and moon-like, swathed in jet-black hair.

". . . any reason to assume that he was lying?"

This cutting through because I knew this word and all it implied: *lying.*

"No, no, I mean, why would he . . ."

"To establish a timeline. I'm thinking. Or to, you know, deflect. You two being the only other people they knew up here.

He might have wanted to be seen to be looking for her. Any reason to think that? Anything unusual?"

"Well, Jesus, the whole thing was fucking un*usual*. None of this is *usual* to us, can I just be crystal clear about that. We do not— In our lives— This is not— Please understand that until about ten fucking days ago I knew nothing about any of this."

"Of course. But it's odd, don't you think? That he would come *here*, of all places?"

"Yes! Yes!" My father, shouting and almost laughing. Almost. "I told him that. In no uncertain terms. Why the hell would he think that she would come *here*?"

"And?"

"He said something about talking it out, woman to woman."

A pause in which I lifted the magazine off my knee and pushed it toward my sister, shaking my head. *This is not working, I still don't understand.*

"Was there a discussion ma'am? Woman to woman?"

"I have already told you—"

"Sir, if you don't mind, I need to hear it from your wife."

Another pause in which the crying/wailing became more subdued and my mother maybe shook her head.

My sister sighing, looking around for inspiration.

"And what about you and your—ah—the husband of the deceased. When was the last time you two had contact?"

A slamming noise which made us jump. My father's hand on the bench. "She answered that already, did she not? She hasn't seen him since that night he came looking for her—for his wife. Christ almighty."

"Again, sir, please, your wife can speak for herself."

Perhaps my mother nodded. I pictured her gesturing toward my father. *What he said.*

"Okay, okay, nearly there. Um, let me think." I heard the policeman flicking through his notebook, turning pages sharply, *snap, snap.* My father had begun to pace. Every few seconds he paced into view, past our door, turned and paced away again, out of view.

Vanessa closed the magazine and laid it beside her on the bed. Thinking.

"Okay, yeah, one more thing. Just—you know—tying up loose ends." He laughed, friendly, as if all the swearing and shouting and my father pacing wasn't happening. "You see, in the police, we don't like coincidences. Coincidences don't sit well with us, you can understand."

"Get to the point."

My father's voice so cold and unfamiliar I thought for a moment a third man had entered the room to join in the conversation.

"Well, okay, for starters. Your daughter finding the deceased. You say she just happened to be out there, poking around, on the other side of the lagoon, quite early in the day, around breakfast time?"

"I do say that, yes. What else are kids going to do, out here? It was the boy anyway, he was the one that found it. Not my daughter."

"Yes, yes, I"—pages snapping—"yes, I have made a note of that. I think you mentioned that last night. Okay, well, I'll be speaking to the young man after this. I assume he'll corroborate what you've told me."

"He will. Are we done?" Pacing into view and stopping, hands on hips. Shoulders rounded and thin—very thin. I hadn't noticed before how very thin my father was. Insubstantial.

"Um, nearly. Ma'am, just one more question."

Vanessa laid a hand on my foot, indicating, *Look at me.*

I looked at her.

She blinked. *Okay, here goes.*

Suicide, she mouthed.

Yes, yes, I nodded, *tell me.*

She pointed at herself, pulling the corners of her mouth down. *Me, sad.*

Yes, yes, I get it. You—sad.

In the lounge: ". . . I'm guessing that's why you decided to spend the summer here? In this place? I mean, all the way back in"—pages snapping—"September? Was that your motive? Sorry, loaded word. Hazard of the job. Was that your reason? For choosing this place?"

I glanced at my father, standing outside our door. I saw his head go down, all the way to his chest. His eyes closed.

Vanessa blinked again, drawing a line under *Me, sad.* Then she held up the two fingers of her right hand and cocked her thumb to make: *Gun.*

Yes, yes, I get it—gun.

A long pause, in which my father stood with his head hanging down and his hands on his hips, recalling perhaps, as I was, that moment way back in September, when my mother had planted her oniony finger on the map.

I want to go to a place with people.

And then Vanessa lifted her two fingers to her temple and jerked back her thumb.

Boom.

~~~~

It took a while for us to realize that we were on our own. That our parents were there but not there. Not behaving as parents. Not behaving as *Mum, Dad*. Not even *husband, wife*. My father had defended my mother from that policeman but as soon as the policeman was gone the mood shifted. He waited until the police car could no longer be heard on the street and then he left the house, not even closing the front door properly, just leaving it to swing there on its hinges. My mother stayed exactly where she was, head in hands. A quick glance into the lounge revealed that the orange sponge she'd been using to clean the coffee table was still sitting damply in her lap.

Vanessa and I stayed on the bed for the longest time, expecting someone else to close the door that was creaking in the breeze. Because we had been raised in a house that had always run smoothly, predictably, carefully, we expected our father to be outside, performing some necessary chore. Sweeping crumbs out of the back seat of the car. Cleaning the barbecue. Readying the boot for all our suitcases, pillows, towels, and the typewriter. In Wellington, when we couldn't find a parent, we looked in the wash house, the shed, the garage, the entrance to the attic. Always we found one or both of them, bent over a tub or bench or cardboard box, sweaty, dishevelled, sleeves rolled up. But when finally Vanessa got off the bed and walked to the front door, closing it, she returned to report that our father was gone. Not outside on the patio. Not at the washing line. Not with his head in the back seat of the car, or the car boot. Just gone. Walked out the front door, leaving it swinging, and then out onto the street, off to who knew where.

Got to tell Mum. Got to rouse her get her moving snap her back.

But by the time we summoned the courage to go to our mother—to tell her that Dad was gone and to ask her what happened to lunch, afternoon tea, dinner—by this time she had moved silently, wordlessly, from the armchair to her bed. It took another hour or so for us to persuade ourselves to push with one finger her bedroom door until it opened enough to reveal her lying on her side in the foetal position facing the wall, on top of the covers, shoes still on.

Hugging herself.

The orange sponge dropped beside her bed on top of the black leather notebook my father had given her.

We took the plate loaded with cold sausages out of the fridge. We carried it into our room, where we had never been allowed to eat dinner before, but it felt too strange to sit at the kitchen table, the two of us—what was left of our family. Instead we returned to the exact spot on my bed where we'd sat with our knees up all afternoon, and we ate the sausages one by one with our fingers. There were twelve sausages on the plate— more than enough for our whole family, but we ate ten. Pushing sausages into our open mouths until our fingers, lips, teeth, cheeks and even wrists were coated with a thick film of cold smoky barbecue fat. It tasted good and it was what we needed but we overdid it and felt sick. Partly I kept eating because in my head I was doing this: *By the time we finish our father will be back. By the time I finish the next sausage. And the next, and the next.* As well, part of me was wondering whether we would have to lose our father, because Lucy had lost her mother. It was only fair, wasn't it? And . . . symmetrical?

Please, I begged God, *let me keep my father, I will be good from now on, I swear, just let me have him back.*

Somewhere, I knew, Lucy would be thinking similar thoughts. Only for her it was impossible—no matter how good she tried to be for the rest of her life, she would never see her mother again.

My father did eventually come back, but it was long after we'd stopped eating sausages. I'd cried a lot by then, into my pillow. I'd lain facing the wall, soaking my pillow with tears and running my finger over the word *Charlotte*, thinking, I wish I was dead like you. I wish I could walk into the ocean like you and just disappear, except that would be wrong. That would be a bad thing to do, like suicide.

When our father came home, he poked his nose into our room and decided we were asleep. He took the plate with its two remaining sausages off our floor and carried it to the kitchen table. We were neither of us asleep. Moments earlier, Vanessa had whispered into the darkness, not expecting a reply, "They better not try to take me back to Wellington before the surf lifesaving party." I felt like sitting up and letting my father know, *Mum has been in her room all afternoon, she hasn't said a word to us since you left*. It felt important that he know. Also, I wanted to say, *We ate five sausages each*. Five! Never in my life before had my parents not cared if, or how, I was fed. My father left our bedroom door ajar and ate the remaining two sausages off the plate. I could hear him eating in the kitchen—his breathing, his wristwatch bumping against the table edge. He ate in the dark, and when he'd finished, he didn't do any of the normal things. Didn't wash the plate, or brush his teeth, or anything like that. Didn't check on my mother. I listened and listened for the sound of his hand on their bedroom door, his footsteps entering their room, but that didn't happen. He just went over to the couch and lay down.

TWENTY-FIVE

My father wanted to go home immediately. A day early—before the surf lifesaving party. This much became apparent the next morning, when we woke to the sound of him emptying the fridge and clearing out the cupboards. He'd risen early, after only a few hours' sleep, to get us out of there, away from that place. To wipe our memories of it. "Last day," he kept saying. "Last day," as he tipped what was left of the orange juice down the sink—even though we could have had it for our breakfast, or for that matter, carried it in the car with us. "Last day," he said, clicking his fingers for us to hand him our dirty washing, even though I was pretty sure my mother would have put it in a plastic bag. She would have said there wasn't time for it to dry, and she'd rather wash it at home in Wellington. But my father was in a frenzy. He was operating at warp-speed, barely in control of his movements, or his thoughts. He put a wash on and then switched off the hot water. He tipped that orange juice down the sink and then turned to us and said, "What can I get you? Toast? Orange juice?" He wasn't thinking. He hadn't eaten, except for two cups of black coffee, because he made the usual amount but my mother didn't emerge, and he didn't want to take the coffee to her, so it sat for the longest time on the bench and then he drank it in his warp-speed, not-thinking way, even though I'm pretty sure it must have been cold by then.

It was scary. I had never seen my father like this. I wanted to put my hand on his arm and smile at him—give him my best, brightest smile to bring him back—but his hands were shaking, and I thought that if I dared to touch him, he'd swat me away like a sand fly.

He got us into the car—the clock on the dashboard said five to eleven. Still no food in his stomach and barely any in ours. My sister was in a state about leaving, crying so hard she couldn't breathe or even form words of complaint. The white dress she had planned to wear to the party was stuffed into a bag—not even the right bag, a different bag, full of toiletries and kitchen essentials. "You realize I will n-never s-s-see my friends again," she stammered. I knew that she would see Crystal again—they went to the same school—and could only assume that the person she was really worried about not seeing again was Josh. That thought set me off crying too, because in that moment I realized what I should have realized earlier—that I had let Kahu go without a word. Without getting his address or even the correct spelling of his last name. Both of us girls wailing in the back seat with all our worldly belongings crammed into the car around us and my father determined, it would seem, not to notice that our mother had *still not emerged*. Had still not unfurled herself from the bed. As far as we knew she was lying there in the same clothes and in her shoes, facing the wall, hugging herself, folding in.

"Wh-wh-what about M-Mum?" I asked. I had to say it more than once, to bring my father to his senses. Finally he did pause, standing in the grass in front of our car, in the same pose I'd seen him in the day before—hands on hips, head down, eyes closed. Was it possible for a person to lose weight, visibly, overnight? We sat in the back of the car suppressing our sobs, watching him through the gaps in the headrests. I suppose he'd been hoping that all his crashing around would draw my mother out of her room. I suppose he thought he could transport her back to Wellington without a word. All that remained to pack, after all, was my mother, her typewriter, the pages of the book she was writing, her suitcase, and her black leather notebook.

It was then—as my father stood with his head down, trying to think what to do about my mother—that we heard footsteps coming around the side of the car.

"Ah, now, not thinking of leaving, I hope?"

We heard this, sitting in the back seat, before my father did. Both of us swivelling round to see the policeman approaching with one hand in his pocket and the other shielding his eyes from the morning sun.

"Not going anywhere, I trust? Only I'm almost certain I had it down in my notes that you were staying put until tomorrow."

Arriving at my father, the policeman extended a hand, but my father ignored it, so the policeman wrapped his hand around my father's upper arm, man to man. "Best you stay put for today at least, if you don't mind. Just while we wrap up a few last-minute loose ends, you know how it is. He-said-she-said and all that."

He turned and lowered his head to wave at us—we were choking down tears in the back seat.

"No, I don't know how it is," my father said. "We're leaving now."

"Best you stay here if that's all the same with you—you're booked until tomorrow, correct?"

"Correct, but under the circumstances—"

"Under the circumstances, best that you stay where I can find you, just in case. Just until tomorrow, seeing as how you're booked anyway. I'm going to be chatting at length to the husband today—the other husband—and you never know, his testimony might bring up something I need to go over with you again."

"His *testimony?*"

"Oh, well, you know. The things he has to say. Especially about the night she went missing and what his actions were after that, you know, coming here and so on. I mean, given the proximity of the . . . ah . . . human remains, to here, to this house, to where he was that night, supposedly searching. We have to look at every possible angle, I'm sure you understand."

"What, he's a *suspect?*"

"Well, not exactly. We've learned that the deceased visited the post office just before she disappeared—she was in a distressed state, by all accounts. We've confirmed she sent a letter

to family back in China. Your equivalent of a note, perhaps."
The policeman folded his arms and looked up, toward the sky,
as if discussing the likelihood of a breeze picking up later in
the day. "We're trying to intercept that letter—latest we have,
it might not have got further than Auckland, which would be
great. But you never know. The letter might not be as conclusive
as we hope, and that might put the husband back in the picture,
so to speak. Who knows, time will tell. Important thing is that
you stay here, so that I can get to you if I need to. Okay?"

My father threw his hands up. "What difference is it going
to make?"

"Exactly. It's one night, so you may as well stay where you
are. As it is, your girls don't look too happy with this plan of
yours. Surf lifesaving party tonight—always a big one for the
youngsters. All hands on deck. Torches at the ready. No, no,
hahaha, it's not that bad, the kids are pretty well behaved on the
whole. We like to patrol the beaches, stop them doing anything
they might regret in later years."

In veering off course, he had lost my father, who was staring
dejectedly at the bonnet of our car. The policeman bent down
again to look at us, at the two empty front seats. "Your wife
not . . . ah . . . included in this high-speed getaway?"

"What? No—it's not a getaway. I simply thought . . ."

"Of course, I'm just teasing. Just teasing," he said, once again
wrapping his big hand around my father's arm. But he wasn't
entirely teasing, because the next thing he said was, "So, your
wife?"

"She's inside."

"Uh-huh."

"Exhausted."

"I'm sure. Still, maybe if I could . . ." He pointed toward the house.

"Why?" my father said, lowering his voice and stepping forward, so that their noses now were almost touching. "You worried I might have thrown her in the lagoon?"

The policeman took a step back, palms raised. "Hey, now, no need for that. You know I'm just doing my job, looking out for all concerned. Perhaps I'll just pop in the house and have a word with her myself."

"Be my guest."

"Okay, okay, I'll do that. You wait here."

The policeman stepped inside, and we waited. I found myself afraid, in that moment, of what he would find. None of us had laid eyes on my mother since the day before. At one point, during the night, I'd thought I heard a stirring from her room—even, I'd imagined, the *tack-tack* of her typewriter. But that can only have been a dream, I thought.

The policeman returned after what seemed like many minutes, shaking his head. "Your wife seems to know nothing of your plans to leave a day early, sir."

"Yeah, well . . ."

"You can't expect her to travel today. Not after the shock she's had. I wouldn't mind calling for a doctor, come to think of it. Has she eaten?"

My father made some small gesture to indicate that no, she had not eaten.

"Look, sir, I understand you're angry, you have every right to be, but you can't just leave her here on her own, with no food in the house, and no way of getting back."

"That was not the plan."

"Okay, well, dragging your family off in a rush like this isn't the answer either. It's Saturday, end of the month, the highway will be clogged up." He stepped forward, stooping down so that he could peer up into my father's face. "What about you? Did you get any sleep? You don't look fit to drive these youngsters anywhere. I have a half a mind to take away your car keys."

At that point, perhaps sensing that my father was defeated, Vanessa opened the car door and stumbled out.

"There now, this one has the right idea," the policeman said, spreading an arm to encompass Vanessa, who ignored him, stomping directly past and into the house. He turned back to my father. "Need help unloading the car?"

My father shook his head.

"All right, if you're sure." He tapped the hood of the car twice, bending down to smile at me. "You too, little lady. Out you get."

I climbed out the other side, walked toward the front of the car, and stood in behind my father—right in his shadow, which was short and close because it was nearly midday.

"Look at that! She's the spitting image of you, sir. Okay, hang tight today, all right? And by that I mean, don't go too far. Stay away from the lagoon, for example. That would be my advice."

"Honestly, what would make you think we would ever want to go near that place again?"

"Yes. Quite. Good. Just asking that you keep a low profile,

that's all. Look, I may as well be straight with you. There's going to be a little gathering at the lagoon today. I suggest you might like to stay away. Keep indoors. Do some more of those jigsaw puzzles I saw the other day when I visited."

"A gathering?"

The policeman nodded. "Some old fellas from the local marae are coming along to do one of their ceremonies, put their, you know, rāhui on the place."

"Their what?"

"Rāhui. It's a kind of . . . well, look, I'm no expert. But the place'll be off limits for a while. No kayaking or mucking around in boats. Out of respect. And I believe the deceased's family are going to be in attendance—the, ah, gentleman and his daughter."

"He's coming here?"

"To the lagoon. Yes, sir. These ceremonies can be very healing for families, and for the local community in general. They can bring a sense of peace to a place. I just ask that you keep a low profile to avoid any awkwardness. That's all. The last thing that little girl needs is . . ."

His voice trailed off.

"Yes," my father said. "Yes."

"Meanwhile, I'm gonna try to pop back later this afternoon, see how things are going"—he nodded toward the house—"check in on your wife."

"She doesn't need you checking on her."

"Ripples, sir."

"I beg your pardon?"

"A thing like this—it can have a ripple effect."

My father blinked maybe three times, and then shook his head at the ground. I stepped closer to him, tucking myself into his backside, and searching around for a hand to hold, which I found. I got a hold of his right hand and dragged it around behind him so that I could grasp it under my chin. The policeman left, and my father and I stood, my father swaying slightly on his feet. For a few moments we stood like that, swaying together in the sun, almost as one.

TWENTY-SIX

Perhaps it would have been better if we'd been allowed to go home. My sister carefully unpacked her white dress and laid it on her bed to flatten out its creases. Otherwise, we left most of our belongings in the car. For lunch we ate warm muesli bars from the glovebox and some packet soups that had been at the house when we arrived. The soup smelled so good we wondered why we didn't eat it more often. "We have to tell Mum to buy this at home," Vanessa said, and I marvelled at her confidence—that we would have a mum to buy us soup in the future. That we would be a normal family again, with a supermarket list on a pad by the telephone. Actually, the soup had a dusty taste, like the inside of a long unopened cupboard. The noodles didn't so much soften as disintegrate. When we'd eaten as much as we could, my father spent a few minutes with his head in his hands while my sister and I tried not to notice. Then he looked around the room and said, "I suppose . . . the beach?"

Sure, we shrugged, but our hearts weren't in it. We'd thought our afternoons at the beach were over, and now that we'd been gifted one back, we didn't really know what to do with it. Besides, our swimming gear was at the bottom of the car boot, damp and salty and folded into our various towels. When our father realized this, his whole body seemed to sag.

"We don't have to swim," Vanessa said.

"We could walk," I said.

But my father was still in a sag and didn't look like he could walk.

"*We* could walk. Us two. We don't need a chaperone," Vanessa said. "I'm fifteen."

My father nodded. "You're right. Of course you don't. When I was fifteen . . ." But he didn't have the energy to complete that thought. "Stick together. Don't be too long."

We couldn't believe our luck, and couldn't get out of there fast enough. We promised our father we wouldn't be long, and that we'd stick together, and then we bolted—trotting, not walking, to the top of Palmer Street. As soon as we got to the grass verge, we turned to face each other.

"I'm going that way," Vanessa said, pointing north, toward the busy end of the beach, where the surf lifesaving flags were.

"I'm going that way," I said, pointing south, toward the lagoon and Kahu's house.

"Okay. Don't do anything stupid."

"You neither," I said.

~~~~

I stayed out all afternoon, in the hope that when I returned, our mother would be restored to us. I waited at Kahu's house, even though it was all locked up. Curtains pulled. Cars gone. Boat and trailer gone. No bikes piled up in a heap, no cousins roaming the lawn. No Dotty and Scottie, slavering on the doorstep. Nothing to be seen but a broken jandal, lying in the grass close to the letterbox. No clues, no messages written in dust—nothing to suggest that Kahu had thought of me on his last day. Still, I hung around, thinking that his uncle might be on one of his fishing trips, and that when he got home, I could ask him for Kahu's address. I went all around the house, putting my nose up to windows, braving cobwebs, and flower beds filled with bees. There was nothing left behind in the house. No trace. The beds were stripped, the bedside tables bare. I remembered Kahu saying that his uncle only used the house in summer—the rest of the year it became a rental, like 32 Palmer Street.

At some point, as I made my way around the windows, a neighbour came out to glare at me, hands on hips. I slunk away then, up the street. The afternoon we'd been gifted back was possibly the hottest of the entire holiday, but the sun and all its heat seemed pointless and garish now, like Christmas decorations on Boxing Day.

When I got home, my father was asleep on the couch and

my mother was still in hiding. I went into my room and found Vanessa there. She had changed into her white dress.

"Did you get in trouble?"

She gave me a questioning look.

"We were supposed to stay together. We promised Dad we would."

She shrugged. "How does the bow look?" she asked, turning, and lifting her hair.

The bow looked lopsided, squashed. Like it had been packed into the boot of a car and unpacked again. "Who cares?" I said. "Your hair covers it anyway."

"Wow, you're in a shitty mood."

I sat heavily on the bed. "Who says you're even going to this party?"

"I do," she said. "I *am*."

She reached into her cotton bag with the woven handles, which was sitting on her bed, and pulled out the tube of stolen mascara. I stared at it—I'd forgotten it existed. She might as well have reached into her bag and pulled out a moment in time, long past. The mascara seemed so harmless now. She tipped the tube toward me. "Want some?"

I scoffed. "Why would *I* need that?"

"I dunno." She grinned. "For Kahu."

"Kahu left. Yesterday."

"Oh yeah, I forgot. You're heartbroken."

"Shut up."

"*You* shut up."

"*You'll* be heartbroken, if you do it with Stuart."

"What?"

"I'm just saying."

"Do what with Stuart? What are you talking about?"

"You don't even like him."

"Shut *up*."

"You like Josh."

She took a step toward me. "Oh my God, shut your face. Shut it, I'm serious."

"You love him."

"I don't."

"You're in love with him. Even more than Crystal is."

She lunged at me, stabbing me with the mascara. I ducked to one side, sliding off the bed. Now I was on the floor at her feet. She lunged again, catching my shoulder with her nails, drawing blood.

"Leave me alone," I shouted. "You're only mad because it's true."

"It's not true, you're wrong."

We went at each other with hands and feet. Pinching, scratching, trying to bite. I grabbed a handful of her hair and pulled. She dug her fingernails into my wrist, scraping them down my arm.

"The madder you get, the truer it must be," I said, taunting her. She was too old for this, and she knew it. But I had got under her skin. She tried to knee me between the legs—I kicked out, upending her. Now she was on the floor, and I was pulling myself up, climbing on the bed to get away from her. "Crystal would kill you if she knew. She would claw your eyes out."

Vanessa caught my foot and tried to pull me down. I reached out for something to grab, striking the wall. "Admit it," I said, "you love him. You'll be doing it with Stuart, but you'll be thinking about *him*."

She bit me then, she was so enraged. She sank her teeth into the fleshy part of my calf. I screamed, banging my head against the wall. There was a crashing sound in the lounge, and our door was thrown open.

"GIRLS."

Our father, with beer spilt all down the front of his shorts. I dragged my legs up, onto the bed, while Vanessa scrambled over to her side of the room. There was blood on her dress—my blood. My father was drawing air into his lungs, preparing to roar at us some more, but then we all heard, from the other side of the wall, the creak of a floorboard. A door swinging open, and light footsteps into the lounge. My father put one hand up: *No one say anything.* We waited, hardly daring to breathe, wondering if the footsteps would return to the bedroom, or if they'd go all the way to the front door and out, away from us for ever.

Then a voice said, "Is everything all right?"

I didn't recognize it at first—it felt like so long since I'd heard her voice. It could have been the voice of a lost child, or a neighbour who wasn't sure if they would be welcome. But, of course, it was my mother's voice. I saw my father's eyes redden, and knew that he had wanted her back as much as we did. He turned toward the kitchen, swiping at his face with the back of his hand. "Everything's fine," he said roughly. I climbed slowly off the bed and walked into the lounge. Blood trickled down the back of my leg, where Vanessa had sunk her teeth in. Our mother was returned to us. She was standing by the armchair, wearing her light blue T-shirt and her denim shorts. She looked pale and worn, but otherwise the same. I moved around her, not speaking. I wanted to see her from all angles. To check that she was complete. I circled right around her, while my father, who was still swiping at his eyes, pretended to be busy in the kitchen. The back of her T-shirt was flattened and creased—she'd been wearing these clothes for some time. I looked into her bedroom, and saw the pillow propped up, also flattened and creased. She'd been sitting up in the bed. Her curtains were drawn back and the window was partially open—the room filled with light, and cool, flowing air. On the bed I saw a stack of papers. Some had their corners folded over. Some had big red lines through them, and notes in the margins. I also saw a pen, lying on top of some pages that were heavily scribbled. My mother had not been sleeping all this time. I moved behind her into the room. She put a hand out toward me, but I ignored it. I walked all the way over to her bed, until I was standing above the stack of papers. Some were face up, some face down. They were very muddled. One of them, I saw, was different from the rest. It had only two words on it, centred in the middle of the page. I reached down and pulled it out of the stack.

THE END.

I turned and looked at her—she smiled.

She had finished her book. That's what she'd been doing on the hottest afternoon of our entire holiday—the very *last* afternoon. While I was out walking, looking for messages in the grime on Kahu's uncle's windows. While we'd eaten packet soup that tasted like dust. While we'd worried about ripples.

My mother took a step toward me, smiling her little half-smile. I let the piece of paper flutter down to the bed, and then I walked past her, back to my own room.

TWENTY-SEVEN

My mother said we had to pull everything out of the car boot. She said there was still a lot of food left over from when she last visited the grocery store and where was it, what had my father done with it? My father said, "Nice of you to join us." My mother said, "One day—I leave you to it for one day and this is how you cope." My father said it wasn't as if she'd gone shopping with her mother. He'd thought she was having some sort of mental breakdown. My mother said, "Oh really, oh really, and yet you didn't think to pop your head around the door."

I put my headphones on, even though there was no cassette tape in my Walkman. I did it just to feel the foam cushions against my ears. On her side of the room, Vanessa did the same.

My mother said she was sorry she couldn't be everything everyone needed, all of the time. She wasn't a robot, she said.

My father said he didn't need a robot, just a wife who wasn't fucking around.

My mother went back to her room.

~~~

There was a knock on the front door. My father was in his arm-chair in front of the television, which was playing horse races. I don't think he was watching the horse races, I think he was just staring at them. He had found another beer somewhere, and he was drinking it.

My mother was in her room.

I thought it would be the policeman. I took off my head-phones, which weren't playing music anyway, and walked to the front door, expecting it to be him with his solid, rubbery shoes. *I'll try to pop back later this afternoon*, he'd said. It was not late afternoon but early evening. He'd been delayed. I opened the door expecting to see his handsome-not-handsome face smiling down at me.

"Good evening," he said.

Not the policeman, and not smiling either.

"Good . . . Hello," I said.

Neither of us smiling.

"Am I early?"

I shook my head, meaning no, not welcome. Meaning go away. But he thought I meant no, he was not early, so he pushed past me, into our house. His body briefly making contact with mine.

The man from next door—our neighbour.

Vanessa's rescuer.

"Your mother did say Saturday."

He walked a few steps into the lounge and stopped. My father sat himself up with some effort, turning in his chair to see. "Ah, hello," he said, uncertain.

The neighbour looked to me for an introduction. I mumbled something about that time on the beach when Vanessa nearly drowned and we all thought it was the worst thing that could ever happen to us. My father leapt up from his chair and came forward with his hand held out. He took the neighbour's hand and then took his forearm too—he had both his hands on the neighbour and he was vigorously shaking his arm up and down, saying, "Good to meet you, neighbour, properly at last." The neighbour said his name was Robert Hooper, but we could call him Bob. He had a bottle of whisky which he gave to my father. I saw that the bottle had been opened and some of the whisky drunk already.

"I met your wife at the grocery store the other morning and she suggested I come around." Bob Hooper looked over at the empty kitchen, the bare bench, the two bedroom doors, closed. "Saturday, I'm pretty sure she said."

"Yes, yes, so she did." My father was pretending to remember. Coming back from the lagoon after showing my father what we'd found, we'd bumped into my mother with grocery bags, and before we could speak she'd told us about the neighbour and about Saturday night, but that had got swept away in everything that had happened since.

My father was in a tight spot because there was no dinner, no wife, only whisky and racing on the telly. *I leave you to it for one day and this is how you cope.* I hoped that he would say, *The dinner is off. My wife is (not) having a mental breakdown.* But instead he gestured to the couch and said, "Please, take a seat." Then he asked me to go fetch two glasses for the whisky.

I went to the kitchen to fetch the glasses. It took me a while because there were all types of glasses and I wasn't used to people drinking whisky. It was something I'd heard of in films but my father never drank it. Something told me I would be laughed at by Bob Hooper if I brought wine glasses for the whisky. I briefly considered coffee mugs, and then teacups, but I had a feeling that whatever you drank whisky from needed to be see-through. Finally I settled on the tumblers we used for fizzy drink. When I reached my father, I offered the tumblers apologetically, half-expecting to be laughed at, but he took them without a word, setting them down on the floor in front of his feet and unscrewing the cap on the bottle. "Ice?" he asked. Bob Hooper shook his head and said, "Neat." This confused me because a head shake could only mean no, but "neat" generally meant yes. My father drank some whisky while the neighbour talked boringly about the horse racing—he seemed to want to watch the races, not just stare at them as my father had been doing. He seemed quite happy sitting on the couch with the horses and his glass of whisky, even though there was nothing cooking in the kitchen, no wife washing lettuce or slicing bread. I saw my father look toward my mother's closed bedroom door several times, clutching his whisky, and chewing the inside of his cheek. After a while, it worked. My mother's door opened, and she came out for the second time that day. This time she was wearing a striped skirt with her light blue T-shirt. Behind her, the bed was tidy—no pages lying about with scribbles on them. "Good evening," she said. I stared at her with my mouth open. Bob Hooper lurched out of his chair and gave a little nod of the head, a bow of sorts. "Good evening," he replied, tipping his glass toward her. "I said to your husband, I hope I'm not too early."

"Not at all. I can't even remember what time I said. We keep it pretty casual out here."

I was still staring with my mouth open. "Darling," my mother said to me. "Go and tell your sister we have company. I'm sure our neighbour will want to see this troublesome girl he risked his life to save."

Bob Hooper laughed and said, "Hardly."

I went to the bedroom I shared with Vanessa. I said, "That old guy's here, the one who pulled you out of the water."

She rolled her eyes aggressively for several moments.

"Come on, please, I don't want to be out there on my own. They're drinking whisky."

"What the hell are we going to eat?" she said.

But my mother had got that sorted. She had gone to the car and dug out all the food items that my father had packed when he'd been operating at warp-speed. He'd packed a chunk of ham still shrink-wrapped in plastic, and some garlic bread in foil and a wheel of cheese coated in orange wax. My mother brought these things to the kitchen and put them on the bench. I saw her touch the ham and heard her mutter, "Perhaps it'll kill us." I waited until she moved away and then I touched it too—it was warm. "A very simple dinner, I hope you don't mind," she said to the room. Bob Hooper held his whisky glass in the air as a reply, because he was in the middle of some boring story about a fast horse. He hadn't even noticed Vanessa, who was standing behind him, looking for something to do with her hands. But my mother noticed.

"You look very lovely, Vanessa dear, but I hope you don't think you're going to any party."

Everybody heard that, even Bob Hooper. Even the horse racing seemed to still itself for a moment after what my mother said.

"I am. I'm going to the surf lifesaving party. You said I could."

"I don't remember ever saying that. It's our last night, and we have a very important guest."

The two men in their chairs had turned slightly, listening. I looked at Vanessa's face, which was hard and glaring, and I knew exactly what she had it in mind to do—she was going to let loose everything we'd heard. In front of our guest she was going to say "suicide" and "mental breakdown" and "fucking around." She was going to ask my mother and father who they thought they were, to tell her what to do, and how to behave, and I wasn't sure if I wanted her to do it, or wanted her not to. But then Bob Hooper said, "Oh, come now, you must let her go. It's the surf lifesaving party, it's the best thing around here for teenagers—in fact it's the only thing. She mustn't miss it on my account, she's all dressed up—look at her!"

I was surprised the neighbour wanted Vanessa to go when she was looking so beautiful in her white dress with the bow at the back of the neck, like she was a gift to be unwrapped. I'd thought all Bob Hooper had dreamed about, all summer, was unwrapping Vanessa, but now she was right in front of him and he was urging her to go.

I think my mother saw it too—what Vanessa had it in mind to say—because she quite quickly backed down. Vanessa could go to the party, after dinner. So long as she sat down in the meantime and behaved herself, making nice, polite conversation with Bob Hooper the neighbour. (My mother didn't say this last part out loud—it was in a look she gave, which Vanessa and I knew well.)

Dinner was, as my mother had predicted, simple. My mother sat at one end of the couch with her plate in her lap and a large glass of whisky balanced on the arm. Bob Hooper sat at the other end. I was invited to join them, in the middle of the couch, but I point-blank refused. The couch was a three-seater, but only ever sat two. The gap between my mother and Bob Hooper might have looked big enough from across the lounge, but I knew that as soon as I tried to get into it, I would feel it close in around me. This had happened to me at previous family gatherings where, being the youngest, I was invited to cram myself into all manner of tight spots, forced to rub shoulders and thighs with elderly uncles and aunties whose faces, up close, bristled with whiskers. I knew that if I was forced to rub thighs with Bob Hooper I would puke right into my warm ham. He was wearing shorts that had seemed a decent enough length standing up, but once he was sitting on the couch, his bottom nestled into the dip at the back, we were treated to at least three inches of goose-pimpled white skin between his plate and the overhang of his belly. I don't think my mother liked being that close to his exposed thigh skin either, because she really tried to make me sit between them, thumping the couch with her hand until my father held up his fork and said, "Why don't we let the girls eat at the table in the kitchen."

Over dinner, Bob Hooper said that he knew the beach like the back of his hand, and that he had watched "many a fool" battle waves they couldn't handle. He said he had lived in the house next door for a lot of years, and had seen families come and go. "Beautiful families," he said, "like yours." My father was working his way through the bottle of whisky, and had acquired a beer as well from somewhere, and my mother was cutting her ham with her knife and fork, her elbows sticking out either side of her like brackets. I think she was torn between believing the ham might kill her and feeling desperately hungry, as I was.

"Beautiful children, playing on the lawn," Bob Hooper was saying. "I do love to hear their playing."

"Who owns this house, do you know?" my father asked.

"This house?"

"Yes, this house. I've only dealt with a PO box address."

"No, I do not know."

From the way he said it, I believed that Bob Hooper did know, but didn't want to say.

"Well," my mother said, "we've had a lovely time."

"I like to open my sliding doors in the morning and listen to the children playing, all day long," He was wearing jandals on his feet and the whole time he talked, he clenched and unclenched his toes, which were cracked and scaly underneath. "Keeps me young. Children keep us young, don't you think?"

"Do you have children, Bob?"

He shook his head. He had a mouthful of ham and wasn't much interested in the question because he had already begun to think of what he would say next. I saw his eyes flick up for a moment, toward the kitchen. They were dull and unseeing, and I wondered if he was drunk. "I do hope my music hasn't bothered you."

My mother said, "I don't believe I've heard it once."

"Sometimes I play music, with the doors open. I trust it hasn't disturbed you."

"We haven't been bothered once, Bob."

I couldn't help thinking that Bob Hooper was trying to tease me about my cassette tape, which I believed he still possessed, and which I had heard playing loudly across the fence from time to time. Or maybe he wasn't—maybe I was living on planet imagination. Other people were allowed to own Split Enz tapes, after all. But once or twice he glanced toward me in the kitchen, as if to see what effect his words were having, and when that happened, I thought, Yes, he is teasing me. By this time I believe he'd had too much whisky, because his eyes were swimming, and he kept putting his knife down and touching the end of his nose with his folded-over napkin. At one point, to test my theory that he was drunk and not really seeing, I stuck my tongue out at him. I thought that if I got caught, I could say I had an ulcer. I was always getting ulcers, and sticking my tongue out to show adults, who would frown and say, "Ouch." I stuck my tongue out at Bob Hooper and he went right on stuffing ham into his mouth, clenching and unclenching his toes.

Later, we realized there was no dessert. My mother acted very surprised about it, when I think she must have known all through dinner that there was nothing else—the cupboards were empty, and we'd eaten all the biscuits, muesli bars and hard jubes from the glovebox of the car. Vanessa had left by this time—gone to meet Crystal at the surf lifesaving club. I think my mother hoped that when he realized there was no dessert, Bob Hooper would go too. But he patted his belly and said, "You're doing me a favour." Then he said, "If you like, I could fetch something from my place. I've got frozen cheesecake, a couple of packets of scorched almonds, some Russian fudge I bought along the highway. We could send the kid—I'm pretty sure I left the house unlocked." Cheesecake, scorched almonds and Russian fudge were three of my favourite things, but my mother shook her head, saying no, it wasn't necessary, we'd filled up on ham, and besides, we needed an early night, we were heading off early in the morning.

She couldn't have made herself any clearer, but still our guest stayed where he was, drinking with my father. My mother began to yawn, which in turn made me yawn. My father waved a hand in our direction. "Go," he said. "You two, go to bed, I'll wait up for Vanessa." His voice was low and growly, and his words were slowing down; getting stuck in places, like a Walkman about to run out of batteries. My mother and I brushed our teeth together in the bathroom, our faces side by side in the mirror, elbows bumping. As soon as I could, I put my toothbrush down and got out of there, so that she couldn't kiss me goodnight, or touch my hair, or do any of those things she usually did.

In bed, I planned to stay awake. I planned to outlast Bob Hooper and to see my sister arrive home. I listened to the clunk of the tumblers hitting the floor, and tried to count the refills, but the bottle of whisky seemed bottomless, and eventually I lost count.

TWENTY-EIGHT

I was woken by a chink of light falling across my bed. Vanessa, I assumed, coming home from the party. I waited for her to close the door and cross the room, but the chink of light stayed as it was, neither widening or narrowing. Nothing was said. All I could hear was a low, steady breathing, thinning from time to time to a kind of rattle.

I realized that it was not Vanessa at the door, and in the same instant became paralysed with fear, so that it took all my courage and strength just to roll a fraction, onto my back. There I saw, out the corner of my eye, a figure standing over me—not moving or speaking, just breathing.

For several seconds we remained that way, and then I heard the smallest creak of the door, and knew that the figure, which was Bob Hooper, was pushing the door open with his foot, and that this was why he'd urged Vanessa to go—so that he could murder me in my bed. Put his hands around my throat and strangle me until my nose bled and my eyes popped out of my head. I thought I might pass out from fear then, or leave my body again, like I had the night Vanessa was caught coming in the window. *Please, please, let me leave this useless body, which has frozen itself right when I need it to move.* But my mind stayed where it was, inside my body, and my body stayed where it was too— lying in the chink of light, unable to do a thing.

~~~~

"Wrong door, Bob."

My father's voice, from across the lounge.

"Further along, off the kitchen, there's a passage. See it?"

The chink of light across my bed, holding still.

"That's it, just to your right."

A grunt, and the light was gone.

~~~~

I dressed quickly, under the covers. While Bob Hooper was making his pretend trip to the bathroom—pretend-flushing the toilet, and pretend-washing his hands.

Pale green knickers with a dark green elastic waistband. Blue terry-cloth shorts with white piping up the sides. A sweater I'd outgrown the previous summer but refused to give up. Clothes I'd worn that day, which I'd left neatly folded in a pile at the bottom of my bed.

I drew my knees up to my chest, feeling my way, working quickly. I was good at getting dressed in tight spaces. At school camp, someone had spread a rumour that boys were watching us through cracks in the walls. After that, I'd dressed every morning in my sleeping bag.

I rolled out of bed. Everything felt itchy and wrong because I hadn't bothered to take my nightie off, I'd just stuffed it into the waistband of my shorts, and stretched my tiny sweater over the top.

Groping around for my muddy sandshoes—they'd slid under my bed. I had to lie face down on the floorboards, sweeping my arms in semicircles to find them, huffing dust and fluff, and all the while, trying to squash the panic, one eye on the crack of light under my bedroom door.

Bob Hooper was going to come back, and when he did, I didn't want to be standing in the middle of my room, half-dressed.

I wanted to be gone.

I climbed onto Vanessa's bed. The window there had never seemed particularly high, at least not from the inside. Not with a bed to stand on, and curtains to grab if I felt myself slipping. I turned the latch and pushed the window out, as far as it would go.

If Vanessa could do it . . .

But as soon as my head was out the window, I saw that it was a long way down the other side; down to where Kahu had stood in his KARATE KID T-shirt. Even in the dark, I could see that. I could see that if I managed to get both legs through, it would take every ounce of strength I possessed to stop myself dropping like a stone to the ground. The window ledge was sharp—it cut into my flesh. I wasn't even sure I *could* hook my legs over. Vanessa was taller, I realized, with longer legs. *My* only option was to launch myself out head first. For several moments I hung there, blinking into the dark. The window ledge cutting into my ribcage.

Was I up to this? Or not?

I thought of that chink of light, widening. My frozen body, unable to move.

I wriggled out, over the ledge, bracing myself for impact—for the crunching of bone. For a few moments anything seemed possible—a broken neck, teeth scattering like pegs from a basket—but my passage was slowed by my flailing legs, my big clumsy feet. A sandshoe caught. I saw a windowsill close to my face and grabbed at it with both hands, wrenching my thumbs, and forcing my body into a kind of slow-motion flip, which I still did not manage to land. In the very end I landed on my back, but it was a fall that I took in stages, and my nightie, bunched around me in folds, acted as a cushion. My injuries: a torn fingernail, a bloody scrape up my shin, and a vague, shifting pain in my hip.

I had done it, I was *gone*.

I craned my neck up. The window jutted out, it glinted in the moonlight. Kahu had held it open the other day, but he was taller than I was, and even if I could have reached up high enough to push it shut, it wouldn't take Bob Hooper long to figure things out. If I stayed where I was—a tight little ball in the grass—soon enough his face would appear at that open window. His arm, reaching out.

Bob Hooper's arms would be long. His legs too—long, like Vanessa's.

I got to my feet, shaking grass and sand from my hair. What choice did I have? Kahu's uncle's house was shut up and empty, and it was a long walk in the dark to the surf lifesaving club, where I might not be allowed in without a ticket, and might not be able to find my sister. Limping, I made my way toward the back of the property. The little rowboat was where it had always been, lying upside down next to the fence with the oars tucked under it. I thought it would make the perfect hiding place—no one had touched it or paid it any attention since the day my father and I had used it to explore the lagoon. But I knew it was too heavy for me to lift alone, and I knew also that underneath was a network of cobwebs. There weren't many things in life I hated as much as I hated Bob Hooper, but spiders were one. Besides, I was thinking of what Kahu had said, the night we'd played hide-and-seek—the night we ruined the game by hiding so well that no one could find us. *They never think to look in their own rooms, or under their own beds.* Bob Hooper was in my house, which meant he wasn't in his own. I looked up at his empty deck, where the white plastic chair glowed in the moonlight. From there, Hooper had watched us all summer long. He'd been there when we arrived, and when Crystal had found us, and when Lucy and I had turned cartwheels in the grass. It was his favourite place in all the universe, his sanctuary. He would never think to look for me there—would he? *It always works,* Kahu had said. *Every time.* Passing the boat, I made my way to the fence, where I ran my fingers along the boards, prodding them, until I felt one of the boards slip and swing. The gap in the fence. Behind me I heard laughter—I turned and saw the lounge windows blazing with light. My father and Bob, working their way to the bottom of the whisky bottle. I lowered my head and ducked through to where it was dark. To Bob's side of the fence.

~~~

As soon as I was through the fence I ran. Across the grass, toward the ranch slider by which I'd entered his house the first time. The house was unlocked—Hooper had said as much, after dinner, when he'd talked about sending me over for dessert. *I've got frozen cheesecake, a couple of packets of scorched almonds, some Russian fudge I bought along the highway.* I ran, almost tripping on a loose paver, and on a length of pink rope, coiled in the grass like a snake. Reaching the door, I didn't hesitate—I grabbed the handle and yanked it, praying that it would open, praying that soon I would be out of that dark, empty night.

And then I was inside. In my neighbour's musty spare room, where there was a bed, an armchair and some type of exercise equipment—a bike, or maybe a treadmill—hulking and silent in the corner.

Up the stairs. Clutter there too—it was worse than when I last visited. Now there were clothes piled up, and big black rubbish bags, bulging. The rubbish bags scared me because they looked like crouching bears, or worse—giant slugs, crawled up from under the earth. I froze for a moment, staring hard at those black shapes, until I saw shiny folds in the plastic. *Not* slugs— I raced past—one of the bags tipped, its contents tumbling down the stairs as I fled, up, toward the landing, toward the lounge with its deck that overlooked our lawn. A clock on the wall at the top of the stairs told me it was ten thirty-five.

(Stopping dead then because there was light coming from the lounge—I hadn't expected that. Had I missed my neighbour's arrival? Had he come home while I was dashing across his back yard? But there was no one there—it took me several seconds to confirm, standing frozen at the lounge entrance, sweeping the room with my eyes. No one there. Just a couple of lamps left on.)

It appeared that Hooper had been in the middle of some activity, or project, when he'd left to come over to our house. In his lounge, the table was in disarray—covered in papers, with a chair pulled out, a mug, half full of something black like Coca-Cola or coffee, and the plastic tray from a packet of biscuits, completely empty and lying on its side. There was a whisky bottle, this one three-quarters full, and a tumbler with light brown fluid at the bottom. Above me, the shark's jaws yawned and the lanterns glowed dimly, but everything seemed smaller than the last time I'd been there—more distant somehow. I was there but I was not really there, I was floating. Somewhere in a high corner I was watching myself. I stopped. Closing my eyes, I said aloud to myself, "It works every time." My voice sounded strange in the empty room but it did the trick—I felt stronger, calm. Kahu was beside me; I wasn't floating any more. All I needed to do was watch the holiday house from the deck. When my father and Hooper reached the bottom of that whisky bottle, I would see Hooper leaving, and would know it was safe to return.

I moved forward, into the lounge. The doors to the deck were across the room, to my right. But I didn't go right. I went left, because there was something else—something I hoped I could do, inside Hooper's house.

In the clutter of his built-in bookcase, I could see Hooper's stereo system. It was the expensive kind: stacked, with lots of knobs, buttons, equalizers and sliders, set between a pair of dusty round speakers. My older boy-cousins owned systems like this one, and were forever playing with the sliders, trying to convince me that there was some difference in the sound, which I could never hear. On Hooper's system there were two tape decks, stacked one on top of the other. This was it, the "something else" I wanted. For weeks, Hooper had been teasing me, playing Split Enz across the fence. What if my cassette tape was in there? The one I'd spent a term's worth of pocket money on—the one I knew by heart? What if I could find it, and steal it back?

I ran to the stereo. Kneeling, I opened the top deck first—it contained a cassette with a white plastic shell and yellow label. I knew instantly it wasn't mine. *True Colours* had a black shell with a white label. I closed that deck and opened the one beneath it.

It was empty. I searched the floor around the machine—put my face down to the floor and peered into the dust underneath. Scoured the shelves either side—there were some cassette tapes lying there, but none were black and white, none of them mine. I saw *Born in the USA* by Bruce Springsteen, and *Hotel California* by the Eagles. I saw classical tapes with obscure names in languages I didn't recognize, but no *True Colours*, no Split Enz. Disappointed, I moved away from the stereo, back across the lounge, past the stained couch and a low coffee table, which held an array of remote controls and several well-thumbed magazines. I was heading in the general direction of the deck, but I was still searching for my cassette tape, scanning every surface for its familiar black-and-white shell. Passing the sideboard, I saw that its doors were open. The photo packets that had filled it last time had been cleared out. I swept my eyes over the dining table, at the papers scattered there, and saw that this is what had become of the photo packets—Hooper must have taken them out of his sideboard in armfuls, tipping their contents into one big pile, so that he could sift through individual photos. Maybe my cassette tape was there too—buried under all that mess. I walked quickly over, and began to push my hands through the heap of glossy paper. I was fishing for anything that felt like the hard plastic shell of a cassette tape, and I was barely looking at the photographs, which were the same boring shots of beaches, the same badly focused patches of grass, that I remembered from last time. Most had words scrawled across their backs. TE HORO, one said, JANUARY '81. WAIKAWA, another said, and another: ŌTAKI RIVER. I was growing impatient, wondering if it was time to abandon my search. Perhaps I needed to accept that I would never find my cassette tape. I pulled my hands out of the pile and turned toward the glass door, but my eye was caught by something that was written on the back of a photograph lying face down on the pile. EMILY, '79. I picked the photograph up, flipped it over, and saw a young girl, perhaps my age, perhaps younger. I turned the photograph over again and studied the words: EMILY, '79.

Hooper had told my mother he had no children—who was Emily?

I threw the photo back on the pile. In the distance I heard cracks like gunfire, and realized it must be nearly eleven, because according to Crystal, the surf lifesaving party finished at eleven, and always closed with fireworks, to mark the end of the season.

I was running out of time.

Stepping back from the table, I noticed that the mess continued on the floor—some of the photos had slipped off the table and were lying on the carpet. Some were face down. I saw EMILY again, and FOXTON BEACH. I stopped a little lower, thinking perhaps my cassette tape had slid off the table too—maybe I still had a chance to find it.

Just one last look, I told myself, and then I'd run out, onto the deck.

That's when I saw, scrawled on the back of a photo that had landed face down on the floor beneath the dining table, my name.

ALIX.

My name wasn't all that unusual, but it wasn't common either. There was only one other girl at my school with the same name as me, and she used a different spelling. Reaching out, I turned the photo over.

I had never seen myself from that angle before—from above. That's not me, I told myself. That's not what the top of my head looks like. But even as I thought it, I knew it was wishful thinking, because there were my red togs, worn through in places, and loose across the hips. There were my skinny legs and narrow feet. My hair, mouse-brown, turning out at the ends. I was standing toward the back of our section, looking down at the ground. My feet were apart, my hands clasped loosely under my chin. Talking to myself, or maybe those were headphones glinting in my hair. Maybe I was singing. In the top left-hand corner of the photo, I saw a triangle of blue. It took me a moment to work out that it was a corner of Vanessa's towel, laid out on the grass for sunbathing. But Vanessa wasn't in the shot. Vanessa wasn't the point of this photograph—I was. Quickly, frantically, I began sorting through the photos—the ones on the floor first, and then the ones on the table, all over again. This time I was looking for my red togs. What I hated most was how small he'd made me look, how babyish. Or perhaps it was the fact that he'd learned my name—I'd never given it to him, or invited him to use it. I puzzled this out for a moment, bent over Hooper's table. Then it came to me—I had etched my name into the back of my Walkman. I had made it extra neat and tidy so that it would be easy to read, should anyone find it.

Five more photos, I found. It was hard, though, because there were flashes of red everywhere, and in some of the pictures I was wearing other clothes, or had my hair pulled back, so that I didn't immediately recognize myself, and had to look hard to know for sure that it was me. My vision was beginning to blur, and my hands were shaking. In the end I resorted to looking at the backs of the photos, grabbing anything with my name on it, flipping photos over, knocking them to the floor, creasing them. I didn't care, I was rushing—I'd been there too long. Vanessa might be home by now. What would happen when she saw my bed empty? Would the police be called? Would I be in trouble? Shoving photos aside, I picked up four more, and then uncovered a bunch that must have come from the same packet—all of them were of me. With both hands I swept them toward me, right to the edge of the table. I had forgotten all about my cassette tape. I only wanted to get my image off his table, off his floor. Some of the photographs fell, and I stooped to grab them, but hair got in my face, and when I tried to hook it behind my ear, photos slipped through my fingers. I was so focused, so determined to get every last one—so that he had none, and could not look at me ever again, or write my name—that I almost missed the sound of the front door opening. Almost missed it, but then the door slammed shut, and I did not miss that. Nor did I miss what it meant—I was going to be caught. I grabbed an empty packet off the floor and stuffed the photographs of me into it, then I turned and looked wildly around. There were footsteps on the stairs now. The man who had wanted to murder me in my bed would now have the pleasure of doing so in his own home—right here, under the table, under the beaches and the riverbanks.

I thought about the deck. Perhaps I could hide in a corner out there until morning. But no, it was too risky, Hooper might go out there himself, even at this late hour, and besides, the sliding door might not open quickly enough for me in my panic. I considered the couch; the shelving unit. Could I hide in the curtains like I had when I was little? Could I tuck myself into the folds and hold myself still all night, until the police came knocking? That nice policeman with the big rubbery shoes— would he be the one sent to find me? A voice on the stairs was rising—it was coming up to meet me, singing loudly and tunelessly, words slurring together. My only choice, the only place I felt I could fit, was right in front of me—Bob Hooper's empty sideboard.

TWENTY-NINE

It had never occurred to me that adults talked to themselves too. I'd thought it was only something children did—children whose families never listened to them. But Bob Hooper talked to himself from the moment he reached the top of the stairs.

"Ho!" he said, as he stepped into the lounge.

(His "Ho!" was so loud, and so spontaneous, that at first I thought I'd been spotted. It'd been hard work squeezing my backside into the sideboard, and in fact, I hadn't quite managed it. I found I couldn't properly shut the door—instead it was pulled to, my arm twisted painfully behind me.)

"Ho, ho, ho!" he said, sounding nothing at all like Father Christmas. He walked over to the dining table, where I had only just been. I was holding my breath in the sideboard, waiting for the explosion of anger that would come when he saw the mess I'd made of his photos. But he seemed not to notice the larger number of photos on the floor, the photos of me that were now missing, or the photos that I had creased in my search.

"There they are," he said, sifting through the photos that remained. "There, there." I closed my eyes, tightening every muscle, and pulling myself inward, so that the door might close. "There you are, my little ones," he said. He was very close to the sideboard, moving around the table, and he was talking to his photos. "There, lovely." I heard small smacking sounds which I realized were kisses. He was kissing the air, or the photos. I heard a shuffle; he was moving further along the table, away from the sideboard. "Perfect, yes." And then a growl, a clearing of the throat. "Bit worse for wear. Smooth you out—there, better. Lovely."

It was harder for me when the talking went away. When he was silent, I had no idea where he was. Was he crouched down at the sideboard, his ear pressed against it, his hand ready to pull the door out of my grasp? For a while there was nothing, and I was too scared even to breathe. Then I heard him moving about in the kitchen. The fridge door opening and closing, and the clatter of a drawer. Eventually I heard a sound like ice, tinkling into glass, and then he began to sing, rolling through Elton John songs I knew from the car radio. "Blue Eyes" and "Nikita" and "I Guess That's Why They Call It the Blues." He seemed to know only one line from each song, and he would sing it, and then his voice would drop into a kind of puddle, where the words and the notes blurred together, and then out of the puddle, a new line from another song would emerge. He would sing each line heartily once, and then let it fall away again. I thought, This is how frustrating life would be if you never took the time to learn the lyrics to your favourite songs. For a while he wandered around the lounge, singing intermittently, and then he returned to my side of the room with a *thunk*—his glass going down on the table. "Right!" he said. "Right, let me see, what do we have." I heard him dragging the chair over, and settling into it with a protracted sigh. "Bloody hell," he muttered. "Bloody hip." My own hip was hurting, and my arm, twisted behind me, had lost all feeling. I was also painfully aware of a metal ring pressing into my thigh—it was the handle of the hatch in the base of the sideboard, the one I'd seen Hooper pull and lift, the day he'd given me back my Walkman.

I thought that I could only last a few more minutes like this. At the dining table Hooper burped loudly, and then fell silent again. After a while I heard a sound like snoring, and I dared to let go of the door behind me, and move my poor, stiff arm around to my front. The door opened a fraction, letting in light, but the snoring continued. I lay there, wondering if this was my best chance. Bob Hooper, face down in his photo collection.

Then, just as quickly as he'd fallen asleep, he woke with a snort. I was glad I hadn't tried to roll out of the cupboard, or crawl past his feet. "My little ones," he said again. "My darlings." I felt hopeless then, as if this moment would never end. Would Hooper sit there all night, drooling over his photo collection? And when he was done enjoying it, would he scoop all the photos up and return them to the sideboard? My heart started beating very fast then, thinking about what he would do to me when he found my hiding place. I covered my ears, but I couldn't block out the banging I could hear, which was my own heartbeat. At last, an even louder sound snapped me out of my panic.

Hooper, pushing his chair back from the table so hard, I was surprised it didn't fall over. I told my heart to remain quiet and still, so I could listen. Hooper was rattling the lock on his sliding glass door. "Come on, you little fucker," he muttered. For an awful moment I thought he meant me. But then there was a great release of air, and a sound like a giant zip opening, and I knew he'd managed to open the door, because I heard him stepping out onto the deck.

~~~~~

At school, the teacher sometimes had us play a memory game. I'm not sure what it was supposed to teach us, but it went like this: our desk neighbours had two minutes to run around the classroom, grabbing a bunch of random items—a stapler, a piece of chalk, a pink paperclip, an apple—while we sat on the mat with our eyes closed. After two minutes the teacher would ring a bell, and those of us on the mat would jump up, run to our neighbours' desk, and stare at the items for ten seconds, committing them to memory, while our neighbours counted, shouting as loud as they could, "Ten, nine, eight, seven . . ." and so on. The teacher would then ring the bell a second time, and as fast as we were able, we had to scribble down as many items as we could remember, in as much detail as possible. The bell-ringing and shouting were an important part of the game, because they were designed to confuse us, to distract us from the job of remembering.

I thought of that game as I tumbled out of Hooper's sideboard, pain shooting through my hip, the photographs I'd stolen, which had been stolen of me, still clutched to my chest. On the deck, Hooper was laughing, leaning out over the glass balustrade, raising his glass high in the air. "Ho!" he was yelling. "Ho, neighbour! What're you doing over there?" But I needed to ignore that, and not to wonder about it, or let it distract me, because as I'd tumbled out of the sideboard I'd caught with my foot the metal ring beneath my thigh. The hatch had dislodged, and now I could see, in the hollow base of the sideboard, the contents of Hooper's wooden box.

A collection of hairclips suitable for a small girl—a white pair of girls' knickers, very small—a purple sun hat, torn and faded— a notebook—a Barbie doll in a gold dress—a handkerchief—a black-and-white cassette tape.

Other things I couldn't identify, or didn't try to. But these things were important, I knew. In all the mess and clutter of his life, Hooper had carefully grouped these things together in a little box he hid in the base of his sideboard. For the life of me, I couldn't figure out why he'd do that. Behind me, Hooper was doing his best to distract me with his shouting and off-kilter laughter. I took a deep breath, and told myself to focus. Firstly, the cassette tape was mine—it was *True Colours.* I grabbed it, stuffing it under my arm with the packet of stolen photos. Secondly, the notebook belonged to my mother. It was the one she'd dropped in the surf the day my sister almost drowned. I didn't have enough hands for that, and my mother had finished her book, so my brain made the split-second decision to leave it behind—as I was clambering to my knees—as outside, Hooper sang, "We come on the Sloop John B." Everything else in that pile I would have to leave. All the strange and precious things hidden there by Hooper. All that stood between me and my neighbour was an open glass door and a net curtain, wafting in the breeze. I needed to be faster than I had ever been in my life. "I feel so broke up," Hooper sang, as at last I scrambled to my feet and lunged for the lounge door.

~~~

I ran down the stairs, kicking rubbish with the toes of my feet, slipping here and there, but not caring, and not afraid, because I was fast and light, and I had got what I wanted—my cassette tape. I ran out the door under the deck, across Hooper's back yard. Everything was quicker and easier going back; I was fast and light, and Hooper was not. He was old and slow and still on his deck, oblivious to what was going on beneath him. Before I knew it, I was at the fence. It took a moment to find the loose board—briefly I thought, Is this it? Will this be my downfall?—but then I was through, to our side of the fence, with Hooper behind me, and the little rowboat lying peacefully at my feet.

I followed the fence right around the house in a counter-clockwise direction, past my still-open bedroom window, along the side of the house that faced the street, to the front door. My father was standing over the little charcoal burner with his back to me; he had lit a fire, and he was blowing on it, fanning it with his hand. I let myself in. My mother's bedroom door was closed, and the room I shared with Vanessa was empty.

It was eleven twenty-five.

I had expected something on my arrival—to be shouted at, or held close, or questioned, or all three. I had expected to have been missed by someone, but my bedroom door, like my mother's, had remained closed, and as far as my father was con-

cerned, I'd been asleep there all evening. I dumped my loot on
my bed and sat down next to it. Picking up my cassette tape, I
checked it over for harm, but it looked exactly as it had when I'd
last seen it. I pulled my Walkman out from under my pillow and
slipped the cassette into the deck. Next, I turned to the packet
of photos. I'd left the front door open, and a light breeze was
sweeping in across the lounge, rustling the curtain at our window, and cooling the scrape on my shin. Outside, I could hear
my father muttering encouragement to his fire, and distantly,
I thought I could hear Hooper, too, laughing and singing, and
firing lunatic questions off his deck. My father had unpacked
the little three-legged barbeque from the car, and had set it up
on the grass away from the house, even though there were no
sausages in the fridge, and nothing else at hand to cook or eat. I
pulled a photo out of the packet and turned it over. The sight of
my name, written there in his hand, made my stomach turn. I
stuffed it back inside with the others, noticing, as I did so, some
words scrawled on the front of the packet:

HOOPER, ph. 289-6002, pick-up Tuesday,
colour, 6x4 gloss, paid.

I placed the packet face down on my bedspread. I was
relieved to have my cassette tape back, and to have taken from
Hooper the photographs he'd taken of me, but I was feeling
regretful about the things I'd left behind—the items Hooper
kept hidden in his sideboard. I knew they were important—but
how? And why?

Why did an old man with no children need hairclips and a Barbie doll?

And where had I heard something before about a Barbie doll?

I stood up, and, limping slightly, walked back across the lounge to the open front door, out onto the patio. Across the fence our neighbour had fallen silent—gone to bed perhaps, or perhaps he was back at his dining-room table, snoring over his collection. My father was crouched down at his barbecue with his back to me, puffing into it, and stoking it with a stick. Next to him on the ground was a stack of papers. I was surprised, because when barbecuing, my father always tried to keep the flames down, but these flames were already quite high, and still he was stoking them, feeding them air.

"Where's Mum?"

If he was surprised to see me standing there with my nightie tucked into my shorts and grazes all over my legs, he didn't show it. His eyes were dark and unfocused. "Where do you think?" he said. "In bed, sleeping, as you should be."

I stepped forward, so that the flames warmed my face. "What about Vanessa? She's late."

"Is she?" he said. "Is she?"

"She's half an hour late."

My father looked at his wrist, where there was no watch. "We'll give her ten more minutes, shall we? Then if she's not back I'll go looking."

I took a step closer. "What are you burning?"

"Everything. The summer."

I nodded. My father stooped down and took a piece of paper from the stack at his feet. Crumpling it in his fist, he tucked it into the flames. I was amazed at how calmly he could touch the fire with his fingertips.

An idea came to me. "Can I burn some stuff too?"

"I guess so," he said, shrugging. "It's only fair."

I ran inside, scooping the packet of photos up from my bed. If I burned the photographs Hooper had taken of me, it would be as if the prints had never existed. He would no longer be connected to me in any way—there would be nothing left between us. By the time I got back to the barbecue my father's fire was high, and I could see he was happy with it. "What you got there?" he asked, but I saw that he didn't really care—his focus was on the flames, which he meant to keep alive until the stack of papers was gone.

"Just rubbish and stuff," I said.

I opened the packet and threw a photo on the fire—at first the flames seemed to move around it, making a little space for it, and I feared it wouldn't burn. But then a greasy bubble opened up on its surface. There was a hiss, and it was swallowed by the flames. *Take that*, I said to Hooper in my head. I fed another photo onto the fire—me, crossing the grass in a T-shirt and shorts. Small, unaware. My father and I took it in turns, saying nothing, just feeding the fire with what remained of our summer. It was wonderful, hypnotic. Image after image I fed to the flames—me with my back turned, me squatted down in the grass. It turned out I had accidentally stolen a photo of a beach hut, and I felt a little bad about burning it, but did it anyway. My father seemed to have an endless supply of paper at his feet. At one point he turned away from the fire to wipe smoke from his eyes, and I thought he was upset.

But he wasn't upset. He was determined.

"The trick is not to crumple the paper too tight," he said. "Gotta let the air circulate."

I nodded. Mostly I wasn't crumpling the photos at all— I was feeding them, flat, onto the fire, because I liked to see them burn. *Take that, and that, and that, Bob Hooper!* I liked watching the edges of the photos curl, and the blackness creep across the lawn toward the feet of the small, babyish girl who didn't know she was being photographed.

But then I threw a photo on the fire and saw that the girl disappearing into flame was not me. It was another girl, pudgier than me, blonde, and wearing a purple sun hat. I looked at the next photo in my hand and, finding the same pudgy, blonde girl, turned it over to see what was written on the back.

I felt cold then, despite my father's fire.

Cold and very still, playing the memory game again, going back over the items that had tumbled out of Hooper's sideboard.

A collection of hairclips suitable for a small girl—a white pair of girls' knickers, very small—a purple sun hat, torn and faded— a notebook—a Barbie doll in a gold dress—a handkerchief—a black-and-white cassette tape.

The name written on the back of the photo was the same as the one written on the wall beside my bed. It was the name Kahu had used the day we'd met, when he'd taken me to see the wooden cross for the very first time.

Her name was Charlotte. She was nine.

And now I remembered where I'd heard something about

a Barbie doll. My mother, sitting on the patio, drinking cask wine, her foot going back and forth through the air.

Apparently she'd lost a doll on the beach. A Disco Barbie, is what I heard.

I squatted down, laying the photos out on the grass. Of the five I had left, two were mine. The rest were hers; they were Charlotte's. I had no right burning them, no more than he had taking them. Above me, my father coughed. "Run out of fuel? Want some of mine?" I gathered the photos and stood up. My father was holding a piece of paper toward me. I shook my head. He fed it to the fire. "Trick is not to crumple it too tight," he slurred. I nodded—he'd said that already. The piece of paper he'd held toward me was lined with neat rows of type. It was a page from my mother's completed book, but I knew that already—I'd figured it out.

"I have to go," I said, dropping the last photos of me onto the fire.

I ran toward the street. I didn't wait to hear my father's response, or to watch my photos burn.

I knew what I had to do.

THIRTY

At the top of Palmer Street someone called my name. Not someone—Josh. He was a block or so away, walking toward me. I hesitated—I didn't want to stop, not even for Josh. But he called my name a second time, and began to jog toward me.

"I can't find her," he said.

"Who?"

He looked me up and down, taking in the clothing bunched around my waist, my grazed shin.

"Jesus, did you get in a fight or something?"

"No, not really. Kind of."

"Are you okay?"

I nodded. We were standing under the glow of a street lamp, and I could see clearly that Josh had taken a shower, washed and brushed his hair, put on every single friendship bracelet he owned, scrubbed the sunblock off his face, and pulled on a pair of ripped jeans and a long-sleeved top, which he wore with white sandshoes and no socks.

I wondered if Vanessa had seen him looking like that, and if it had really ruined her evening with Stuart.

"I don't know where Crystal is," I said.

He shook his head. "I'm not looking for Crystal."

"Okay."

"I'm looking for Vanessa."

"Oh, well, I don't know where she is either."

"She didn't come home?"

"Nope."

"Stuart was walking her home."

I made a face like, *Well, there's your answer then.*

"What does that mean?"

"Nothing."

"Hey, kiddo," he said, touching my elbow. "Come on, you know something. Spill."

I sighed. "You're supposed to be with Crystal, and she's supposed to be with Stuart."

"She likes Stuart?"

"No, not really. But there's this whole, um, agreement. Between Crystal and Vanessa."

"An agreement?"

"Yeah, like a pact." I was squirming, clutching the packet of photos in my hand, and shifting my feet around on the spot.

Josh took a step toward me. "Tell me about the agreement."

I shook my head—no way.

He moved even closer, cupping his hands over my shoulders, causing my head to spin. "Please," he said, "tell me."

I looked down at his sandshoes and mumbled, in my smallest voice, out the corner of my mouth, "Crystal said she'd do it with you, if Vanessa did it with Stuart."

I'd expected him to say, *Do what?* I'd expected to have to explain it—what *it* was, the way I'd had to explain it to myself, with the magazine that Vanessa hid under her pillow. But Josh dropped his hands and took a step back, puffing air out of his lungs, and hanging his head. I knew that he knew what *it* was.

After a few moments he said, "Did she actually want to, do you think? With Stuart?"

I said nothing, just shook my head. He ran his hands through his hair. "I broke up with Crystal," he said. "Just now."

I stared at him.

"I was never . . . I never said I'd do that with her. I've been trying to break up with her all summer. I kept telling her, she's too young. She just wouldn't, you know, she wouldn't . . ."

I nodded—of course she wouldn't. Who would? Who would let Josh go?

"I wanted to see Vanessa. To tell her."

"Why?"

"Because." He had his hands on his hips, and he was looking toward the ridge of pines, not because there was anything going on over there, but because he didn't want to have to look me in the eye. "I like her, I guess."

I nodded.

"Where do you think they went?"

I shrugged. "Out there somewhere, on the beach."

"Okay, shit, what a mess." He ran his hands through his hair again. "Well, shit. I'm gonna try to stop her. I'm gonna go back to the surf club and look for her. If you see her . . ."

"I'll tell her," I said.

"Thanks." He turned and started jogging back.

"Josh," I said.

He stopped, turning back to face me.

"She likes you too," I said.

He nodded. "I know."

~~~

The wooden cross was hard to find in the dark, away from the road, where there were no street lamps, and pines overhead. I went back and forth along the narrow path, looking for a gap in the dunes. Beer cans lay discarded among the pine needles—cigarette butts and crumpled party tickets. From the beach I heard young men shouting, mocking each other, and girls screaming and giggling, and everywhere, from every direction, the pop and fizz of cheap fireworks—Double Happys and sparklers, left over from New Year's Eve, and sold for a couple of dollars at the local store. In the end I had to close my eyes and count my steps from the path entrance to where I thought I would find Charlotte's cross—about fifteen steps in, and a couple of metres off to the right.

The first thing I noticed was that the flowers at the base of the cross were dry and wilted. I was pleased, because this meant that very soon, within the next day or two, Charlotte's mother would be back to replace them. The next thing I noticed was that there was something new adorning the cross, something I'd never seen there before. As I moved in for a closer look, a couple of girls came along the path, giggling and chatting. Either of them could have been my sister, with their long hair, and their short, floaty skirts. I ducked back, into the dunes, but they saw me, falling silent for a few moments, and then bursting into laughter when they'd passed. I guess I must have looked like a pretty weird kid, hanging around in the dunes late at night with my nightie tucked into my shorts and my tiny sweater stretched across my chest. I waited until the path was empty, and then I stepped forward, dropping to my knees in the sand in front of the cross.

It was Kahu's pendant hanging there—his pounamu. In all the time I'd known him, I'd never seen him take it off, or go anywhere without it. *I'd be in so much trouble if I lost it*, he'd said to me once. I reached out to touch it, turning it over in my hand. The greenstone felt warm between my fingers. I was kneeling there, wondering if Kahu had left his pounamu there for me, or for Charlotte, when I heard a female voice, very close to my ear.

I jumped, dropping the pounamu. The voice spoke again, further away this time. I couldn't make out the words. I checked all around me, in the grasses surrounding the cross, and between the pine trees. There was no one in the little clearing but me. Still, the voice kept coming back to me, tickling my ear, and laughter too—not full-throated laughter like I'd heard on the beach, but a shy, tinkling laughter, uncertain about itself, and accompanying it, a sad sound like a sigh, which made the hairs stand up on my arms. It was the wind, I told myself—the wind was blowing the voice toward me, and then, in a change of direction, pulling it away again. I stumbled out of the little clearing, onto the path that snaked through the trees, disorientated by the voice that was one minute in my ear, and the next far away.

I could have sworn that it belonged to my sister.

"Vanessa!" I said, loudly. "Vanessa!"

The voice stopped—not gradually, as if carried away by the wind, but abruptly.

"Vanessa?" I hurried along the path toward the beach. "It's me, where are you?"

I had reached the beige sand at the top of the beach. In front of me a small group of teenagers stood around, drinking from cans. In unison they turned to look at me, and, seeing that I was small and unimportant, turned away again. Every now and then one of them—a girl—would break away from the group, dashing into the surf, and another one—a boy—would drop his can in the sand and run after her, grabbing her around the waist and hoisting her in the air, twirling her around as she screamed and shouted. I turned to the north, where the floating voice had come from, and began to pick my way through the sand, which was damp underfoot and heavy. "Vanessa!" I called. "I have a message! Where are you?" It was hard work, trudging through that thick sand. The voice that had sounded like Vanessa's had fallen silent, but other sounds came to me on the wind—fireworks landing right on my shoulder, small, tinny snatches of music, and something that sounded like vomiting. I pushed on, passing a dark mass in the sand that could have been a bathing seal, or a giant, twisting piece of driftwood. I peered into the mass as I skirted it, only realizing when I had almost passed it that it was a couple, wrapped in each other's arms, denim jackets draped over their heads for privacy. It was the girl's pale, naked legs that made it human. They were not Vanessa's legs, so I moved on.

Finally, in a dip in the sand, between two large clumps of grass, I found my sister. She was easy to spot in her bright white dress. Sitting up, looking toward me. I guessed that she had heard me calling her, and had been waiting for me to show up. Stuart was sitting next to her, wrapped around her with his back to me—so close that he was almost on top of her. My sister's legs were stretched out in front of her, pressed together and stiff, her white dress pushed into her lap. An empty beer bottle lay close to her feet. Stuart had one hand in the sand behind her, supporting his weight, and the other was inside her skirt.

She said nothing when she saw me. Her eyes were wide and watchful. I wondered if she thought I was an apparition, carried on the wind.

"Vanessa," I said. I couldn't be cool—couldn't get the urgency out of my voice. The information I had was burning a hole in my chest. "Vanessa, I saw Josh."

Slowly, sleepily, Stuart turned to look at me. "What are you?" he said. "The search party?" He turned back, laughing into Vanessa's hair. I saw that the hand he had pushed up her skirt was squeezing her flesh, kneading it like dough. I hated how big and tanned his hand looked on her thigh—how close it was to the edge of her knickers. "Piss off, kid," he drawled.

"Vanessa," I said, ignoring him, "Josh broke up with Crystal."

My sister's eyes seemed to flicker. She blinked. I waited for her to push that big ugly hand away, but she didn't.

"Did you hear me?" I said. "Josh is looking for you."

I had seen my sister angry before. I had been shouted at by her, and ridiculed, and told to go away, to shrivel up and die, get lost, eat shit. I was ten years old, and used to the feeling of not being wanted. That was not the feeling I got, standing there in the sand, not ten feet from where a boy was pushing his hand up under her skirt. I looked into Vanessa's eyes and I wasn't sure what I saw, but I felt that she was listening.

"You don't have to do this," I said, more quietly this time. "Josh is looking for you."

"Jesus *Christ!*" Stuart said, whipping his hand out of my sister's skirt and lunging toward me, forcing me two steps back in the sand. "Seriously, kid, get the fuck out of here. Get off the beach—go away, go home! Your sister's with me now, I'm looking after her. Go away, she can talk to Josh in the morning."

"We're leaving in the morning."

With one giant stride Stuart pushed his face into mine. "All the more reason for you to go away and let us finish what we fucking started," he growled. He put one hand on my chest and pushed—a short, sharp shove that sent me stumbling back, into the sand, where I landed with a thud. Standing over me, he waited for me to scramble back up, his arms hanging at his sides, fists clenched. Still, I took my time getting to my feet, in the hope that Vanessa would use this opportunity to get away— that she would jump up and run home through the dunes, or calmly walk around him to join me. *You know what, Stuart? I think I've changed my mind.* But Vanessa stayed where she was, and when finally I was back on my feet, I saw her give me the smallest tilt of the head—a nod, or a shake, I couldn't tell which.

I knew then that it was over. I had done all I could—the rest was up to her.

I turned and ran, back the way I'd come.

Back to the wooden cross.

~~~

I took Kahu's pounamu for myself. I lifted it off the cross and slipped it over my own head. In exchange, I left behind the blue packet with the three photos of Charlotte inside. I was careful to tuck the packet deep into the loop of wire, where it would be held snug, and protected from the wind and rain, until Charlotte's mother came back with fresh flowers. Each photo showed a small blonde girl in a purple sun hat, and each was inscribed with the word CHARLOTTE on the back. On the outside of the packet, scrawled in black, were the words:

HOOPER, ph. 289-6002, pick-up Tuesday,
colour, 6x4 gloss, paid.

I figured it was a fair trade.

THIRTY-ONE

In the car on the way back to Wellington the next morning, I left my Walkman sitting on the seat between Vanessa and me. We sailed past two antique shops—both times my father glanced at my mother and both times my mother, who was wearing sunglasses, stared straight ahead. I decided that if we passed a third antique shop I would say, "Mum, antiques," because I knew she'd be sad if we got all the way home without adding to any of her collections.

Then my father pulled up at a store selling ice-blocks and summer fruits in brown paper bags. "Refreshments," he said, killing the engine. Vanessa shrugged when he asked her what flavour ice-block she wanted, but when I said, "Lemonade please," she said, "Yeah, me too."

My mother said she wouldn't say no to a bag of plums.

While my father was paying, I decided to stretch my legs. It was a relief to be out of the car that had been racing in a straight, silent line all the way from the holiday house. Vanessa joined me, but at first we didn't talk, we just pushed our feet through the fine gravel at the side of the road. Dust turned the tips of our toes grey.

When we were about halfway through our ice-blocks, Vanessa pointed at my neck and said, "What's that?" I shook my head. She reached out anyway, pulling the pounamu from where I'd been hiding it under my shirt. I held my breath, but my sister didn't tease me, or tell me off for having something that wasn't mine. She held the pounamu for the longest time, and then she tucked it carefully back inside my shirt, where it fell against my chest with a pleasing weight.

Back in the car, my mother passed around the bag of plums. I didn't want one, but I took one because I wanted to say yes and not no. Vanessa said no, but she added a thank you. My mother said in a very quiet voice that they were the best plums she'd ever tasted. "Half what you'd pay in Wellington," my father replied. I was relieved that he'd heard what she said, because she'd said it so quietly. We waited a long time for a break in traffic, and then we pulled out, onto the highway that would eventually take us home.

Acknowledgements

I thank my lucky stars for Felicity Blunt, without whom this book might never have seen the light of day. Thank you, Felicity, for picking up the phone and calling me on the other side of the world; for bearing with me as I flapped around in shock and disbelief; and for bringing on board the wonderful Grace Heifetz and Christy Fletcher. I will forever be grateful for your guidance and compassion, and for the work you have done, collectively, to find the book a home.

I'm so lucky to have three passionate and talented editors, Madeleine O'Shea, Carolyn Williams, and Cate Paterson, who understand the book deeply, and trust me to deliver it. To have been trusted in this way has been a gift.

To my first readers—Anna Jaquiery, Christy Menzies, Emma Robinson, and Mandy Joseph—a very heartfelt thank you for your encouraging words and astute observations. And to my writing group—the aforementioned Anna, Guy Randall, Alex McKinnon, Bruce Miller, Lauren Hayes, and Margot McLean—you have sustained me through years of toil and doubt. Without your support I'm not sure I'd still be writing.

This novel was awarded an assessment through the New Zealand Society of Authors CompleteMS programme, an initiative supported by Creative New Zealand. I am very grateful for this, and for the subsequent assessment, provided by Geoff Walker, which gave me the encouragement I needed to send the book out.

Finally, a huge thank you to my mother, Judith, my husband, Geoff, and my two amazing children, Sam and Tessa, for always believing in me, and for convincing me, on more than one occasion, not to give up.

A B O U T   T H E   A U T H O R

With a background in photography and children's publish-
ing, Jennifer Trevelyan is now a full-time writer living in
Wellington, New Zealand, with her husband, son, daughter,
dog and cat. When not at her writing desk, Jennifer can usually be found in the garden.